Oh, Bury Me Not

An eye for an eye? That's how it looked to Conan Flagg. At least that's how it looked when he arrived at his friend's huge ranch in eastern Oregon. With the McFalls and their neighbours the Drinkwaters carrying on an old-fashioned feud, a range vendetta, cutting fences, burning haystacks, poisoning cattle, everything seemed to be pretty petty, if costly and vicious. *An eye for an eye.* Until the vendetta turned bloody, and murder became the ultimate act of revenge, and Conan Flagg, proprietor of an esoteric bookshop on the Oregon coast, and sometime private eye, found himself caught in the crossfire, desperately trying to stop another murder in which the victim might be himself.

By M. K. Wren

OH, BURY ME NOT
A MULTITUDE OF SINS
CURIOSITY DIDN'T KILL THE CAT

Oh, Bury Me Not

M. K. WREN

ROBERT HALE · LONDON

ISBN 0 7091 6531 5

Robert Hale Limited
Clerkenwell House
Clerkenwell Green
London EC1R 0HT

Printed in Great Britain by
Lowe & Brydone Printers Limited, Thetford, Norfolk
Bound by James Burn Limited, Esher, Surrey

Dedicated with thanks to Mildred and Leonard Davis of the
White Horse Ranch, and Lani Davis of the Alvord Ranch; with
hearty appreciation to Sam Burt; with sorrow to Bridgie Sitz,
who will never read it; and with love to Cassie Drinkwater,
the gentle and generous abiding spirit of Harney County.

Oh, Bury Me Not

Oh, Bury Me Not

CHAPTER 1.

The rain should make Mr. Flagg feel right at home.

Beatrice Dobie trudged the half block from the bookshop to the post office, galoshed, raincoated, her freshly permanented and auburned hair preserved in plastic. Just yesterday. She squinted ahead through spattered bifocals. She'd had her hair done yesterday, so what could she expect but rain today?

It was a fine rain that seemed half fog, but could soak the unprepared to the skin in a few minutes, and Holliday Beach, which tourists inevitably called "charming" in the summer, looked like a woebegone rural slum on this late September day. She passed the Gold Star Realty office, anticipating the space separating it from the beauty shop where her determined pace allowed her a brief glance between the buildings and over a jumble of roofs to the rim of the sea. She looked out at the ocean washing this Oregon shore and thought of Conan Flagg, thousands of miles away in Kyoto on the opposite shore.

Metaphorically, of course. On the authority of Rand McNally, she knew Kyoto didn't literally overlook the sea. Anyway, Mr. Flagg wasn't there now. He was on his way home, perhaps approaching Hawaii. . . .

The post office floor was puddled with water. She picked her way across it, smiling at Mrs. Higgins, nearly unrecognizable in her rain gear except for her astonishing girth balanced so irrationally on thin-shanked legs.

"Mornin', Miss Dobie. Wet 'nough for you?"

"Well, we needed the rain; it was a dry summer. At least, for the coast." She went to the bookshop box; the combination was too familiar to necessitate concentration.

"Junk mail," Mrs. Higgins sighed. "How ever does a person get on so many mailing lists? But I guess junk's better'n an empty box. You heard from Mr. Flagg lately?"

Miss Dobie smiled faintly as she examined the bookshop mail. She'd answered that question for the ladies of Holliday Beach, young and old, in weary repetition during her employer's two-week absence.

"He'll be home this afternoon, Mrs. Higgins."

"About time. Never knowed a young feller to wander around so much. Where'd you say he was off to this time?"

"Japan. He was . . ." She paused, distracted by the red-inked message "Private and Urgent" on one of the letters, finishing vaguely, "He was on a consultation project."

"In Japan? What was he consulting about over *there?*"

"Oh, it had to do with some Hokusai woodcuts. Art works. By the way, I got in some new Phyllis Whitneys for the rental shelves."

Mrs. Higgins beamed. "Well, I'll come look 'em over."

When Miss Dobie had the bookshop open and Mrs. Higgins ensconced among the Gothics, she unlocked the door behind the counter: Mr. Flagg's office. *He* called it that; she privately referred to it as his lair. A Hepplewhite desk; a Louis Quinze commode accommodating a small bar and stereo tape deck; paneled walls crowded with paintings; a richly patterned Kerman on the floor. Meg's favorite claw-sharpening spot. One snagged corner was evidence of his indulgence.

But Miss Dobie didn't begrudge Conan Flagg his indulgences or extravagances. He could afford them, and she knew that the Holliday Beach Book Shop—and, ergo, Beatrice Dobie—must be counted among them.

His chief extravagance came trotting in then, announcing herself with a hoarse, demanding meow. Miss Dobie, preoccupied with sorting the mail, assured her, "Meg, I'll get your breakfast in a minute," but the cat wasn't convinced. She jumped up onto the desk, knocking the neat stacks of mail into shambles.

And that was purposeful. Meg could walk a two-by-four laden with crystal without disturbing one precious piece if she were so minded. The *grande dame* of the bookshop—so Miss Dobie regarded this sapphire-eyed, blue-point Siamese aristocrat, as did Meg's faithful following. But she had a lot to learn about noblesse oblige.

"*Shoo!*" A shout and clapping of hands sent her out into the shop, ears flat, and Miss Dobie irritably began resorting the mail, her frown deepening when she came across the letter that had caught her eye at the post office; the one marked "Personal and Urgent."

It was for Mr. Flagg; the return address, G. W. McFall, Black Stallion Ranch, Star Route, Drewsey, Oregon. The slanted Running S brand was emblazoned above it.

The Black Stallion was a name to conjure with in the annals of Oregon history; half a million acres in Harney County, the largest ranch in the state, for a century the domain of the McFalls, and Aaron McFall was as much a legend in his own time as Henry Flagg —Conan Flagg's father and the founder of the Ten-Mile Ranch— had been.

G. W. McFall. That would be George, Aaron's oldest son. Mr. Flagg had been best man at his wedding, but that remembrance didn't elicit her frown, nor was this the first time his name had come to her attention lately.

The frown was for the red-inked "Urgent," for the repeated phone calls, and for the clippings she'd carefully extracted from the Portland *Oregonian* during the last two weeks.

She separated the clippings, reading the headlines. FRONTIER FEUD ERUPTS IN HARNEY COUNTY. SHADES OF HATFIELDS AND MCCOYS. This a clever and condescending column written by a man whom she doubted had ever ventured out of the slurbs of Portland. The last one, dated yesterday, included a photograph of a stackyard, the mountains of hay reduced to smoking ruin. MCFALL-DRINKWATER FEUD FIRED BY ARSON.

She sighed prodigiously. Mr. Flagg just might have to get out his private investigator's license.

◈◈◈

The black XK-E pulled up to the curb at four-thirty. Beatrice Dobie, at her post behind the counter, put aside *The Antiquarian* and looked out through the front windows, smiling to herself. Before Mr. Flagg could cross the short distance from his car to the shop, the Daimler sisters, Adalie and Coraline, cornered him, joined a minute later by Marcie Hopkins, a nubile fifteen-year-old. Even crotchety Olaf Svensen paused for a grumbling greeting, while inside the shop, the remaining customers emerged from the nooks and crannies and gravitated toward the entrance.

Miss Dobie knew Conan Flagg's secret: he was kind to old ladies, truly kind, and to ladies in general, actually. His country boyhood was betrayed in that. She'd grown up on a farm in Iowa where children were taught to say—and think—"Yes, ma'am" and "Yes, sir," and she understood that courtesy, which was so ingrained as to seem innate.

But he didn't show his rural upbringing outwardly. In fact, he looked out of place here, stepping out of that low, sleek car. Another of his indulgences. She was convinced he wouldn't know a carburetor from a carbuncle; he simply considered the XK-E beautiful.

He was still dressed for travel, and rather elegantly, she decided. She seldom saw him in anything but comfortable slacks and sweaters, and perhaps that was why he looked so intriguingly foreign now; lean and dark, high cheekbones, raven-black hair, and eyes with a slight Oriental cast. But that was his Nez Percé heritage, and it so submerged the Irish, it should have stamped him irrefutably American; *true* American.

He escaped Marcie and the sisters Daimler and retreated into the shop, only to be met by more well-wishers, and while he dealt with the friendly onslaught, Miss Dobie let her thoughts wander into a small fantasy. Conan Flagg freshly returned not from an esoteric inquiry into the authenticity of a series of Japanese woodcuts, but from a romantically secret foray as a special agent of G-2, Army Intelligence.

That was years behind him, he always insisted. Still, it was one of the few personal secrets her employer shared with her. That and his private investigator's license.

At length, catching the look of appeal he sent her between smiling pleasantries, she bestirred herself to disperse the last of the greeting party, while he escaped to the privacy of his office, where he stripped off his coat and tie and sank into the leather chair behind his desk, venting a sigh of relief when the front door finally closed. Miss Dobie secured it by putting up the "closed" sign, then crossed to the office door and paused there.

"Well, Mr. Flagg, it may be redundant, but welcome home."

He called up a smile. "Thanks, Miss Dobie. How are you? And where's Meg? Snubbing me?"

"I'm fine, and Meg's probably sulking upstairs. The Duchess is displeased, you know, with your absence."

"As usual. Well, I'll bring some chicken liver tomorrow. That should put me back in her good graces."

"Probably. How about a cup of coffee? The pot's on."

"If it weren't, I'd know the Apocalypse was approaching. Yes, I'll have some coffee." He looked around the room with a curious sense of mental vertigo, seeking some elusive touchstone in this accumulation of cherished products of work and pleasure and years.

Jet lag. He surveyed the waiting stacks of mail and found the prospect of sorting through them mindboggling. By tomorrow morning, this intimately familiar world would be itself again, but now it seemed paradoxically alien. He watched Miss Dobie as she handed him a mug of coffee and settled in the chair across the desk from him. He could anticipate almost every laconic comment and weighty sigh, yet she seemed a virtual stranger.

"Well, Miss Dobie, any news?"

Her shoulders came up in a predictable shrug.

"Well . . . that depends on what you consider newsworthy. How was your trip? Did you connect with Mr. Morishi?"

"Yes. He made all the crooked ways straight, and fortunately speaks beautiful English. With an Oxford accent. I'll have to call Halsey." He frowned at his watch. "Tomorrow. It's the middle of the night in New York."

"Not quite, but he can wait another day for his report. The prints are authentic?"

"Definitely. Morishi nearly wept when I left with them. If Halsey's interested, he could triple his investment." He paused, his attention caught by the words "Personal and Urgent" on one of the envelopes. At first he dismissed it as another missive from his cousin, Avery Flagg. Conan had made him chairman of the board when the Ten-Mile Ranch was incorporated, which spared him the mental drudgery of running the business, but not Avery's periodic outbursts of fiscal hysteria.

Then he recognized the Running S brand.

"What's this?"

"Well, I guess that's one item you could call news. I was going to tell you about it as soon as you caught your breath. It's from George McFall."

That was self-evident and told him nothing. He tore open the envelope. The letter wasn't typed, although the stationery was a businesslike bond with the Black Stallion address printed at the top.

"He's called three time this week," Miss Dobie added. "He would've called you in Kyoto if I'd had a phone number."

Conan didn't comment on that barb, too distracted by the cramped irregularity of the writing.

Miss Dobie elaborated: "He wasn't just being friendly, either. He sounded like a man with his back to the wall."

"George? I find that hard to imagine."

"Well, everybody gets his back to a wall sooner or later," she observed sagely. "Anyway, he wants you to call him as soon as you can, and he doesn't care what time of the day or night it is."

That kind of insistence from a man notable for a calm, unruffled approach to life was alarming. Conan began reading the letter, but Miss Dobie wasn't through yet.

"It probably has something to do with that feud. I saved some clippings for you."

"What feud?" He glanced at the clippings, but they seemed as meaningless to him as a Japanese headline.

"Well, the McFalls and the Drinkwaters—I guess their ranch is close to the Black Stallion—"

"Yes, the Double D. It borders the Black Stallion on the west."

"That's it, the Double D. Anyway, they're having a good old-fashioned feud; cutting fences, flooding hay fields, even poisoning cattle."

He raised an eyebrow skeptically. "Sounds like some reporter's been watching too many Westerns."

"I'm afraid not, and it's getting serious. That last item, the arson, I saw a film story on the news yesterday. A thousand tons of hay went up in smoke."

He felt a chill at that, and "serious" struck him as a sadly inadequate term for a disaster. The fall stores of hay were put aside to see the herds through bitterly cold winters. Losing them could mean starvation for hundreds of head of cattle and bankruptcy for a rancher.

He returned to the letter, and apparently Miss Dobie had had her say; she remained silent while he read it.

Dear Conan,

This is sort of like a Dear Abby letter—I never thought I'd be writing one, and I never thought I'd be looking for a private eye, but I am now. I need help, and you're the only private eye I know, and I figure if you can't trust your best man, who can you trust?

I've been trying to phone you, and I asked Miss Dobie to tell you to call me as soon as you get home, but thought I'd better write in case she forgets. It's about this feud. Sounds outlandish, I know, but I guess that's the only way to describe it. You know Pa, and Alvin Drinkwater is just as stubborn and cantankerous as he is. I don't know what's really going on, but I'm afraid if I don't get this thing straightened out, somebody will end up dead.

I'll need help to get to the bottom of this. I want to hire you to do some proper investigating, and I'm not just after some friendly advice or sympathy. I need some answers and I'm willing to pay whatever it costs to get them.

I know this probably doesn't make much sense, but there's no use trying to explain the whole thing in a letter. Just call me as soon as possible—please.

Thanks,

George

It *didn't* make much sense. Conan read the letter again, then methodically folded it. George McFall afraid and freely admitting it—

that was what didn't make sense. He studied the clippings briefly, then put them in the envelope with the letter.

"I'll have to call George this evening."

Miss Dobie nodded over her cup, with the hound-on-a-scent look she always got when he was on a case. He didn't bother to remind her that he hadn't taken any cases yet.

"When did you first meet George McFall?" she asked. "Playing Cupid at Stanford?"

He managed a laugh. "There was no Cupid involved. Fate, perhaps, in the shape of George's ineptitude on the ski slopes, and Laura was rather spectacular in white."

"You mean nursing white or wedding white?"

"Both." Five years ago. It seemed longer, and it had always seemed a paradox that he and George hadn't been brought together by the common experience of being scions of two of the largest ranches in the state. They'd met in a totally different environment, and even in another state; Stanford University, where Conan was auditing a course in ethology conducted by a visiting European scientist. But George wasn't a passing sampler in the groves of academe; he was working conscientiously toward a degree in business administration. As heir apparent to a domain conservatively valued at three million dollars, he took his responsibilities very seriously.

Conan sometimes wondered if George hadn't considered Laura part of that responsibility; that it behooved him to bring home a bride to ensure the continuity of the dynasty. Not that he hadn't been thoroughly in love with her. In that, perhaps, he lost sight of his obligations to a degree. The dynasty might have been better served by a bride bred to the land.

The red alarm of the word "Urgent" drew and held his eye. *You know Pa, and Alvin Drinkwater is just as stubborn and cantankerous as he is.* Pa. The form of address was typical, and he did know Aaron McFall. He'd met him formally only once, at George and Laura's wedding, which took place at the Black Stallion, inevitably. But he knew him in another sense. His own father had been of the same mold: men accurately described as cattle barons. The allusion to hereditary title was apt, yet Aaron McFall considered himself a pillar of democracy. His wife had borne him three sons, and they were named by the lord of the demesne George Washington McFall, Abraham Lincoln McFall, and Theodore Roosevelt McFall. The third birth had cost Carlotta McFall her life.

Conan had never met Alvin Drinkwater, but if he was in fact as stubborn and cantankerous as Aaron, he could understand the frayed and anxious tone of George's letter.

Finally, he rose and surveyed the stacks of mail.

"Miss Dobie, I can't contend with all this now. Any crises here will have to wait until morning."

She smiled tolerantly. "There's nothing imminent. Oh, I called Mrs. Early this morning and told her you were on your way. She said she'd get the house aired out and warmed up for you."

He went out into the shop, savoring the musty, attic flavor of it, and turned at the entrance with a parting smile.

"Miss Dobie, you're a rare gem. Thanks for taking such good care of the shop. And me."

CHAPTER 2.

The housekeeper par excellence, Conan thought as he peered into the refrigerator. Not only was the house shining clean and comfortably warm, but Mrs. Early was ever solicitous of his stomach. On the counter was a loaf of homemade bread and an apple pie—Gravensteins, no doubt—and in the refrigerator a platter of fried chicken done to a crisp turn.

He smiled at this offering but didn't partake of it; his internal clock was still at odds with the one on the wall. He went into the living room and tossed his coat onto the couch, then irritably crossed to the windows that made up the west wall. Mrs. Early did have one shortcoming. She was continually lowering shades and closing curtains.

It was a soft, mist-blue light that filled the room as he opened the drapes. The autumn equinox inevitably brought rain, a preview of winter. The ocean was gray and running high, breakers spilling in masses of foam. The sound seeped into his consciousness, a balm he never realized he missed so desperately until he returned to it.

But in his mind's eye, another vista was taking shape. Arid hills clothed in the velvet of sagebrush, an open sky overwhelming in its grandeur, dry air that stretched distance and dwarfed sensibility. He started to take George's letter out of his shirt pocket, then with a vague feeling of rebellion, thrust it back. He hadn't even been home long enough for his body and mind to adjust to his spatial location.

The rebellion persisted while he went to the bar to mix a light bourbon and water, then returned with it to the windows to watch the light fade from the breakers. But by the time he reached the halfway mark on his glass, he was perched on a bar stool, the letter open in front of him, trying to convince a telephone operator of the existence of Harney County and G. W. McFall. The Black Stallion, at least, seemed to make some sense to her, and finally the electronic link was established.

"George, this is Conan. I just got home a—"

"Oh, thank God. I've been chewin' nails for . . . but I can't—look, just sit tight a minute. I'll call you back. Okay?" Conan didn't have a chance to answer before he was cut off with a sharp click.

George's reason for returning the call was no mystery—he wanted to go to a more private phone—but the raw tension in his tone was unnerving. Conan lit a cigarette, taking three spaced, slow puffs before the phone rang.

"Sorry for the delay, Conan." He was a little more relaxed now, but his laugh was strained. "Figured I better put this on my bill since I asked you to call; it might be a long talk."

"If you're going to explain what prompted this letter, it probably *will* be long."

"Afraid so. Well, it's this . . . this *feud*. Hell, what else do you call it? Sounds like it's straight out of Hollywood, only there's no ridin' into the sunset with this; it just keeps gettin' worse."

Conan was looking down at the letter, finding a parallel between the erratic, crabbed lines and his tense voice. Not even the rural accent took the edge off that.

"Maybe you'd better start at the beginning, George."

"I'm not even sure where that is." He paused for a deep, audible sigh. "Well, it goes way back. Part of it, anyhow. Pa and Alvin Drinkwater never did get along; sort of a tradition in both families. There was a time, fifty years back, when the Double D and Runnin' S were about neck and neck in land and stock."

"But the Running S took the lead?" The use of the brand in lieu of the ranch name came naturally; in the cattle business they were virtually, and sometimes actually, synonymous. "That sort of competition doesn't usually involve cutting fences or burning stackyards."

"No, and it never did until lately. I don't know, Conan, it just doesn't make sense. I mean, Pa and Alvin threw talk off and on since they were kids, and I guess they got into a big jackpot over Emily Drinkwater before she married Alvin, but that was over thirty years ago. Since then, if they had any real squabbles, they always talked it out face to face, even if it wasn't exactly peaceful. Like that Spring Crick rezzavoy. Alvin wanted to put in a dam; he needed a rezzavoy for his winter pastures, but the crick runs over our land, too, and Pa set his heels over losin' most of the stream flow. Well, they chewed around on it for a few years, then finally got together with the county watermaster and set up an agreement so we get enough water for our irrigation ditches. You see what I mean? Water's your life's blood out here, and they had some hard words over it, but that's all. It was never anything like this."

"You'd better tell me more about what it's like, then." He frowned as George prefaced his reply with another weary and atypical sigh.

"Well, it's been goin' on for about a year. It started off so easy, nobody paid much attention. Just damn fool stunts like leavin' gates open, or takin' off the wire hooks so you couldn't shut 'em. Maybe half a dozen times somebody opened the horse corrals in the night, and the whole cavvy spread out to hell and gone. Then we started findin' our irrigation ditches clogged up with junk; weeds and rocks, or even garbage. At first we figured it was just hunters or those damn ORV nuts. Even when the fence cuttin' started, we weren't sure. That was last fall, and huntin' season was on. But last spring somebody broke some of the ditch walls and flooded the fields. Then they shot holes in our waterin' troughs up in the high pastures. This summer we had cattle turned into the alfalfa fields before harvest, and lately the fences on some of the stackyards were cut. Hell, one herd went through five hundred ton of hay before we saw the fence was down. We've had so many fences cut and gates left open, we'll never separate the strays, and when they get mixed with Double D cows, you need a U.N. negotiator along to sort 'em out." He paused, his tone an uncertain mix of bewilderment and resentment. "Then it got really dirty, Conan. A month ago we lost thirty head of cattle because somebody shot a salt block full of cyanide, and I guess you heard about the grand finale."

"The arson?"

"Yes. Thank God it was only the one stackyard, and we had a good harvest this year; we'll have enough hay for the winter. If somebody doesn't get to the rest of it."

"George, you keep talking about 'somebody.' Do you mean Drinkwater?"

The answer was long in coming.

"Yes, I guess so."

"You *guess*?"

"I don't really know. That's what's got me so rattled. The trouble is, if you talked to Alvin, he'd give you a list of damages as long as ours. Cut fences, broken ditches, cattle poisoned—the whole shit-taree. Maybe we've got him topped off with the arson, but that's about all."

Conan's hand stopped in midair as he reached for the cigarette burning itself out in the ashtray.

"An eye for an eye?"

George said dully, "That's how it looks, doesn't it? On both sides."

Conan picked up the cigarette and took a puff.

"At first glance, yes. Is that how it is?"

"I can only tell you how it is on one side. Nobody at the Runnin' S has authorized any forays on Drinkwater property, and I'm in a position to know."

As business manager of the Black Stallion, he was justified in that assertion, but Conan was remembering Aaron McFall, whom George himself characterized as stubborn and cantankerous.

He asked cautiously, "What about your father?"

"You think he'd carry on this little war behind my back?"

"I'm just asking."

"No. Not Pa," he said stiffly. "Anyhow, he'd have a hard time keepin' me from gettin' wind of it. I don't spend all my time in this damn office. I still get out and work the cattle when we're shorthanded, or just to keep up the calluses on my butt. I know what's goin' on around here."

"Still, you can't keep track of all the hands all the time."

"No, but we've only got ten full-time employees on the payroll now, and I have a pretty good idea what any one of 'em is up to at any given time. And only five of 'em—well, six, countin' our foreman —are buckaroos. This little war's taken some hard ridin'."

Buckaroos. Conan smiled reminiscently at the term. In other regions, they might be called cowboys or cowpunchers, but it had been left to the cattlemen of the Northwest to bastardize the Spanish *vaquero* into buckaroo.

"Only six? It sounds like you're shorthanded *now*."

George laughed. "Times have changed since you took off for the woods. We're mechanized these days. We just put in a new branding corral. Sixty head in an hour, Conan; branding, dehorning, castration, vaccination, and dipping. Give us another ten years and we'll be automated."

"When you get a computer willing to ride fence in the middle of a blizzard—well, don't tell me about it. Leave me my romantic delusions."

"It's the dude ridin' fence who's deluded. Or nuts." The spark of life in his voice faded as he seemed to recall himself to the subject under discussion. "Anyhow, we're not shorthanded. Linc and Ted do their share of buckarooin', and Pa hasn't retired from the saddle yet. And we're not exactly out of touch with what's goin' on around here."

"All right. What about Alvin Drinkwater? Is he cantankerous enough to wage a war like this personally?"

"Conan, two years ago I'd have sworn on a Bible he wasn't, but now I'm just not sure. I'm not sure of anything."

"Has all this been kept between the warring camps, or has anyone called in the law?"

George gave a short, caustic laugh.

"Joe Tate's spent enough time up at this end of the county to stake a homestead claim, but he—"

"Joe Tate?"

"Oh—sorry. He's the county sheriff, and I've never had any reason to think he was dealin' off the bottom."

"But he's come up with nothing to help you?"

"Not a damn thing. I think right now he's sorry he ever won the election. He spends half his time between the Runnin' S and the Double D, with Pa and Alvin both hollerin' at him to lock the other up."

Conan didn't envy Joe Tate, and he had the uneasy feeling he was being drawn into a similarly uncomfortable position.

"I suppose you've considered the possibility that neither of them is guilty?"

"You mean some outsider's playin' both ends against the middle? Sure, but who'd have the opportunity or enough of a grudge against both Pa and Alvin? Still, there might be something to it; something to explain part of it, at least. I think . . . well, there may be some rustlin' goin' on. I guess that sounds like it's out of Hollywood, too."

"Times haven't changed that much, George. You don't need to convince me of the existence of cattle rustlers."

"No, I suppose not. Well, most of it's penny ante. Dudes cadgin' a side of beef to help out on the food budget, and a lot of hunters go home with white-faced deer all dressed out in the field. But some of it's big business with organization and equipment behind it. Joe Tate says there's an outfit workin' out of a packin' plant in Winnemucca. Both the Oregon and Nevada law been after 'em for years and never laid a hand on 'em."

"You think they might be involved in the feud? How? As a diversionary tactic?"

"Maybe." He hesitated, then went on more confidently, "With all the trouble here, and Pa and Alvin ready to hold a neck-tie party for each other—well, it makes a damn good diversion. Trouble is, we're just bringin' the herds down from the summer pastures, so we don't have a full head count yet. Right now, it looks like it's runnin' low, but we've got eight hundred square miles to cover, and God knows how many strays are still left up in the hills." Then he added bit-

terly, "Or how many carcasses we'll find if somebody put out more
of those cyanide salt blocks."

"What makes you think you've lost cattle to rustlers? Just the low
head count?"

"No. Something Bert Kimmons saw. He ran the K-Bar to the
south of us. He was an old friend of both Pa's and Alvin's, and it really hurt him seein' them lock horns like this. Anyhow, one night—
let's see, it was a couple of months ago—Bert was drivin' back to his
place late. There's a county road runs along the line between his
property and ours. Well, he come up to a cattle truck headed east. It
had a Nevada plate, and it was a big rig—big enough for twenty-five
or thirty head—and he says it was loaded."

"I don't suppose he could see any brands."

"No. Maybe some trucker was just takin' a shortcut on that road,
but I'm damned if I can figure where to, and those cows weren't
bought from any spread within fifty miles of here."

Conan was frowning, but his tone was ironically light as he said,
"Well, that *would* make a person wonder."

"It sure made Bert wonder. He decided to talk to Pa and Alvin
about it. I guess he thought it might be one way to get them together, and then he felt obliged to tell them they might be furnishin'
free steaks for somebody."

"Did he get them together?"

"No. Damn it, sometimes I think this whole thing—it's like Fate.
There's not a damn thing *anybody* can do to . . ."

Conan felt a tautening thread of alarm as the words choked off;
the desperation was so naked in his voice, the following silence so
long.

"George?"

"I—I'm sorry. I guess my nerves are kind of raveled out. Well, to
finish the story, the day after Bert saw that truck, he went over to
the Double D to talk to Alvin. What he wanted was for the three of
them—Bert and Alvin and Pa—to compare notes and see if they had
any other evidence of rustlin', then they'd all go to Sheriff Tate.
Well, he finally got Alvin to agree to that."

"Did Alvin have any evidence to offer?"

"I don't know. It never got that far. Bert spent most of the afternoon with Alvin, then he drove on out here to the house to talk to
Pa."

"Were you in on that conversation?"

"We all were. I mean, the family and Gil Potts, our foreman.
Bert had supper with us, and we hashed it out at the table. That's
the way this place is run most of the time."

"Did Aaron agree to this summit meeting?"

"Yes, finally. I was so relieved I could've kissed ol' Bert. I didn't give a damn about losin' a few cows if Pa and Alvin would at least talk about it. About *anything*."

"And what happened?"

"Bert . . . well, he died."

The words were so mumbled, Conan wasn't sure he understood them correctly.

"He died?"

"Yes. Right here at the ranch. He had a bad heart. Doc Maxwell said he'd been runnin' on borrowed time for years. When we finished talkin', it was late. We could see Bert was worn out, and it's a long drive to his place, so we asked him to stay the night. I guess we didn't realize . . . anyhow, he died durin' the night. Heart failure, Doc said."

"I'm sorry, George. Was Kimmons a close friend?"

After a moment he answered dully, "Yes. Bert was sort of like an uncle to Linc and Ted and me. It just seemed to take the wind out of everybody, especially Pa. He's at the age where all his friends seem to be droppin' around him, and I don't think it did much for him, knowin' he has the same kind of heart condition."

"Is it serious?"

"Pa's? No. Nothing like Bert's. A couple of years ago he had a mild attack and spent two weeks in the Burns hospital. Doc gave him some pills and a diet and told him to take it easy, all of which he ignored."

Conan was reminded, again, of his own father, whose distrust of orthodox medicine was atavistically abiding.

"Did anyone talk to Sheriff Tate about that cattle truck?"

"I did, but there wasn't anything he could get his teeth into." Another long, weary sigh. "If there *is* some rustlin', it might explain part of what's goin' on here. But not all of it, Conan. Not by a hell of a long shot."

"And you want me to explain the rest of it?" He put out his cigarette with impatient thrusts, well aware that the task he was considering was possibly hopeless and probably thankless. "I'm not sure I can explain anything."

"I'm not askin' for miracles, but I have to do something. I don't hold it against him, but Tate can't handle it. I guess I could find plenty of private investigators in any city phonebook, but they wouldn't know their hind end from the fore around here. You grew up in this business." He tried a brief laugh. "At least you know how to stay on top of a horse if you have to do any ridin'. Unless you've forgotten how, after sittin' on that pile of books all these years."

"That would be like forgetting how to walk." He took a swallow of his drink as if he needed it to firm his resolve. Curiosity shaped his decision as much as George's desperation. Someone was invoking lex talionis on Drinkwater even if no one at the Running S had authorized it. He wondered what Drinkwater's side of the story would be.

"All right, George, you've hired yourself an investigator, but I want a couple of things understood. First, the odds are against my coming with anything conclusive, and even if I do, you may not like it."

"Maybe, but I don't like what's going on now, either."

"I know. Another thing: I'd rather you didn't spread it around that I'm there as a private eye."

For once, George's laugh came easily.

"Yes, I know; you take that 'private' seriously. I'll do my best to keep it in the family."

"I hope the family goes along. On that and my mission in general."

"If you're worried about Pa, don't. He'll holler about callin' in an outsider, but I can talk him around."

"Do you have any influence with Sheriff Tate?"

"Enough. But I can't help you with Alvin."

"I didn't expect that. All right, this is . . . Thursday?" He'd lost a day in his peregrinations across the international date line. "I have a few loose ends to tie up here before—"

"Conan, please—I mean, I know I'm already asking a lot, but I . . . I need you here tomorrow. Tomorrow morning."

"Tomorrow morning? But it's a six-hour drive, and I—"

"We have an airfield. It's not fancy; no facilities except a fuel pump. But there must be someplace out there where you can charter a plane."

His harried insistence was disconcerting, and Conan relinquished the prospect of a recuperative late rising in the morning.

"The plane's no problem. Times have changed at the Ten-Mile, too; we have a plane, a helicopter, and a full-time pilot. But what's happening tomorrow that's so important?"

"Nothing. I mean, nothing connected with the feud, but I have to leave tomorrow afternoon for Portland. There's an Oregon Cattlemen's convention, and I can't very well get out of it since I'm treasurer of the damn thing. That's why I was tryin' so hard to get hold of you. I wanted you here and dug in before I left. I'll be gone a week, and I—" There was an odd, tight break in his voice. "I guess I'm afraid to be away from the ranch that long without . . . I don't know. Makin' some sort of provision, I suppose."

A provision for disaster, Conan realized, and wondered what George expected him to do to avert it.

"All right. I don't know when I'll be arriving, but I'll make it as early as possible."

"Thanks, Conan. You don't know what this means to me. It's helped already just to—well, to talk about it."

"I charge extra for therapy, but don't get your hopes too high."

"Any hope is a relief now. I'll see you tomorrow, then, and get you set up here. Better dig out your boots."

"I will, but unfortunately my saddle's in storage in Pendleton." He paused, the forced humor fading, and wondered why it was he who had to ask the question. "How's Laura?"

"What? Oh. She . . . she's fine. Pretty as ever. She'll be glad to see you."

Conan was on the verge of asking if there was a George or Laura *fils* or *filles*, but thought better of it. That news would have been heralded with engraved air-mail fanfares. Besides, something in George's noncommittal tone discouraged further questions.

"Well, give her my love. I'll see you tomorrow."

After he hung up, he sat immobile in the twilight gray for some time, enduring the creeping doubts and second thoughts that came inevitably at this stage of the game. At length, he reached over the bar for the bourbon bottle and added a little color to his drink; quite a little color.

CHAPTER 3.

Johnnie Moss was one of those graceful, golden young men of twenty-five who, entirely unwittingly, could make a man of thirty feel old and incompetent. The great passion of his life was flying, and it was typical that he made an enviably good living doing exactly what he most enjoyed.

Johnnie had one characteristic that particularly endeared him to Conan: he didn't find it necessary to talk about his passion, or anything else, while indulging it. He spoke only those words requisite to his function or to basic courtesy, a profound relief to Conan, who considered flight an aesthetic privilege wasted on the bird brain.

The Cessna 150 took to the air in a lavender dawn from an airstrip near Holliday Beach, turned sunward over the Coast Range where wizard worlds of mossy rain forests smoothed the contours of the hills, then idled across the wide trough between the Coast Range and the Cascades. The Willamette Valley, incredibly green through drifts of cloud, patched with multitudes of small, rich farms; the Promised Land at the end of the Oregon Trail. Most of the residents of the state crowded into this valley, their cities proliferating like intricately structured fungi.

Then the plane nosed up through the clouds, striking out with a certain bravado toward the bulwarks of the Cascades. Set against the dark velvet of the forested foothills rose the glacier-carved peaks, pearls unstrung along the spine of the range. In their youth they had shaped themselves with awesome outpourings of lava, but now they entered middle age serenely, crowned with white.

Beyond the crest of the Cascades, the forest changed color and texture, fir and hemlock giving way to ponderosa, that in turn surrendering to the tenacious, tough juniper. The land seemed to stretch itself to a retreating horizon, the sky became more intensely blue, the sun a dry, white glare that made dark glasses a necessity and bleached the colors of the land to subtle, grayed siennas and ochres. Even the juniper at length retreated to the heights, giving way to sagebrush. There were always mountains in view, low ranges of hills or fault block ridges, but the expanses between them reached into flat, blued distances; old lake beds, many of them, floored with alkali like unseasonable snow.

On the map, Harney and Malheur counties made two vertical rectangles side by side in the southeast corner of Oregon. The Forgotten Corner, it had been called; twenty thousand square miles, a fifth of the area of the state, yet it supported only a small fraction of its population. This was a Promised Land only for the hardy, courageous, persistent, and lucky. It was the kind of land Conan had grown up in, and he respected and even loved it, but he'd left it by choice because he understood the demands it made on the human psyche; because survival required too much of a man's resources and left too little of his soul intact.

It was exactly 9 A.M. when they passed over Burns, the seat of Harney County. With a population of less than four thousand, it contained more than half the county's inhabitants. Its main distinction in Conan's mind was that some literate pioneer founder had named it for Robert Burns. He always wondered how the poet would have felt about having this outpost in a land he'd never seen—and probably couldn't have imagined—named in his honor.

Past Burns, Johnnie took the plane down to a lower altitude, following the fragile line of Highway 20, Burns's link with both east and west, drawn ruler-straight across the fossil lake bed of Harney Valley, then curling up over a range of hills named Stinkingwater Mountain. Singular. Then the highway straightened again, striking north-northeast across another basin, through which the Malheur River threaded its way eastward toward Hell's Canyon. A lonely cluster of houses and trees on the river marked the site of Drewsey, but Johnnie turned due east before they reached it, following a dirt road that struck off the highway. He gestured downward once, shouting the word "Drinkwater" against the roar of the engine.

Conan nodded, looking down at the tiny patch of trees and buildings, the headquarters of the Double D. This survey was part of the flight plan he had outlined on Johnnie's navigational maps before their departure. Three miles past the Double D was the border between the two warring domains, marked by the thin line of a barbed wire fence. It was a long border, stretching south ten miles, and north five miles to the Malheur River. A long border to patrol or defend.

A flash of light reflected from an oval of dull copper to the south caught his eye. That would be the Spring Creek reservoir George had told him about. It was on Drinkwater land, but within a mile of the property line.

Then he frowned, shading his eyes with one hand. The reservoir seemed nearly empty, a brown puddle ringed with darker brown, wet earth. And the dam—

He touched Johnnie's shoulder, shouting his instructions, receiving a wordless nod as the right wing tipped down and the plane made a long arc over the reservoir.

And Conan stared numbly down.

The reservoir *was* nearly empty, and soon would be entirely empty. Dark earth sprayed in radiating lines that converged at what had once been the center of the dam.

It had been blown up; dynamited.

A minor disaster it might seem. It had been a simple earthen dam no more than fifty feet across; the reservoir couldn't have been more than half a mile long.

But in a land with an annual rainfall of ten inches, and in autumn, when there would be little precipitation except in the form of snow until the following spring, it was a disaster of major proportion for the rancher who depended on it to water his cattle in their winter pastures.

George had told him that only the burning of the Black Stallion stackyard put them ahead of the Double D in total damages sustained in this miniature war. Now the score had been evened. With a vengeance.

Conan gestured to Johnnie to continue their course, grateful for his reticence and the engine noise; he was too distracted by the implications of that disaster to discuss it.

It was only seven miles via the dirt road from the Double D's headquarters to the Black Stallion's. He saw the trees first; an improbably lush grove, green shading to gold with the season. Cottonwoods, most of them, but soaring over them, the golden plumes of Lombardy poplars, as nobly defiant as Cyrano's white plume. They shaded every ranch house more than fifty years old in the region, lovingly nurtured in a land where water was precious. Untended, they died and their white skeletons marked the graves of countless homesteads. Well tended, they flourished, creating green oases, barriers against dust, sun, wind, and snow.

In and around this grove was a small community, its prosperity evident in its orderly arrangement and white-painted buildings and fences. The main house and the barn were separated by an open graveled area perhaps a hundred yards across, the house putting its side to it and facing west, the barn opening onto it, facing north. These and the pump house were the oldest structures, but the windmill atop the latter had been rendered impotent by the advent of electric power, the vanes gone, and the rudder only an indicator of wind direction. The cookhouse, bunkhouse, and three private residences for familied employees were more recent additions, but still verging on middle age. The newest additions were three house trailers, two matched pairs of tall metal cylinders—silos and propane tanks—and a large building housing the shop, a totally modern, elaborately equipped automotive repair depot Conan remembered well from his last visit. The sun glared from its metal roof, glittered on the machines in the yard behind it; pickups, tractors, road graders, backhoes, and the mechanical dinosaurs that harvested, baled, and stacked the hay and alfalfa crops.

Johnnie made a circle into the wind as Conan looked down at the main house, wondering at the number of cars parked in front of it. From the air, it looked like a child's building block to which had been added a low, pyramidal roof, but on the ground, he knew, it was quite impressive despite its prudent austerity; two stories high, built of beautifully dressed tan stone, fronted with a wide porch, it was a rare example of ostentatious display for the area. Few families of its period were prosperous enough to build stone houses, usually satisfying themselves with clapboard copies of the houses left behind east of the Mississippi.

The airstrip east of the buildings was only a bulldozed length of 'dobe, but Johnnie Moss put the plane down as smoothly as if it were new paving and taxied toward the only observable gate.

"I thought your friend had a pump. Oh—there it is."

Conan scarcely heard him, but not because of the engine noise. There was no one in sight. Yet, George was expecting him, and the approach of the plane couldn't have gone unnoticed.

"Are you low on fuel?" he asked absently.

"Yes, but I can make it to the Burns field if there's a problem here. It's only thirty miles."

There *was* a problem here; one that had nothing to do with the availability of fuel. The conviction was only reinforced when the plane came to a stop near the gate and he finally saw a sign of life.

It came in the person of a uniformed man who approached at a measured, determined pace. The uniform was brown and tan, and included a flat-brimmed Stetson and a .38 revolver in a belt holster. From the county sheriff's office.

Johnnie asked dryly, "That the kind of welcoming committee you were expecting?"

"Not exactly. Will you get my luggage out while I see how welcoming this committee is?"

His ears rang in the baked silence as he went out to meet the uniformed man. The light wind was cool, but it had only to stop for a moment and the heat of the sun closed in. The man squinted at Conan, his arms hanging in a ready curve. When they were within six feet of each other and came to a mutual halt, he turned his attention to the plane.

"You from the Circle-Ten?"

The Ten-Mile Ranch name was also lettered on the plane, yet he chose the brand by which to identify its owner. But Conan didn't smile at that; he was too overwhelmed with a sense of dread to notice colloquial subtleties.

"Yes. I'm Conan Flagg. Where's George?"

The man gave him a look in which suspicion vied with shock, then glanced back toward the ranch buildings.

"You mean George McFall. He . . . he's dead."

CHAPTER 4.

Deputy Sheriff Harley Ross's refusal to answer any questions was not to be construed as discourtesy to a stranger. He made that clear by offering to call someone to refuel the plane and by helping Conan with his luggage. Duty stilled his tongue. It was up to Sheriff Tate to decide whether Conan's questions should be answered.

After the first shock, Conan accepted that. He sent Johnnie Moss on to Burns to take care of the plane, then walked beside Deputy Ross past the house trailers, the bunkhouse, the cookhouse, and through the graveled yard between the barn and the main house, seeing nothing and feeling nothing except the breathless heat of the morning sun.

It seemed a long way and a long time, yet he was grateful for Ross's silence. It gave him a chance to gear his mind to rational function again; to pass the "only" stage. "If only," and "only yesterday," and "only thirty years old."

Deputy Ross took him around to the front of the house, past the white picket fence, and up the five steps to the porch. The door was open, and the foyer seemed crowded, but when Ross disappeared through the double doors on the right into the living room, Conan realized there were only two other people in this shadowed passage.

He took off his sunglasses, meeting the curious stare of another of Harney County's finest, posted by the front door. At the foot of the stairs, a dark-haired girl sat hugging her knees, black eyes mirroring the outside light. She was Chicano, and he wondered how much English she spoke, and how much of the tragedy visited on this house she understood.

More than he, perhaps.

There were voices from the living room; Deputy Ross explaining the visitor, then a rush of footsteps, and Conan turned to see Laura McFall in the doorway, gazing at him in bewilderment.

He looked for symptoms of shock and grief, but found them hidden. Pretty as ever, George had said, and it was true; the kind of perfectly structured face that makes models famous with the right lighting, yet in normal contexts attracts little attention. One was more likely to notice her copper-red hair, or her translucent, amber-brown eyes. She wore her hair short now, and it seemed paler, faded.

"Conan? Is it—oh, Conan . . ." She moved toward him in an unthinking rush, but stopped short of his offered embrace.

"No, I . . . I'm all right."

She wasn't all right; it was only that she had herself under control now and knew that a sympathetic embrace would be enough to jeopardize it. The girl on the stairs had risen.

"*Señora?*"

"Oh, Ginger . . . where's Mano?"

"Outside with one of the sheriffs, I think." Then, unexpectedly, tears spilled from her dark eyes. "*Señora*, I have no words . . ."

Laura could risk a comforting embrace with this young woman; she was giving as much as accepting the comfort.

"I know; I understand." Her reassuring smile was almost convincing. "You'd better go out to the cookhouse and help Mrs. Mosely. She'll need . . . someone."

"And you?"

"I'm all right. I'm fine. Thank you, Ginger."

She nodded, then turned and nearly ran to the door at the far end of the vestibule.

"Her name's Gabriella," Laura murmured absently in the wake of her retreat. "I nicknamed her Ginger, or Irene would've called her Gabby. *Oh, Conan—*" Abruptly, she turned away, hands making small fists. He reached out to her, but at the tense negative shake of her head, he withdrew his hand, watching helplessly until she had restored her stern self-mastery. She looked around at him perplexedly.

"But, Conan, what are you—how did you find out?"

"About George? Deputy Ross just told me."

"Then, you didn't know he—he was . . ."

Voices were still audible from the living room. One, in its cutting asperity, carried over the others; Aaron McFall's.

"No, I didn't know. Didn't George tell you I was coming? That he asked me to come?"

"What? No. He didn't say anything about you at all; not recently. Conan, I don't understand."

"Neither do I." Then he glanced at the attentive deputy by the door and added vaguely, "He thought I could help him with something."

Her eyes narrowed. "The feud? That's right, you used to do some sleuthing on the side. He *did* talk about hiring an investigator. I guess he should've called you sooner. He might still be . . ."

"Please, Laura," he said gently, "don't start that."

She managed a brief smile and nodded.

"Might-have-beens are dangerous. So is self-pity."

There was something subtly out of character in her tone, but he couldn't pinpoint it, and he reminded himself that he'd never known her well, nor had he talked to her face to face for five years. Since the wedding.

"Laura, do you feel up to telling me what happened? Ross wouldn't tell me anything."

"Yes. I can tell you what I know, anyway. I'm all right, Conan. Really I am. Besides, maybe *you* can . . ." She didn't finish that speculation, instead reciting coolly, "At this point, all we're sure of is that the dam on Alvin Drinkwater's Spring Creek reservoir was blown up."

"Yes, I saw it." And recognized it as a disaster, but not a tragedy. Then, at her questioning look, he explained, "When we were flying in. How was George involved in that?"

"I don't know. I mean, I don't know why he was there, but he was found—his body was half buried in the debris. He was probably killed by a blow to the head. The left parietal bone was fractured."

The terminology made him pause, and reminded him that she was a registered nurse. Perhaps that explained in part her objective calm.

"Fractured by what?"

"A rock, apparently. That's what Sheriff Tate says."

"Flying debris from the explosion?"

She shrugged, staring down at the floor.

"I suppose so."

"All right, Laura. Do you know when it happened?"

"Probably about eleven last night. Some of the Drinkwater hands told Tate they heard an explosion then. But the reservoir is quite a distance from the ranch house, and they just passed it off as a sonic boom. There's an Air Force base in Boise, and I guess they consider this uninhabited country; they keep making practice runs over us."

"How did George get out to the reservoir?"

"On horseback. His horse wandered back to the barn. I saw her there this morning, still saddled. That's when I first realized something was wrong."

"Not till this morning?"

She nodded mechanically. "Yes. Early. A little after five. Last night George said he wanted to work in the office to get ahead on the books, since he was going . . . there's a Cattlemen's convention. Oh, Lord, I'll have to call someone—"

"Sheriff Tate can take care of the notifications."

"Yes, of course. Anyway, I went out to the house—we moved into the foreman's house a year ago; Gil Potts has no family and doesn't need the room." She frowned, seeming to find it difficult to keep track of her narrative. "I read for a while, then went to bed. It didn't occur to me to worry about George. I slept right through until five, then I realized he hadn't even been to bed. I was on my way to see if he'd fallen asleep in the office, when I saw his horse, and of course he wasn't in the office. It was locked. I sounded a general alarm, and Aaron and the boys and the buckaroos rode out to look for him."

"Could they trail his horse?"

"I didn't go along, but I doubt it; it's been pretty dry lately. *They* didn't find him, anyway."

"Who did?"

"A couple of Drinkwater hands. They were just out riding fence. Spring Creek crosses the property line, and the fence was cut there."

He raised an eyebrow. "The reservoir's a long way from the fence line. On horseback, at least."

"Yes, but all that water had come down the creek, so they rode up to investigate. All that water. Conan, that was Alvin's main reservoir for his winter pastures. I just can't believe . . ." She swallowed hard, throat constricted.

"You can't believe George would blow up the dam? Is that the way it's being interpreted?"

"Oh, Tate has to consider that possibility, since it's rather obvious. Naturally, Aaron won't accept it."

"I find it a little hard to swallow, myself. Who called Tate?"

"Alvin. The two men who found—one of them rode to the ranch house to tell Alvin. He called Tate, then went out to the reservoir. Aaron and the Running S crew arrived on the scene about the same time as Tate and his deputies. I guess it's a good thing Tate was on hand, or someone else might've been killed." Her breath came out in a long sigh. "That's all I know. Tate's in the living room now, trying to get some answers out of Aaron and the boys. Conan, what are you going to do?"

He looked at her blankly, taken off guard.

"I don't know."

"Laura?"

They both turned toward the living room door. The young man standing there seemed made all of supple, tough brown leather. The Western-style shirt and Levis clung to his lean body as if they'd been tailored; a practical consideration, Conan knew, for someone to whom riding was a living, not a pleasure. His hair was nearly black, slipping down over his forehead to shadow eyes of an unusually bright blue. George had had the same intensely blue eyes, although his hair had been a tawny, sun-bleached brown.

Abraham Lincoln McFall. Conan recognized him easily enough. He would be about twenty-two now.

But Linc didn't seem to recognize him. The blue eyes reflected both suspicion and a curiously defensive attitude. It was Laura who evoked the latter; Conan didn't realize that until she spoke and Linc's attention shifted to her.

"It's all right, Linc," she said, answering a question he hadn't voiced. "You remember Conan Flagg, don't you?"

Linc admitted the memory, but almost reluctantly, asking warily, "What brings you out here?"

"An SOS of sorts, and I liked the circumstances of my last visit better. I . . . just heard about George." Linc's unresponsive stare discouraged any expression of condolence, and Conan turned uncomfortably to Laura. "I should talk to Sheriff Tate."

She nodded and led the way to the living room doors.

"Come on, I'll introduce you."

Conan remembered the stone fireplace on the wall opposite the door; the entire room had an air of familiarity the memories from his one visit here didn't explain. It was very much like the living room of the old house at the Ten-Mile; a totally masculine room whose furnishings were chosen solely for their function, and if among the overstuffed, mail-order styles there were a few fine old pieces left by previous generations, it was only because they had proved themselves in terms of utility.

It was a room without books. The shelves on either side of the window on the right wall were occupied with trophies, symbols of prowess in riding, cattle breeding, or shooting. On the left wall in a glass-fronted case by the office door was a rack of hunting guns of various makes and calibers. All the walls were hung with animal heads, glass eyes staring out in a morbid facsimile of life. It was also a room without paintings. The wall over the mantel, which might have held a portrait of an ancestor, was occupied by the head of an elk with a magnificent spread of antlers.

Between the glass-eyed hunting trophies and the curious human occupants of the room, Conan felt as if he'd suddenly stepped onto a stage. Or mounted a scaffold.

The two men sitting on the couch to his right were both strangers. The older of them wore a tie and conservative business suit, which with his thin-soled shoes marked him as a town dweller. The other wore dusty boots and Levis and a curled-brim Stetson.

Conan found himself giving this man a second look, and wondering why. One of the buckaroos, or, more likely, the foreman. A weather-worn face caged in prominent bones, sage gray eyes set in a squint made permanent by years under the sun.

The man in the chair to the right of the fireplace was uniformed, complete with star, Stetson, and revolver. He'd done his share of riding at one time or another; his hands showed it, but with the arrival of middle age, he was putting on weight, most of it accumulating in the area just above his low-slung belt. This would be Sheriff Joe Tate.

Conan looked for Deputy Harley Ross and found him in the corner to his left, leaning against a high counter. No. A bar. A new addition, and an unexpected one.

The young man slumped in the chair near the bar could only be Ted. Theodore Roosevelt McFall. He was fourteen when Conan had last seen him, still a boy, but he was a grown man now, with big, sun-browned, capable hands and shoulders that strained the seams of his shirt. Conan wasn't prepared for his resemblance to George. The same tawny hair, strong cheekbones and jawline, and intense blue eyes. He wondered if Ted had the same slow, wry smile.

He wondered, too, if he'd been purposely avoiding, or delaying, recognizing Aaron McFall.

The elder McFall sat in an armchair to the left of the fireplace, and the genetic source of his three sons' blue eyes was obvious; Aaron's burned incandescent from under white brows. Unlike the sheriff, he hadn't gone to paunch with age. He might be a little thicker in the torso, but his posture and general physical condition were at odds with his hair, still thick, but white as snow—or ice.

Yet the last five years had exacted more of a toll than would be expected, incising the lines in his face, sinking his eyes deeper into their sockets. Perhaps it was only the last year, or the last few hours.

"I know you," he said sharply. "You're Henry Flagg's boy. What the hell're you doin' here?"

CHAPTER 5.

At that abrupt greeting, Laura stiffened as if she'd been slapped.

"He's here because George *asked* him to come."

That was something Conan would have preferred to reveal himself, in his own time, but the damage was done.

Aaron said curtly, "George never said a damn thing to *me* about him."

Laura sighed as she went to the chair Ted vacated and silently offered her.

"Thanks, Ted. Aaron, he didn't say anything about it to me, either. Oh—I've neglected the introductions. Dr. Walter Maxwell . . ." This was the elderly man in the business suit; then the man at the other end of the couch, "Gil Potts, our foreman. And Sheriff Joe Tate. Conan Flagg, an old friend of George's and mine." Then she looked up at Ted, standing by her chair, and added, "You met Ted, of course, Conan, but that was a few years ago."

As the small ceremonies of shaking hands and exchanging guarded amenities were observed, Conan noted that Linc was standing near the door, arms folded, watching everyone's every move, particularly his.

When the courtesies were concluded, Joe Tate resettled his hat on his head and himself in his chair and squinted up at Conan.

"You say George asked you to come, Mr. Flagg? Mebbe you can clear up a little question of a phone call we been wonderin' about. You call him yesterday evenin'?"

Conan found both that deduction and his cool, thoughtful tone impressive.

"Yes, I called him. It was about six."

"Tallies. Jest a friendly call?"

"No. A business call."

"I s'pose George had some dealin's with the Ten-Mile."

Conan hesitated, not because he was reluctant to explain George's call to Tate; he simply objected to doing so in such public surroundings. But there was an alternative to verbal explanation. He took George's letter from his breast pocket and handed it to Tate.

"I think this will answer your questions, Sheriff."

"Well, I'm obliged, Mr. Flagg."

"That from George?" Aaron demanded. "What's it about?"

"Can't say yet." Tate donned bifocals and read the letter, frowning all the while, then took time to put his glasses back into his shirt pocket before turning a speculative eye on Conan.

"This what you and George talked about on the phone?"

But Aaron cut in impatiently, "Hand it here, Joe."

Tate went up a few notches in Conan's estimation when, with a questioning look, he left it to Conan to decide whether that sharp command should be obeyed, and when Conan reached for the letter, returned it to him without hesitation.

"Thank you, Sheriff. Yes, this is what we talked about."

Aaron shot to the edge of his chair.

"Jest a gawdamned minute! That letter come from George, didn't it? He was my *son*, and if it's got anythin' to do—"

"Aaron, please," Dr. Maxwell put in, quietly insistent. "If you don't simmer down, you'll work yourself up to another heart attack."

That possibility didn't seem to concern Aaron, but it distracted him enough for Tate to resume his low-key interrogation.

"Well, Mr. Flagg, an honest-to-God private detective is somethin' we don't often run into in these parts."

Conan restrained any overt expression of annoyance at that oblique but revealing query as he opened his wallet to his private investigator's license.

"Honest enough," he quipped as he handed it to Tate. "But if you want a character reference, try Steve Travers. He's chief of detectives for the Salem division of the state police."

"I've had some dealin's with Travers. He come from around Pendleton, too, didn't he?" Then he frowned. "This address says Holliday Beach. I thought you was from the Ten-Mile."

"I am, but Holliday Beach is my home now."

Tate mulled that over, appraising him with a skeptical squint as he returned the billfold.

"What do you intend to do now, Mr. Flagg? I mean, now that George is . . ." He didn't finish that, glancing uncomfortably at Laura, but she was intent on Conan, waiting for his answer.

"I'm obligated to George, alive or dead. If I can, I'll meet that obligation."

"*Obligation!*" Aaron repeated contemptuously. "Damn it, we got trouble enough already, so you can jest take your obligation and chuck it! George is dead, and he don't need you no more, and *we* sure as hell don't."

"Aaron!" Laura came to her feet, white and trembling. "Conan was a friend of George's, and he's here at his invitation. He's also *my* friend, and I won't have a friend of mine treated that way."

Aaron seemed vaguely confused at that charged protest, but it served to cool his antagonism, at least temporarily. His pride precluded a direct apology to Conan, but not a lamely placating gesture.

"I said we got enough trouble, but it ain't of your makin'. You're welcome to stay on here if you want."

Conan managed to keep a straight face. "Thank you."

"But if this here obligation has anything to do with George bein' murdered"—he sent Tate an accusing glance—"I wanta know about it."

"Oh, Aaron . . ." Laura sank back into her chair with a disspirited sigh.

"Well, I got a right to know," he insisted. "He was my son. Now, what was that letter about?"

"I don't recognize your right to know," Conan said tightly, "simply because George was your son. I *will* discuss it with you because it concerns the ranch, but only in private."

"In private!" The color began moving up into his face. "Listen, Flagg, this ain't one of your fancy corporation ranches. This here's a *family* business. Always has been and always will be. I got no secrets from the family." He seemed to realize the room was a little crowded then, and added, "Joe and Harley Ross got a right to know 'cause they're the law. As for Walt . . ." This with a glance at Dr. Maxwell. "Well, he's jest about one of the family."

Conan said nothing, only sending a questioning look at the foreman, Gil Potts, who met it with a level confidence soon explained by Aaron's response.

"Gil's one of the family, too."

Conan shrugged at that. "You run your business your way, I'll run mine my way. I'll discuss it with you in private."

"*Discuss* it in perdition, then, for all I care!"

"Oh, Conan, you may as well tell him now," Laura put in dully. "He'll spread it all over the county anyway, if he wants to."

Aaron said reproachfully, "Now, Laura, you got no call to say that."

"Don't I? Conan, please. I can't . . . there's been too much to deal with at once."

He studied her taut, pallid face, and recognizing the futility of further resistance and the price it was exacting from her, he surrendered the letter to Aaron, putting an ironic emphasis on the last word as he said, "I'll at least ask that this be kept in the family."

Aaron ignored that and for some time frowned over the letter, his intentness revealing not only his emotional state, but a myopia he refused to recognize by wearing glasses.

"'. . . or somebody will end up dead.'" He read the words numbly, as if they didn't make sense, then roused himself and looked up at Conan, his suspicion apparently unallayed.

"So, George hired you to play private detective."

Conan's temper was getting short.

"I don't *play* private detective."

"Whatever you call it, then. He says here he wants you to help him 'get to the bottom of this.' The trouble between me and Alvin? Is that what he meant?"

"Obviously. Now this 'trouble' includes his death."

Aaron snorted derisively and tossed the letter onto the table by his chair.

"How much was George aimin' to *pay* you for gettin' to the bottom?" Then, perhaps recognizing a danger signal in Conan's eyes, he went on defensively, "Well, it don't take no detective to figger out what's plain as day."

Conan went to the table and retrieved the letter.

"Apparently George didn't agree."

"And look what come of that. If he'd listened to me—" He paused, the muscles of his jaw swelling. "Anyhow, it don't take no detective to figger out who killed him."

This shaft was aimed at Tate, who was occupied with unwrapping and lighting a formidable cigar, a task he finished before he responded.

"So, you got it all figgered out, Aaron?"

"Damn right, and so've you, so how come you're sittin' here jawin' while that sonofabitch gets off free as a bird?"

Tate emitted a leisurely puff of smoke.

"You mean Alvin?"

"Who'd you *think* I meant? The President of the United States?"

"Well, y'know, I gotta be sure I have a case before I take a man to court. If Alvin *did* kill him, I need a motive. The only one I can come up with now is he must've found George foolin' around with his dam and flew mad over it."

"What d'you mean, foolin' around with his dam?"

"*Somebody* blew it up, Aaron."

"It sure as hell wasn't *George!*"

"Then what was he doin' out to the rezzavoy?"

"I don't *know!* But him bein' there don't mean he dynamited the dam. That's what that bassard *wants* you to think. Mebbe he blew it up hisself so's ever' damn fool 'round here *would* figger it that way!"

Tate apparently took no insult at being lumped with local damn fools.

"Well, that could be," he conceded, "but it still don't tell me why Alvin would wanta kill him."

"For the same reason he's been poisonin' my cattle and burnin' my haystacks! You want a sensible reason for *anything* from a man like *that?*"

"But you ain't the only spread around here had trouble lately."

"I *told* you, I don't know a damn thing about the trouble Alvin's had. I never so much as set foot on his land."

Tate only nodded. "Funny, though, Alvin told me the same thing about the trouble *you* been havin'."

For a moment, Conan thought Aaron would attack Tate physically, but before he could even get a coherent word out, he was distracted.

"Pa, you know Joe has to get court proof." It was Ted, miserably apologetic, pleading not so much for agreement as for peace. But he was looking to the wrong source for that.

Aaron turned on him, his features rigid and crimsoned.

"Who're you speakin' for? Me? Or your brother? Why the hell don't you jest go on and move in with that little piece of skirt? You can't even show any loyalty at a time like this! But I guess you already showed your colors when you took—"

"Aaron, for God's sake!" Laura pressed her clenched hands to her forehead. "At a time like this—can't you show any—any *feeling* for anyone? Any vestige of human—" Then abruptly she rose and ran to the door. "I can't stand this! I can't *stand* it!"

She was gone before anyone could stop her, and in the ensuing silence Linc glared at his father.

"You satisfied now, Pa?"

He didn't stay to hear any answer Aaron might have made, but turned on his heel and exited, calling Laura's name. Afterward, there were a few uncomfortable shiftings and exchanges of glances in the room, but Aaron was oblivious to them, staring blankly at the space where Linc had been. Yet if he regretted his behavior, it was obvious he had no intention of admitting it. Conan watched him settle back in his chair in bristling silence, and wondered when Aaron McFall would weep for his son. Only in solitude, if then.

"So, you figger you got an obligation to George?" After the tense silence, that abrupt charge was startling.

Conan nodded. "Yes."

"Then you wanta pl—to get to the bottom of this thing, like George said?"

"If I'm not stopped."

"What could stop you?"

"Either you or Sheriff Tate. Especially you."

"Well now, I can't speak for Joe, here, but I won't put nothin' in your way."

Conan studied him skeptically.

"So. Why the change of heart, Aaron?"

"Why? Look, I figger it this way, Flagg: you and me is headed up the same pass. We both wanta nail the man who killed George. Right? I *know* who killed him, but Joe needs his court proof. So, mebbe you can come up with it."

"Maybe. Apparently, you haven't considered the possibility that Drinkwater is innocent."

His eyes narrowed until the blue was invisible.

"Consider all you damn please, but if you get the man who killed George, it'll be Alvin."

"I can't argue that now." He pulled in a deep breath, then nodded. "So, we're in agreement. Momentarily. But before I go ahead with an investigation, you'd better be sure you understand my terms. First, George is still my client. Not you. Second, this 'court proof' you're so willing to let me search for may *not* point to Drinkwater, but I won't ignore or change any facts to satisfy you."

"It'll point to Alvin."

"Another thing, you said—" He stopped as Linc returned, gave his father a single cold glance, then resumed his position by the door like a sentry.

It was Dr. Maxwell who asked, "How's Laura?"

"She's all right. Said she'd be out to the cookhouse."

Aaron seemed even less inclined to show any remorse in Linc's presence, ignoring his return entirely.

"So, what's the other thing?" he asked of Conan.

"You said you wouldn't put anything in my way. I'll interpret that as an offer of full cooperation."

"Whatever you want. I mean, within reason."

"No. Not if you expect to draw the boundaries of reason. You have my word, I won't ask anything I don't consider necessary to the investigation, but *I'll* draw the lines."

Before Aaron could protest, Linc burst out, "Investigation? What's goin' on here?"

Aaron said curtly, "George hired Flagg to get to the bottom of this trouble. I know who's at the bottom, so if he can come up with any proof of it, well and good."

"What? Damn it, we don't need some outsider stickin' his nose into—"

"Listen, boy, it ain't up to you to decide what we need." Then as Linc lapsed into smoldering silence, he turned to Conan. "All right, you got your cooperation."

Conan made no response to that, addressing his next question to Joe Tate.

"Laura told me George worked late in the office last night. Did anyone see him leave it?"

"No, but Morgan Hayes—he's one of the buckaroos—says he seen a light in the office right before he turned in. That was about eight."

"The door was locked when Laura came looking for George early this morning. Has anyone been in the office since?"

"Don't guess anybody's had time to. Far 's I know, it's still locked. Harley, give that door a try."

The deputy went to the door on the left-hand wall; when it refused to open, Conan turned to Aaron.

"Who has keys to it?"

"Well, I do, and the boys. And Gil, naturally."

"May I have them?" It wasn't a request; it was a demand and a test, and Aaron seemed to recognize both.

"Now listen here, I got a ranch to run, and I can't—"

"George spent the last few hours before he died in that room; there may be evidence bearing on his death in there, and if so, I want to be sure no one gets to it before I do. And that's the last time I'll explain myself to you. You offered cooperation, and I'm calling you."

Aaron's mouth tightened into a thin, hard line, but at length he reached into his pants pocket, removed a key from a jangling ring, and tossed it to him. It fell short, forcing Conan to pick it up off the floor. Gil Potts was more courteous, rising to dig into his pocket, even offering a brief smile as he presented his key.

"Don't have much use for the thing, anyhow."

Ted was equally cooperative; it was Linc who threatened real resistance.

"He's got no right comin' in here and—"

"I give him the right," Aaron said testily. "Let him have your key." Then, when Linc had complied, "All right, Flagg, anything else you want in the way of *cooperation?*"

"Not at the moment. Sheriff, what about George's horse? Where is it?"

"Out to the barn. Nobody's touched it 'cept my deppity. I had him look her over."

"Did he find anything?"

"Don't know yet. Haven't talked to Ollie." He rose, took a last puff on his cigar, and tossed it into the fireplace. "Come on, we'll take a look. Aaron, you can go ahead with the funeral arrangements. Have Roy get in touch with me. Doc, any idea when you'll be finished?"

Walter Maxwell had also risen and stood working the brim of his hat in his hands, regarding Aaron with the tired, cognizant eyes of one familiar with every form of grief.

"I'll take care of the autopsy today. Aaron, I'm going out to see Laura, and I'll leave some pills with her; something for both of you, to help you sleep." Then with a glance at Ted and Linc, "You boys, too. Won't hurt you, and it might help."

Ted said, "Thanks, Doc."

"Sure. Aaron . . . I'm sorry." Then with a long sigh he turned to the door. "Just don't get yourself riled up."

As he shuffled away, an unknowing observer would guess him to be the bereaved father, not Aaron McFall.

CHAPTER 6.

"Mr. Flagg, I don't know you from Adam," Tate observed as they crossed the graveled yard between the house and the barn with a pair of shaggy, mongrel dogs tagging along curiously. "Guess I better give Steve Travers a call."

"I don't think you have any alternative, in your position, Sheriff." The wind had died and the air felt hot to the touch. Conan looked ahead to the barn, eyes aching with the harsh sunglare reflected from its whitewashed walls.

It was an old building of beautiful proportions, the roof coming to a point over the loft in the center, then breaking into a shallower angle at each side. A louvered cupola sat the ridgepole, graced by a weather vane on which an ebony-enameled stallion pranced. Surrounding the barn on three sides was a maze of corrals with skinned posts weathered to satiny silver. To his left, beyond the corrals, Conan saw a pair of buckaroos lounging on the bunkhouse porch, but no one else was visible except the deputy standing in the barn door by a sorrel mare.

"Guess Ollie unsaddled her," Tate commented. "Told him to keep ever'body away from her. Yep, I better have a word with Travers, but I don't figger it'll change my mind none."

"I suppose I'd have to know how your mind's set before I take any encouragement from that."

Tate shrugged. "Well, I wouldn't usually take to any outsider hornin' in on somethin' like this, but y'know, I always admired young George. Smart as a whip, but he kep' both feet square on the ground. So, I figger he had his reasons for callin' you, and they'd be good ones. And then—how much did he tell you about the trouble here?"

"Quite a bit in general terms, but not much in detail."

"I can give you plenty of *de*tails; got a file a foot thick on this jackpot, and I never got a handhold on it. Like chasin' smoke. But you, now, mebbe you can get a bead on it from another slant. I figger it's worth a try."

Conan smiled obliquely. "Desperation makes strange alliances. Well, I'll try not to get in your way, and if I can help you, that's only fair. I won't get far without *your* help."

"Well now, that's sorta what I was hopin' you'd say. Mebbe we can scratch each other's back." He tilted his head to give Conan an amiable grin. "But you take one step out of line, Mr. Flagg, you'll find out your welcome in Harney County's run out."

Conan nodded acceptance, knowing full well the threat wasn't idle. The sheriff was on home turf here; he could close almost any door at which Conan might knock.

"Ho, Ollie." Tate touched his fingers to his hat brim as they approached the deputy. "This here's Conan Flagg. He was a friend of George's. Ollie Cartwright."

The deputy offered a terse acknowledgment while Tate ran a hand along the horse's neck.

"Easy, girl. Got herself purty well lathered up sometime or 'nother. Where's her saddle and riggin', Ollie?"

"Jest inside the barn there. I looked it over."

"You find anything on it?"

"Nope. If George left here carryin' anything, it was in his pockets. Wasn't even a lariat on the saddle."

Conan frowned at the white mud caked on the hooves.

"Was she curried before George took her out last night?"

Cartwright glanced at Tate before answering.

"She took outa here clean. I asked some of the hands."

Tate pushed his hat back to scratch his forehead.

"Wonder where she got into all that mud. Mebbe the rezzavoy. Almost have to be; most of the cricks is dried up this time of year, and we didn't have no rain last night."

Conan searched his pockets for a container, but the plastic evidence bags he usually used were still in his luggage. Finally, he took out the envelope containing George's letter.

"Sheriff, I want to get a sample of that mud. Will you hold her head for me?"

He reached for the reins, cautioning, "Jest don't move too quick and get her spooked." Then he added with a short laugh, "Sorry, forgot you ain't a greenhorn."

Conan kept a wary eye on the mare's hind legs as he scraped some mud from her forefoot into the envelope. She wasn't pleased at a stranger taking such liberties, but restrained herself to nervous shiftings. He gave her shoulder a grateful pat as he straightened and turned to Tate.

"Thanks, Sheriff. I'd like to see that saddle now."

"Come on, we'll both take a look."

If Ollie Cartwright had missed anything, it also escaped Conan's eye. There were no saddlebags, nor even a toolbag tied to the leather strings; nothing in which anything might be carried. Finally he rose, frowning.

"You know, if George went to the reservoir intending to blow up the dam, he couldn't have gone empty-handed."

Tate nodded agreement. "I know. Course, I'm not so sure it was him who blowed it up. It looks bad, the way this damn feud's been goin'. Most folks'll figger it that way. But there wasn't nothin' in his pockets 'cept a pack of cigarettes. If he *did* handle any dynamite, though, we can mebbe get some traces off his hands."

"What about gloves?"

"We didn't find none on him nor anywheres near. Ollie, get somebody to see to that mare, then round up Harley and Cece. We better get back to town." He began walking toward the two county cars parked in front of the house.

"'Nother queer thing, Mr. Flagg, somethin' else we didn't find. Wire cutters."

Conan looked at him sharply, no doubt asking the same question Tate had already asked himself. How did the fence crossing Spring Creek get cut if George didn't do it?

"Interesting, Sheriff, but a pair of wire cutters could get lost in the debris from the explosion, and when was the fence last seen intact?"

"I know. I could give you half a dozen mebbes for that. For almost ever'thing that's happened 'round here this last year."

"Right now I'd just like a maybe to explain why George went to the reservoir. When I talked to him last night, he mentioned it, but only as an example of past cooperation between Aaron and Drinkwater. He didn't seem at all concerned about it, and he said nothing to suggest he intended going out there." He sank into musing silence for a moment, then, "How long a ride is it to the reservoir?"

"A good hour 'n a half at a walk, and there ain't many stretches you could go any faster 'less you wanta break your horse's leg. 'Specially at night. There was a full moon, but it'd still be a slow ride."

"One of the hands saw a light in the office at eight o'clock. Did anyone see a light later, or see or hear George ride out?"

"If they did, they ain't sayin' so."

"Have you some idea where everyone was after eight?"

"You mean like alibis? Well, the buckaroos was in the bunkhouse. Some of 'em got up a poker game, but they'd all turned in by nine. Days start before sunup out here; ain't many night owls around. Lessee, Laura went out to her house at seven-thirty, and Aaron and Ted turned in 'bout then, too. Wil Mosely was down to Jenturer to pick up some auto parts."

Conan was having a hard time translating, "Jenturer," finally connecting it with the nearby town of Juntura.

"What—oh, yes, Wil Mosely. Shop foreman, isn't he?"

"Yep. His wife Irene's ranch cook. She went to bed soon as she got supper cleaned up; little before eight. She says Wil come home 'bout nine-thirty. The Moselys been workin' here for near twenty years, y'know, and they never would even listen to a bad word 'gainst the McFalls."

"Was George in the office when Wil came home?"

"He says he didn't see a light in the windah. Lessee, the Messican couple turned in at eight, too, but they're out anyhow. Neither one ever sat a horse; scared pink of 'em."

"And that leaves Linc and Gil Potts."

"They went into town last night. Left here at seven."

"Into Burns? Why?"

"Oh, jest to kick up their heels, mostly." He came to a stop, putting his back to the house, frowning absently up at the sky. "Anything I despise, it's gossip, but you'll be hearin' plenty of that. 'Specially 'bout Linc."

Conan nodded. "When I was here five years ago, George was wondering when—or if—Linc was going to settle down."

"Well, he ain't settled yet. Fact is, he's jest got wilder. Aaron sent him off to Oregon State a couple years back. Prob'ly George's idea. He took so well to college, guess he figgered it'd be good for Linc, too."

"That's usually an error. What happened?"

"Oh, Linc come home after two quarters. It ain't that he's dumb; jest seems like a fish outa water wherever he happens to be. And he had somethin' eatin' at him then. Y'see, Linc and Alvin's oldest girl, Charlotte, used to see a lot of each other."

Conan raised an eyebrow. "When was that?"

"Since they was kids, really. I always sorta hoped Charl would settle him down, and I still think she might've, but Aaron and Alvin weren't neither one too happy 'bout them pairin' up. I don't know what happened, but they split up right before Linc went off to college, then while he was gone, she come down with diabeteez. Real bad, too. Doc said she was walkin' a tightrope ever' minute of her life with the ins'lin and all that." He paused, briefly distracted. "I guess she finally took a step the wrong way."

"What do you mean?"

"Well, she died. That was two years ago, right after Linc come home from college. He took it hard, too. I figger that's one reason he's got so wild since."

"You said they parted company before he went to college; did they get back together afterwards? Before she died?"

"Well, I don't rightly know. If they did, they kep' it quiet. Course, Aaron and Alvin was dead set against it. Damn fools, both of 'em. First, Alvin sayin' Linc's too wild; never make a fit husband for *his* girl. Then Aaron takin' insult and sayin' Charl wasn't good enough for *his* son. In the end, it didn't matter a damn; not with Charl dead." He turned at the sound of distant voices, watching his deputies, Aaron, Linc, and Gil Potts leave the house and walk together to the cars.

"There's somethin' else you'll prob'ly be hearin' about, Mr. Flagg. Before this feud got fired up, Ted was romancin' Bridgie Drinkwater. That's Alvin's youngest, and the only one left home. He has a boy, Austin, but he didn't stick with the ranch. Career Army, and a major by now. He's over in Germany some'eres."

Conan looked across at Aaron, remembering his caustic attack on Ted. That "little piece of skirt" was Alvin Drinkwater's daughter. But something else in that tirade was still unexplained: Ted had already shown his colors. In courting Bridgie? Or was there more to it? But he deferred that inquiry for the moment.

"Sheriff, just how 'wild' is Linc?"

"Well, I never had to th'ow him in jail." Tate resumed his ambling walk toward the cars. "Thought I would once on an A and B, but it turned out the other feller swang first. Mostly, he jest hits the booze and commences to holler and whoop, and when he starts dragstrippin' in that fancy for'n car, he's a menace. And I ain't had any complaints wrote out, y'understand, but I guess he's a menace with women, too, and he don't seem to mind much if they're married. Now, that worries me. He's li'ble to end up ventilated with a shotgun. But sometimes I ain't sure he'd care."

They were nearing the cars where the deputies, Aaron, and the subject of their conversation were standing, and Tate lowered his voice slightly.

"Anyhow, what got me off on all this was alibis. Like I said, Linc and Gil was in town, and neither one of 'em is sure exac'ly when they come home, but it wasn't before three A.M. They saw the bars in town closed."

"Does Potts often join Linc in the heel-kicking?" He frowned as he realized the foreman had disappeared from the group ahead.

"Matter of fact, he does, but it ain't what you might think. Gil's took a likin' to the boy, and he's smarter'n Aaron or even George was about him. Keeps an easy rein, y'know, but never lets him get his head down so's he can really start buckin'. Since Gil come to the Runnin' S, I ain't had nearly so much trouble keepin' Linc outa jail."

"When did Potts join the Running S?"

"Oh, 'bout a year and a half ago." Then he gave Conan a crooked smile. "Gil used to ride for the Double D."

"He what?"

"Yep. Damn small world 'round these parts. Howdy, Aaron. Me and the boys'll take outa here and leave you be. Ollie, you and Cece might as well get goin'." Then as the two deputies departed with a slamming of doors and a rattling roar, Tate sauntered over to the other car, motioning Ross in, talking over the roof to Aaron. "I'm sorry as hell about this, you know that."

"I know, Joe." He turned a suspicious squint on Conan. "All I want is to see it done with."

"I'm doin' my best, and Mr. Flagg and me sorta come to an agreement. Can't say I like an outsider nosin' 'round in this, but if George hired him, and you go along . . . well, all right. Him and me'll work together."

That assurance obviously did nothing to brighten Linc's day, but however transparent his feelings, he wasn't prepared to voice them again in Aaron's presence. Conan almost regretted that; it would have kept Aaron in his camp out of sheer perverseness, and the elder McFall was having second thoughts.

"Glad to hear you two hit it off so good," Aaron said to Tate, but, like Linc, his eyes never strayed from Conan.

But Joe Tate was a man of rare good sense. He favored Conan with a cool look and replied, "Well, now, I never said we was signin' up to be friends for life. I don't b'lieve in payin' out on a nag till I seen it run. Talk to you later, Aaron."

When he had departed in a spray of dust and gravel, Aaron stalked away with the curt announcement, "Me and Linc's goin' into town to see Roy Caplin about the funeral."

Neither of them looked back, Linc following his father to the long, metal-roofed shed extending from the corner of the picket fence. Conan wondered if Aaron would choose the shining black Continental for this occasion. He didn't. Linc drove him away in the black Buick station wagon.

CHAPTER 7.

Ted McFall was waiting at the front door. He looked pale and haggard, but managed a constrained smile.

"I'll help you get your stuff up to your room."

He took the suitcase while Conan perched the Stetson on his

head, draped the sheepskin jacket over one arm, and with the brief-case in his free hand followed him up the stairs. As they reached the top, he glanced into the open doors ahead. The boys' bedrooms, probably, each taking up a corner of the house.

"Where's Laura, Ted?"

"She's still out to the cookhouse. Your room's down this way." He made an about-face and led Conan along the balustrade surrounding the stairwell toward the front of the house. "She likes to work in the cookhouse. I mean, she always did, and mebbe now . . ." He con-cluded with an expressive shrug, then, "Here it is."

A door opened off each side of the hall; as Ted turned into the one on the left, Conan glanced into the other. The master bed-room, no doubt, and only Aaron would occupy that.

But the guest room was impressive enough; a spacious, airy room the same size as the living room, which was directly below it. The windows were in the same relative positions, two on the long wall opposite the door, and a big double one looking out over the front porch. The room was obviously a repository for several generations' "good" furniture, including a beautifully carved bedstead, probably a gift to an ancestral McFall couple on the occasion of their wedding.

Ted put the suitcase down by the bed and waved in the direction of the door on the left wall.

"The bathroom's in there. Laura said to tell you if you need any-thing, jest holler."

Conan deposited his load and went to one of the windows on the opposite wall; it looked across to the barn through a mosaic of leaves. Then he turned, studying Ted, who waited uncertainly, hands thrust in his pockets. He'd rather be elsewhere, Conan knew, and alone.

"Is this the first . . . the first time you've lost someone close?"

Ted stiffened, immediately on the defensive, but after giving Conan a close scrutiny, he seemed to relax a little.

"I guess it is. Ma died when—when I was born. There never was anybody I was really close to. Bert Kimmons, mebbe, but it wasn't like he was family." An uncomfortable pause, then, "Mr. Flagg, did you . . . was you and George close?"

"No. We were friends. It isn't hurting me as much as it is you." He looked away, then down at his watch; the morning was nearly gone, and in any case, he had no more desire than Ted did to pursue the subject of grief.

"Ted, I want to see the reservoir. Do you know if that fence is still down?"

"Guess so. Joe Tate said nobody was to touch it."

"I'll need a horse. Can you take care of that?"

"Well, you can have Molly. She's mine. Sort of a pet horse, I guess; no good for workin', but she's gentle as a milk pen calf." He stopped, his face going red. "I don't mean to say you'd need a—a gentle . . . I mean . . ."

Conan laughed as he lifted his suitcase onto the bed.

"It's a long time since I looked a bronc in the eye. Give me a few minutes to change clothes."

Ted waited patiently through the transformation, and Conan refrained from questioning him; he needed a little time to get used to this stranger in their midst.

But as he buttoned the trim-waisted shirt and belted the hip-hugging Levis, Conan felt himself less a stranger. The metamorphosis went deeper than costuming. It was not only a step into a familiar river of remembered experience, but a recognition of his present context.

The boots seemed to epitomize that. Last night, when he took them from their storage place, they struck him as vaguely ridiculous; thirteen inches high, toes molded to a cramping point, high heels sloping in rakishly. But now, with the prospect of a long ride before him, they begin to make sense. They were designed for function, not effect; to assure a man's efficiency and survival on horseback, and for some tasks, there was still no viable substitute for the horse; not in this country or in this business.

The Stetson was of the same ilk; dust-colored beaver felt with a wide, curling brim. It could serve as protection from sun, rain, or snow, as a goad or semaphore, or even as a water bucket. Vanity couldn't be separated from function in clothing, and a buckaroo might spend a month's wages on his hat and boots, but function was of necessity his primary concern. These were tools more than adornment, and as Conan settled the hat on his head he found its uncompromising weight and sturdiness eminently reassuring.

He nodded to Ted. "Let's go have a look at Molly."

When they passed from the white, hot morning sunlight into the cavernous darkness of the barn, Conan took a deep breath, savoring the cool, earth-animal-hay smell. Ted led the way into the tack room, where the scent of leather was added to the rich mélange. The walls were festooned with bridles, halters, hackamores, reins, and lariats, among them a few of braided rawhide, masterworks of an unrecognized folk art. Ten saddles draped with blankets and chaps straddled wooden jacks.

"You—uh, mind usin' George's saddle?" Ted asked. "You could

use my rig, but I'll need it if I'm gonna take you out to the rezzavoy." It was an awkward situation for him; he was reluctant to ask Conan to use something belonging to a dead friend, but found it equally unthinkable to offer any saddle other than his own.

"No, I don't mind, Ted." Conan found the situation awkward for another reason: he wasn't planning on an escort.

Ted took a bridle from a hook and swung the saddle onto his back, bending a little under its forty pounds.

"Molly, now, you can use her anytime you want. She's a good ridin' horse. Laura takes her out a lot."

Most of the stalls were empty, but a few horses were always kept in the barn so they'd be available on short notice. Night horses, these reserves were called. Ted opened one of the stalls to be greeted affectionately by a blue roan Appaloosa mare. He laughed as she nuzzled his hip pocket until he produced a few dusty cubes of sugar.

"That's Laura's doin'. Got her spoilt rotten. Hey, Mol, you pineared plug."

Molly, an elegant little creature who could never honestly be called a plug, submitted graciously to having the blanket and saddle flung upon her back. In the stall opposite, a muffled whinnie attracted Conan to another piece of horseflesh that was anything but a plug; a tall, black stallion, its coat gleaming silkily in the soft light.

"This another pet horse?" he asked.

Ted looked up from threading the latigo and gave a curt laugh as he glanced across at the stallion.

"Don't let Linc hear you say that. That's Domino. Pa put out five thousand for that stud; give it to Linc for graduation. And I wouldn't think too serious about takin' him out for a run. Linc's sorta short-fused when it comes to Domino. He ain't one of the cavvy."

"I'll remember that. Besides, I don't like the way he shows the whites of his eyes. Let me put on her bridle."

"Sure. Jest give her a little sweet talk."

Molly was remarkably amenable. At first she set her teeth against the bit, but apparently decided she liked what he was saying, or at least the way he said it. The bridle in place, he smoothed her mane, then turned to Ted.

"I don't think you should go to the reservoir with me."

He frowned questionably. "What d'you mean?"

"Well, I *should* get permission from Drinkwater before I cross that fence line. I know that, but I also know I have no legal authority, and I doubt he'll put out a welcome mat for me. I want to see the reservoir before anyone else gets in there and tramps around. I

won't disturb anything or make trouble, but if anyone's going to tres-
pass on Drinkwater land, it's better if I do it. Alone."

Ted leaned against the stall gate, intent on the toe of his boot
scuffing out a bare strip of dirt in the straw.

"Well, I guess so, but it don't seem—"

"Are you afraid I'll get lost?"

He was, but he called up a laugh.

"If you do, jest give Mol her head; she'll come back to the barn
sooner or later. Well, I s'pose if you jest follered Spring Crick—it
crosses the road a half mile down—it'll take you to the rezzavoy. It's
about six miles."

"That doesn't sound like too difficult a navigational problem.
Come on, Molly."

He led her outside to mount, an elementary precaution so ingrained it wasn't a conscious decision. If a horse was going to buck,
the rider was well advised to be clear of walls, posts, or gates. The
same unconscious caution dictated his method of mounting, turning
the stirrup around, facing Molly's hindquarters, then making a 180-
degree turn as he swung up into the saddle. Ted laughed at that.

"You can mount up squaw-style with ol' Mol. Never bucked a
jump." Then he frowned, shading his eyes with one hand as he
peered into the distance. "Oh, damn."

Conan found the object of his chargin: a plume of dust rising
from the road.

"What is it, Ted?"

"Cattle truck from the feedlot at Boise. I forgot they was due
today, and I guess Pa did too." For a moment, the reason for that
forgetfulness seemed to overwhelm him, then his mouth thinned
into a firm line. "We got a contract to meet, and them damn cows
should be in the corral already." He started to turn away, then, "You
sure you'll be—"

"I have absolute faith in Molly's homing instinct."

"Okay. Luck." And with that he struck off toward the bunkhouse,
his peremptory orders flushing buckaroos and sending them about
their business at a run.

Conan watched curiously. The foreman, Gil Potts, was among the
hands galvanized into action, and he toed Ted's mark with as much
alacrity as the others. But it was Ted's confident competence that interested Conan. It was so much at odds with his attitude and behavior up to this point.

CHAPTER 8.

The wide, parched bed of Spring Creek wound the path of least resistance through gullied hills and across alkali flats in an indifferent silence. As the sun reached zenith, more prudent creatures sought the shade of juniper and sage, but Conan wore his own shade—the Stetson and his sunglasses.

The flood unleashed by the demolished dam was increasingly evident as he rode upstream, first in swaths of wet 'dobe already crazed under the searing sun, then in glistening sinks of mud, and finally in linking strands of moving water reddened by its burden of iron-stained earth. It was like seeing someone bleeding to death.

He stopped when he reached the property line. The sheared barbed wire spiraled across a morass of mud threaded with an indecipherable tangle of tracks. Hopeless. The reservoir would, no doubt, be equally hopeless.

In this spirit of pessimism, he dismounted to examine the broken fence. The wires showed off-center ridges in cross-section, the mark of a tool in common use in this country, but seldom individually owned. Wire cutters were ranch tools, available to any ranch hand who needed them.

As he continued upstream, he kept Molly near the bank to avoid the treacherous mud. At times he had to leave the stream bed, but he stayed in it as much as possible, hoping for the miracle of something overlooked, and trying to make sense of the tracks. Between the Double D, the Black Stallion, and the county sheriff's office, at least twenty men and horses had tramped the mile between the fence and the reservoir.

He saw the grove of junipers ahead and guessed they grew on the banks of the reservoir, but he was intent on the ground. There was no sound to warn him; he was enjoying the quiet peculiar to places uninhabited by men and machines, lulled by the steady thuds of Molly's hooves and the leathery creaking of the saddle. He was only a few hundred yards from the ruins of the dam when the shot ruptured the silence.

Molly screamed alarm and reared as a spray of dirt sprang up near her forefeet, and Conan felt himself plunging backward. He checked his instinctive impulse to pull on the reins, grabbed for the saddle-horn, Molly's mane whipping his face as he strained forward, then rocked back when she lurched into a staggering run, stumbled, and nearly threw him again before she fell into the creek bank.

He was too consumed with anger to consider his good fortune in getting pinned against the soft bank rather than a rockier surface. He shouted Molly to her feet and up the bank, heels in her flanks, and urged her into a dead run.

The sniper was in clear view, mounted on a bay whose shadowy color blended all too well with the junipers. At his sudden charge, she turned and spurred north in full retreat, but Conan had the advantage of both surprise and momentum, and it was a short chase. And a damn fool one on ground this rough.

But his temper remained at full boil, disdaining caution, until he caught up with the bay, grabbed the reins, and brought both horses to a halt in a cloud of dust. When it cleared, he was looking down the barrel of a .22 rifle at a dark-haired girl whose steel-gray eyes served notice that the gun was no bluff.

"Mister, you let go them reins or I'll blow you to kingdom come."

"An unarmed man? Bridgie, whatever happened to the code of the West?"

The muzzle came down a few inches as determination gave way to surprise. But there was no lessening of suspicion.

"I never seen you 'round here. How'd you know my name?"

He laughed and freed her reins. Who else of her sex and age would be acting sentinel here but Alvin Drinkwater's daughter?

"No, you've never seen me, so is that any reason to fire on me without a word of warning? I'd hate to have to walk back to the Running S and tell Ted I broke Molly's leg."

That disarmed her, literally. She cradled the gun properly on her arm, but it seemed more reflexive than intentional.

"That's Ted's horse," she said, eyes widening, then narrowing again. "You ridin' for the Runnin' S?"

"Not in the usual sense. At least, not on Molly."

She relaxed enough for a brief laugh.

"No, I guess not. But you ain't no greenhorn, mister, or you'd still be coughin' up mud in that crick. And in case nobody told you, that fence you crossed a ways back is a property line, and you're tres-passin'."

"Yes, I am, and you had every right to put a bullet between my eyes, which I'm sure you're capable of doing."

"Well, if I'd been aimin' for you, you'd know it."

He nodded, taking time to remove his dark glasses.

"I'm Conan Flagg. I was a friend of George McFall's."

Her response was equivocal: antagonism mixed with an uncomfortable awareness of the respect due the dead.

"You . . . uh, come to see where he . . . passed on?"

"Yes, but not out of sentiment." He looked back at the junipers edging the reservoir. "Bridgie, I make a sort of business of finding answers for people. George asked me to find some answers for him. He's dead now, but that just means I have one more answer to look for."

"Findin' answers? You mean like a detective?"

"Yes."

She waited for him to elaborate, and when he didn't, she asked caustically, "So, you hired on with Aaron McFall?"

"No. I hired on with George. Aaron has decided to tolerate me for the time being."

"Why?"

"Because he thinks I might be useful to him. I have no control over what he thinks; I doubt anyone does."

"Sher'ff Tate know you're detectin', or whatever?"

"Yes. He thinks I might be useful, too."

She paused to consider that, then, "How come you wanta look at the rezzavoy?"

"It's the scene of the crime. Or perhaps I should say possible crime."

"Possible! Mister, there ain't nothin' *possible* about that dam—" Then she subsided, a little embarrassed. "Oh. You was thinkin' about George." When he nodded, she frowned dubiously. "You figger somebody killed him on purpose?"

"I don't know."

"Is that what Aaron told you? I s'pose he's sayin' Pa killed him."

"Bridgie, I told you I have no control over what Aaron thinks. Or says. What do *you* think?"

She tossed her brown hair back over her shoulder.

"Well, I don't figger you'll like what I think, 'cause the way I see it, there was only one crime done here."

"The reservoir?"

"Believe it, mister. You got any idea what it'll mean to Pa, losin' that rezzavoy this time of year?"

"Yes, I do. I grew up on a ranch."

"Oh. Well, then you know there's more down the drain here than the money to put up a new dam. And this ain't the first piece of dirty business 'round here."

"I know about the feud, too."

"Do you, now?" Then she shrugged. "Okay, you asked, so here's what I think: George jest didn't know enough about handlin' dyna-mite."

"You think he intended to blow up the dam, but made an error in judgment and got caught in the explosion?"

"That's how I figger it. I'm sorry. I mean, you said he was a friend, but you asked me."

"Well, it's a logical theory."

"But you don't believe it? What's *your* theory?"

"I don't have one yet."

She eyed him doubtfully, head tilted to one side.

"What's ol' Aaron gonna say if you find out I'm right?"

"I don't give a damn. I want the truth, and in this business it comes in the form of facts. Aaron's opinions won't alter facts. Nor will yours. I have no interest in this vendetta except as the context of George's death."

She mulled over that declaration, apparently impressed.

"If you ain't workin' for Aaron, nobody at the Double D's gonna make trouble for you. We got nothin' to hide."

"I'm not working for Aaron," he assured her. "I wouldn't last a day. We're both too stiff-necked."

"I can see that." She laughed and turned her horse toward the reservoir. "Come on, you might as well have a look around since you come this far."

She pointed out where George's body had been found, but Conan could have guessed it from the concentration of footprints. While he examined the scene of the disaster, Bridgie held Molly's reins and watched him intently. The survey occupied nearly half an hour, but he had nothing to show for it except a pair of mud-caked boots. He took a sample of the mud before he again pronounced it hopeless and returned to Molly.

Bridgie asked, "You find somethin' out there?"

"A lot of wet 'dobe." He frowned, looking back. "I can see one thing, though. This whole area is volcanic ash; a very fine-grained soil."

"So, what does that tell you?"

"Only that there aren't any rocks of any size; nothing more than pebbles. The dam was simply 'dozed out of the ground. Nothing was brought in for fill. Am I right?"

"Right."

"George's skull was crushed by a large rock, and if your theory is correct, that rock was here of natural causes, so to speak; available to be hurled at his head by the force of the explosion."

She shrugged. "Must've been."

"Bridgie, it would have to be the only large rock within miles.

Have you any idea of the odds against one lone rock flying at random and hitting George squarely enough to kill him? They're astronomical. For the sake of your theory, I'm sorry."

"What d'you mean?"

"I mean that it's virtually impossible that his head and that rock collided accidentally." He looked up at her. "I mean George was murdered."

She stared at him, alarm flashing in her gray eyes.

"Who . . . who would want to *murder* him?"

"I don't know." He took Molly's reins and mounted. "Bridgie, I'd like to talk to your father."

One eyebrow shot up. "Well now, I ain't sure he'll wanta talk to *you*."

"Probably not, but it might help if you'd introduce me."

"Might not, too. You won't get around him as easy as you did me."

"Easy? Does 'hard' mean that bullet between the eyes?" Her responding laugh was a little constrained, and he went on soberly, "You know if this isn't interpreted as an accident, your father will be the prime suspect."

"Mister, Pa would *never*—"

"I'm only telling you how it will look. Your father found George preparing to blow up his dam, killed him in a fit of rage, then tried to cover the murder by dynamiting the dam himself. Another logical theory."

"Pa wouldn't *kill* him. He might rough him up a little—" She stopped as if caught in a damning confession, then insisted, "He'd never take a *rock* to him. His fists, maybe, but I know Pa, and he don't have it in him to kill anybody, not even a McFall, and if you try to hang him for this—"

"Bridgie, I'm not trying to hang him. I told you, all I want is the truth. That can't hang him if he's innocent."

She studied him for a long moment, then finally turned her horse, spurred boots nudging its flanks.

"Come on, then. Pa's at the house."

Conan let the silence grow as they left the reservoir behind and rode north up the shoulder of a low ridge. Bridgie sat her horse with easy grace, relaxed, reins loose; she'd probably learned to ride while she learned to walk. And he was thinking what an error it was for Aaron McFall to oppose a union between Ted and this strong young woman. She would be a bride bred to this land.

It was Bridgie who finally broke the silence. Something was worrying her, but it took a little time for her to make up her mind to voice it.

"Did Joe Tate—did he tell you he'd been askin' where ever'body was last night?"

"He gave me a rundown of alibis for everyone at the Black Stallion. Why? Wasn't your father home last night?"

That shaft hit the mark and called up a wary frown.

"No. But he didn't have anything to do with—with what happened to George."

Conan smiled. "All right, Bridgie. Where was he?"

"Well, he'd been out all day workin' cattle. We can't keep enough buckaroos on with the feud and the Runnin' S hirin' away all our hands. Pa can't pay the wages Aaron does. Anyhow, Jerry and Pete come home to supper, but Pa was clear out to Cabel Basin roundin' up some strays, and he found a piece of fence down, so he had to fix that. He didn't start home till after sundown, then that bowlegged roan of his got spooked and throwed him. Took off like a jackrabbit and left him knocked cold."

"Was he badly hurt?"

"Oh, he's limpin' around some, but Ma couldn't get him to call Doc Maxwell. Anyhow, when he come to, he had a long walk home. Ma got worried and rousted the hands. They were headin' out to look for him when he finally come in."

"What time was that?"

She gave him a defiant look, then turned away.

"Nearly midnight. Mebbe a quarter to."

"In other words, time enough for him to ride back from the reservoir after eleven?" He laughed and held up a calming hand. "I know, he probably came from the opposite direction, but that's what's worrying you, isn't it?"

"Well, yes. It don't look good."

"What about his horse? Did it come back to the barn?"

"Sure, but . . ." She took a deep breath. "Willful plug, that roan. Don't know why Pa likes him. He didn't come back to the barn till this mornin'."

Conan frowned. If the horse had returned before eleven, the probable time of the explosion, that would give credence to Drinkwater's story; he couldn't walk the five miles from the reservoir in forty-five minutes. But as it was, he might have *ridden* from the reservoir, released the horse near the ranch and walked in, and his injuries could have been acquired in a struggle with George or in the explosion.

"Pa wouldn't lie," Bridgie insisted, "and if he had a mind to, he'd come up with somethin' better'n that."

Like what, Conan wondered, under the circumstances.

"The other hands are accounted for?"

"Yes, and me and Ma are, too. We were both home."

He smiled at that, then hesitated, choosing his words.

"Bridgie, I'm going to ask you to take my word on something; to believe I'm no more welcome at the Running S than I am here. That means I'll have a hard time getting any straight answers there."

"And you figger *I'll* give 'em to you?"

"I hope so."

"Well, I guess that depends on the questions."

"Fair enough. What can you tell me about Linc, for instance?"

She tossed her hair back, mouth going tight.

"Linc's got a likin' for music, booze, and women, and he's never been out of trouble long as I can remember."

"Music? I've heard about the booze and women, but not the music."

"I guess he's purty good at it; singin' and gittar. Ted says he even wrote some songs himself, but he didn't stick with it; he never sticks with anything. He don't really belong here, y'know, but I guess he jest don't have what it takes to pull up stakes and leave."

"He used to date your sister, Charlotte, didn't he?"

She looked at him sharply, pausing before she answered.

"They saw a lot of each other when they was in high school, but they broke up before he went off to college."

"And afterwards?"

"There wasn't any afterwards," she snapped, a little too positively. Then she looked away, gray eyes clouding. "Anyhow, it wasn't long after he come home till she died. That was two years ago."

"Was she in love with Linc?"

"Yes, I guess so. She always was willful." Then a wistful smile. "Charl was the purty one. Red hair like a sunset and skin like cream. Never could take the sun."

"Your parents didn't like her dating Linc, did they?"

"Well, ol' Aaron didn't take to it much, either. Jest spite. That's what makes him run. Jest plain spite."

Conan didn't attempt to argue that.

"How do your parents feel about you and Ted?"

That brought her chin up, but the sharp reply that was her first response died unspoken, and her eyes clouded with regret like the hint of grief displayed for her sister.

"Ma always liked Ted, and Pa never set his heels like he did with Linc and Charl. We were . . . well, we talked about gettin' married, but then this feud started up. Pa's half out of his mind, and he can't see me tied up with anything havin' to do with the Runnin' S."

"Has the feud changed the way you and Ted feel about each other?"

"No, not what's between Ted and me, but you can't really fence it off by itself."

A remarkably wise observation, he thought, from someone so young, and bitterly sad.

"Do you need your parents' approval to get married?"

"You mean by law? I don't know. We never talked about runnin' away." She looked into the distance to a juniper where a klatch of cattle ruminated in its shade. "Y'know, some people are born to this business. I mean, they're born knowin' when a horse'll buck, or how much hay they'll need for a winter, or when a bad storm's comin' down, or where some cow is lost up on a mountain havin' trouble droppin' a calf. They jest *know*. Ted's like that. Most kids around here can't wait to get loose and find some soft, reg'lar job in the city, but he'd go crazy if he tried that. He couldn't ever leave ranchin', and anymore, you can't jest go out and homestead yourself a place. It takes a lot of money to get a start in this business; more'n he'd put together in a lifetime ridin' for other people."

"You think Aaron would cut him out of the ranch if he married you?"

"I know he would; he told Ted so. That was when he set him down about that money."

Conan's eyes narrowed briefly at that.

"What about your father? Would he cut *you* off?"

She concentrated on tightening the knot at the end of her reins, nodding finally.

"He wouldn't take to havin' a McFall run the Double D, and that's what it'd come to since my brother decided to go into the Army. If Ted and me got married, we couldn't stay here. That's why I never put it up to him. I guess you could say we're in love, but it ain't smart to push a person further'n he can go. I know good and well if he ever had to choose between me and the ranch, he'd tell *me* good-bye first. At least, he *ought* to. Never make a life together startin' off on a lie."

Conan turned away, looking ahead to the plumed grove of poplars in the distance.

"I hope Ted never has to make that choice. You said Aaron set him down about some money. What money was that?"

She seemed suddenly older, any trace of the child that always shadows youth chilled in adult bitterness.

"It was a year ago August. Aaron put aside some money for Ted to buy breedin' stock, but when they counted ever'thing up, he was a couple of thousand short, and Aaron flew mad; said he stole it." She turned her angry eyes on Conan. "That was jest plain senseless. I mean, Ted—it'd never enter his head to steal from the ranch. He'd as likely rob a—a church."

"Ted couldn't explain the loss?"

"No. He's got no head for figures. That was George's job, with his fancy business degree." Then she qualified her sarcasm apologetically, "But George had a feel for ranchin', too. I guess nowadays you have to be half lawyer and half bookkeeper jest to keep up with the IRS."

He laughed at that. "Accountants will inherit the earth, Bridgie. Tate told me Gil Potts used to work for your father." He watched her and caught a glint of uncertain suspicion.

"Sure, Gil rode for Pa for about six months."

"Why did he leave the Double D?"

She gave a short laugh. "Well, the way Gil tells it, he left because Aaron was offerin' better wages."

"How do you tell it?"

"Pa fired him. Run him off our place."

"Why?"

"Oh, they jest never did hit it off good; had a couple of real set-to's, and Pa got it in his head Gil was dippin' into the till. Never had any proof, though, and Gil's been at the Runnin' S a year and a half now, and Ted says he's about the best foreman they ever had."

Conan nodded, wondering where the truth lay in Potts's disagreements with Alvin Drinkwater. The poplar grove was closer now, the ranch buildings visible in its dappled shade. Fenced fields stretched to the north and west, peppered with cattle, red, black, and tan.

"Mr. Flagg, what about Laura? How's she takin' it?"

"I don't know. She seems to be taking it fairly well."

Bridgie sighed. "I s'pose she'll go back to California. Her home's there, ain't it?"

"Yes. San Francisco."

"Jest as well, in a way."

"What do you mean?"

"Oh . . . she don't really belong here. I think she tried real hard at first. Y'know, the Grange and 4-H and all that. She still teaches a first-aid class down to the high school in Burns. That's for 4-H."

"Has she given up trying to belong?"

"Well, I don't know, really. We never saw much of each other when I was in school, and then this feud started up. But she's a city girl, and you couldn't expect her to be satisfied with country life or a country husband."

That had slipped out, and Bridgie's cheeks went red as she sent him a quick glance. He managed to contain his surprise at that insinuation while she made a hasty verbal retreat.

"I didn't mean nothin' against Laura. I jest meant—well, a country husband goes along with country life, don't it? And anyhow, the ol' biddies 'round here'll gossip 'bout anybody, y'know, 'specially when . . . I mean, even if there ain't anything to . . ." Finally she stopped, perhaps realizing that she was only compounding the damage.

Conan laughed, focusing his attention on the ranch buildings ahead.

"I know what you mean about gossips; I live in a small town myself. Well, after this long ride, I hope your father's home."

She accepted the change of subject gratefully.

"Prob'ly is. He was purty stove up from last night. Anyhow, he'll have to see about puttin' in a new dam." At that, she became soberly preoccupied. "Wonder if ol' Foley will stand him for a loan. Tight-fisted cuss. But I guess that's why they got him runnin' the bank."

Conan didn't question her on that subject; it would undoubtedly be a sore one, and she had already given him more answers than he had anticipated or even hoped for.

CHAPTER 9.

The headquarters of the Double D weren't as impressive as the Black Stallion's, but far more typical of Eastern Oregon ranches. There were fewer buildings, none painted except the house; some stone walls, but most of raw board weathered the rich, black-streaked gold peculiar to pine in this climate. The hoary-trunked poplars cast a welcome shade in the afternoon heat; no wind moved the leaves; the close stillness was punctuated only by the lackadaisical barking of a brindle dog and the distant cackling of a hen.

The house was old enough to show its age with a certain pride; a bit of Victorian gingerbread graced the porch and eavecorners, and its wood siding was painted an uncompromising white. The picket-enclosed yard would take no prizes for landscaping, but the borders of zinnias and marigolds were bountifully cheerful. Conan saw a saddled horse tied near the gate, where the only human beings in sight, both female, chatted amiably across the fence.

"That looks like Jesse Broadbent," Bridgie said, and Conan assumed she meant the woman outside the fence; the one within it, plump but small-boned, wearing a wistfully faded print dress, suited her surroundings so well, she could only be Emily Drinkwater.

Her visitor was a sturdy woman whom he might have termed matronly except for her baggy Levis, blazing, red-flowered blouse, and alert, ready stance.

"A friend of your mother's?" he asked.

"Yes. Guess you might say Jesse's a friend of the family. She runs the newspaper down to Burns; the *Clarion*."

He gave Jesse Broadbent a closer look; a representative of the press was one complication he preferred to avoid, and he found his scrutiny fully reciprocated.

"That's Pa's roan there. He must be in the house," Bridgie said, giving Conan a nervous glance. She wasn't looking forward, he knew, to explaining him to her father.

Emily Drinkwater called out a greeting to her daughter as they reached the fence and dismounted. Conan was just looping his reins around a picket when the silence was shattered by a sound so much like a gunshot, his first inclination was to drop to the ground.

It was the front door of the house. The screen door slammed with a lighter report, and Alvin Drinkwater stormed into the pastoral quiet in a quivering rage. A tall man, thin, every movement all angles, but too wirily tough to be called emaciated, his sparse hair, still dark, seemed to fly under the static impulses of his anger; heavy brows loomed over black eyes whose crackling flash was contained only by a tight squint.

"That gawdamned, sidewindin' sonofabitch! Collateral! I'll stuff his— Emmy!" He didn't pause for her to respond, and she seemed too shocked to do so. "Emmy, Foley won't back a loan! Twenty years runnin' this place and by God payin' ever' cent I ever owed, and that white-livered bassard calls me a bad risk!" He came to a halt, towering over her, oblivious to the other witnesses to this outburst.

"Foley got *told*! Aaron McFall's behind this, and if he figgers he can run me off my own place, he's gonna get hisself pruned up. Before I let him set name or foot to the Double D, I'll see that sonofabitch *dead*!"

With that final pronouncement, he seemed to run out of steam, his wide, angular shoulders sagging, and Emily took the opportunity to make a waving gesture that vaguely included Bridgie, Conan, and Jesse Broadbent.

"Uh . . . Alvin, we . . . we got company."

He glowered at them impartially, then apparently Jesse registered, and he started to touch his fingers to his hat brim, realized his hat was still crushed in his left hand, and hastily put it on.

"Sorry, Jesse. Didn't mean to scald your ears like that."

She only laughed. "Well, they been scalded worse, and don't worry, I won't print none of it. I'd have me an X-rated newspaper."

He wasn't up to laughing, but tried a smile, then hurriedly pushed out of the gate and stalked over to the roan.

"Emmy, I'll talk to you later."

Bridgie came out of her daze as he passed her.

"Pa, wait—Pa . . ." She glanced at Conan hopelessly; then, with a resolute lift of her chin, "Pa, this is Conan Flagg. He . . . he was a friend of George's."

Drinkwater tossed the reins over the saddlehorn, eyeing Conan warily, but it was Jesse Broadbent who spoke first.

"*Flagg?* Why, I know you. You're ol' Henry Flagg's son, ain't you?"

Nonplussed, Conan conceded that, reading with some foreboding an intimation of further recognition in her speculative gaze as she amplified for Drinkwater, "Alvin, you remember Henry Flagg, don't you? Ran the Ten-Mile up to Pendleton till he got th'owed off a bronc and busted his neck."

The relationship seemed to incline Drinkwater to regard Conan as something possibly of a higher order than a coiled rattlesnake, but not to stay and chat. He swung up into the saddle, sparing him a curt nod.

"I'm sorry about young George, you bein' a friend of his. Emmy, I'll be over to Cabel Basin. Afternoon, Jesse." With that, he spurred the roan into an easy trot, leaving behind a silence in which Bridgie's sigh was clearly audible.

"Well, Mr. Flagg, you said you wanted to meet my pa. You met him."

That revelatory hint at his purpose didn't escape Jesse Broadbent, he noted. Probably very little did.

"I'm afraid my timing wasn't very good. Mrs. Drinkwater, I owe you an apology for that."

"Well, Mr. Flagg, I guess *we* should be doin' the apologizin'." Her smile was reserved by habit, yet it almost succeeded in hiding the strained anxiety. "Don't take ever'thing Alvin says to heart. He—well, he's jest a little tight-wound today."

Conan smiled and nodded understandingly, although it was a little difficult not to take that outburst to heart. Particularly the part about seeing Aaron dead.

"A man has to blow off steam occasionally," he said, "especially in circumstances like these."

But if he hoped to draw her into any sort of revealing exchange with that vague allusion to the "circumstances," he hadn't reckoned on Harney County's representative of the Third Estate.

Jesse Broadbent came to Emily's rescue and assumed command with the wry comment, "If ever'body 'round here stuck to hollerin', there wouldn't be no 'circumstances.' You're stayin' with the McFalls?" Then, as if to explain her clairvoyance, she cocked her head at Molly. "That's Ted's horse, ain't it? By the way, I'm Jesse Broadbent. 'Jessica' when I was christened, but ever'body calls me Jesse."

He shook the hard brown hand she offered, but wasn't given an opportunity for even a polite acknowledgment.

"Oh, damn." This with a glance at her watch and a show of consternation. "Look at the time. Never get that paper put to bed at this rate; and, Emmy, I know you got plenty to do. Didn't mean to stay so long. Where'd I put my car key?"

While she delved into a paper-stuffed saddlebag of a purse, Emily murmured regrets through a sigh of relief, and Bridgie grabbed the bay's reins and made a hurried exit.

"I better take care of this horse," she said over her shoulder. "Jesse, it was good to see you." And in a more restrained tone, "Nice meetin' you, Mr. Flagg."

"The pleasure was mine," he responded absently.

"There's a real gentleman for you," Jesse noted. "You take care, Bridgie. I swear, Emmy, that girl gets purtier ever' day." Then, taking a firm grip on Conan's arm, "Well now, how 'bout givin' an old lady a thrill seein' her to her car? 'Bye, Emmy. Holler if you need anything from town."

Conan bid Emily Drinkwater a brief farewell as he took Molly's reins, well aware that he had entirely lost control of the situation. But he didn't protest. The patent relief with which Emily greeted the prospect of his departure made it obvious that further conversation with her now would only serve to put her on the defensive.

She smiled and waved across the fence. " 'Bye, Jesse. Nice meetin' you, Mr. Flagg."

He withheld comment as Jesse led him toward an old Plymouth that seemed to be blue under a thick coating of dust, but when they reached the car he politely extricated his arm.

"That was a very adroit maneuver, Mrs. Broadbent, but—"

"Oh, for pete's sake, it's Jesse."

"Jesse, then. If you're worried about my staking a claim in your reportorial territory, I promise you, you have no cause for concern."

She gave him a crinkly grin as she leaned back against the car, arms folded across her generous bosom. Pioneer stock, he was thinking;

the kind like they don't make anymore. A freckled, nut-brown face; short hair a salt-and-pepper mix merging into tarnished silver. Past fifty, he guessed, and no doubt he'd be surprised if he knew how far past.

" 'Reportorial territory.' By damn, Conan, I like that; might use it sometime. But I ain't worried about you hornin' in, nor anybody else. Burns is chuck full of reporters, but I got a few advantages here. Joe Tate put a man on the gate out yonder to keep the gawkers out, but you notice I got in. Folks is sorta used to me, I guess."

Conan laughed, assuming that to be an understatement.

"I suppose you got into the Black Stallion, too."

"I was there when they brung George in, 'bout eight this mornin'." Then her eyes narrowed. "But *you* wasn't there. Now, I'll tell you the truth, I *did* cut you out jest now on purpose, but not 'cause I figgered you was a reporter. I was jest wonderin' what brings a feller like you out here to Harney County."

He rubbed Molly's head; she was nuzzling his pockets in search of sugar.

"Well, Jesse, George was a friend of mine."

"I know he was, but how much of a friend? Last time you paid a visit here was five years ago, at the weddin'. Right? But today—lessee, you rode in with Bridgie from the south; from the rezzavoy, prob'ly. That means you had to ride out there first from the Runnin' S, and altogether, that's a lot of ridin', so I figger you showed up at the Runnin' S about nine or ten this mornin', jest a few hours after they found George. That's what I call *fast* friendship."

Conan began a demurrer, but she didn't pause to hear it.

"Mebbe you thought I was kiddin' when I said I knowed you, Mr. Conan Joseph Flagg. Last time I seen you, you was knee-high to a grasshopper, but I ain't likely to forget a name like Flagg, and you're the spittin' image of your ma. Course, she was purtier."

If Jesse's intent was to mystify him, she was successful. He studied her, trying to call up a memory.

"You knew my mother?"

"Sure did. A real lady, she was. Folks 'round Pendleton used to give her a bad time, her bein' full-blood Indian, but she only made *them* look bad." Then finally she laughed and took pity on his bewilderment. "Well, I'll tell you how I come to know your folks. Me and my husband worked for the paper in Pendleton—the *Eagle* it was, back then. About twenty years ago we bought the *Clarion*. That was always Sam's dream, runnin' his own paper, but we wasn't here three years when he lost an argument with a cattle truck up on Stinkingwater Pass." She paused for a stoic sigh. "I took over the *Clarion* then. Wasn't nothin' else to do; we was mortgaged up to our ears.

Anyhow, that's how I happened to recognize you." Then she added slyly, "And I'm a friend of your aunt Dolly Flagg; Avery's ma."

At that, Conan murmured a premonitory, "Oh, no . . ."

"Yep, me and Dolly still keep in touch. She talks about you a lot."

"I was afraid of that."

She grinned crookedly. "Uh-huh. Well, Dolly told me you done a stint spyin' for the CIA or somethin'.'"

"It was G-2," he noted dully.

"Oh, yes. She told me somethin' else, too: said you're a private detective, licensed proper and official. Course, she says you don't exac'ly advertise yourself."

"Stop it, Molly." He irritably pushed the mare away from her futile search for sugar, thinking dark thoughts about what he'd have to say to Dolly Flagg next time he saw her.

Jesse said sharply, "Conan, I can check that with one call to Salem. Now, you wanta tell me more about this here friendly visit of yours to the Runnin' S?"

He studied her a moment, then shrugged.

"If I *did* come here for professional purposes, I'd be a damn fool to advertise myself. I'm an outsider. I'll have a hard enough time getting any information around here as it is without headlining my investigator's license in a newspaper."

She nodded soberly. "Well, I never made a habit out of printin' ever'thing I know. Besides, it jest might be I could help you out on gettin' that information."

"I'm sure you could," he agreed cautiously.

"Damn right, but you're wonderin' what it'll cost you."

"Yes."

"Not so much, mebbe. Y'know, this feud's a real jackpot. I never could make sense out of it, and neither can Joe Tate." She looked back toward the house, her mouth drawn with regret. "What I mean is, this thing's more important than a headline in the *Clarion*. I've known the Drinkwaters and McFalls for years, and I like to think of 'em as friends. If you can make head or tail of this mess, well, I figger I owe it to my friends to give you a hand. Then, if it works out, mebbe you can give me a hand by lettin' me know what you come up with *before* you tell any of them city reporters."

Conan laughed at that. "Done, Jesse. Anyway, I seldom confide in city reporters. I can guarantee you an exclusive, but I can't guarantee I'll come up with anything."

"I learnt a long time ago not to ask for gar'ntees. Well, I better get back to town. You know where the *Clarion* is? Right on the main street. Can't miss it."

He opened the car door for her, waiting for the roar to subside as she started the engine with a full-throttle burst.

"You'll be hearing from me, Jesse."

"Figger I will. Luck."

Molly shied as the Plymouth launched itself down the road, leaving a contrail of dust. Conan mounted, looking back over his shoulder. The ranch seemed deserted, but he had no doubt his departure was closely observed from behind some curtain or shade.

CHAPTER 10.

Even by the road it was a long ride back to the Black Stallion. Conan was feeling the heat and the effects of his unintentional fast; it was nearly five when he reached the ranch, and breakfast was twelve hours behind him. He was also feeling the effects of a day in the saddle, an experience he hadn't endured for some years.

Ginger's husband, Mano Vasquez, armed with a shotgun, was posted at the gate to discourage overeager journalists. He opened it for Conan with a noncommittal nod. Apparently, Aaron and Linc had returned from Burns; the station wagon was back in the openfronted shed with the Continental, the Buick Skylark, the Ford Mustang, and the Mercedes 450SL. The latter was a lustrous red; the other cars, like all the pickups and trucks belonging to the ranch, were black with the ranch name and brand on the doors.

The two dogs, barking and prancing, heralded Conan across the graveled yard, but his arrival had already been duly noted. Three of the buckaroos were gathered at the barn door with Ted, Gil Potts, and Linc, who was lounging astride his black stallion, one knee crooked around the saddlehorn. When he dropped lithely to the ground for a secretive conference with Potts and the hands, an exchange accompanied with sly grins and covert glances in his direction, Conan was warned. The greenhorn was in for it. Ted, he noted, stood aloof, or was excluded, from the conference.

Conan reined near the barn door, and Linc's saccharine, sardonic smile was a further warning.

"Well, looks like you had yourself a long ride, Flagg."

"Looks like it," he agreed as he dismounted, annoyed to discover his muscles were already stiffening.

"Hope that sugar pony didn't give you no trouble." The hands bandied knowing grins at that. Ted didn't share them. He walked over to Conan and took the reins.

"I'll take care of her, Mr. Flagg."

"Thanks, Ted. She was a perfect lady."

Linc snorted, ignoring the angry glance Ted sent him as he led Molly into the barn.

"Well, some people *like* lady ponies," Linc drawled. "Sort of suits 'em. That right, Flagg?"

Conan almost laughed. This little game was probably inevitable; every functioning social unit has its rites of passage. He looked directly at Linc, matching his cool smile and even his casual drawl.

"Maybe. And maybe some people don't need a stud under them to prove what's in the saddle."

Linc's face reddened when the men gave that thrust a round of laughter. Still, he held on to his smile while he stroked the stallion's head to quiet its restive fidgeting.

"Ho, boy, easy now. Well, Flagg, mebbe a person don't know if he's got what it takes to handle a stud till he's had a real horse under him. Like ol' Domino, here."

"Ol' Domino," nostrils flared, shifted nervously from one foot to the other with the leashed grace and contained power of a Nureyev warming up. Conan ran a hand along his neck, moving slowly, keeping his voice low.

"He's a beautiful animal. Is this a García bit?"

That should have alerted Linc to the fact that he wasn't dealing with a rank tenderfoot, but it was too late for him to back down; Potts and the other men were waiting, sunburned faces creased in anticipatory squints.

"It's a García. Set me back a hunderd 'n fifty bucks."

Conan didn't doubt that. Blued steel engraved with a floral motif, a minor work of art. And a spade bit. Few horses were unmanageable enough to need such a severe bit.

"He's a good horse, ol' Domino," Linc went on, inevitably. "Got a little spirit, y'might say. Mebbe you'd like to give him a run." A weighted pause, then, " 'Less you figger lady ponies like Mol is more your style."

The gauntlet had been dropped, and Conan was sharply aware of the expectant faces surrounding him. He didn't consider his willingness to risk a broken leg or following his father's example to an early grave relevant to his courage or manhood, but he knew the rules of the game. Among buckaroos, a man was reduced to pariah status with the succinct phrase, "He's afraid of his horse." The outsider

would have to prove himself, on their terms, if he hoped for cooperation, or even the truth, from these men.

"Well, Linc, I get the feeling Domino's sort of a one-man horse.
I'm surprised you'd offer to let me ride him."

Linc grinned frostily. "I wouldn't ordinar'ly, but seein' as how
you're a friend of the family, so to speak . . ."

Conan took a long breath and reached for the reins.

"Well now, I can't turn down a *friendly* gesture like that. Domino
. . ." I hope you and I end up friends, he concluded privately, his
throat constricting dryly as Domino's ears swiveled back.

He didn't miss the buckaroos' surreptitious shifts away from the
horse as he mounted, but he was concentrating on Domino, hearing
his nervous snort, seeing the warning crescent of white around his
eye. He kept a tight rein—he wanted Domino's ears in sight—and
swung up into the saddle, numbly aware of the muscles coiling under
the withers.

The shout came as expected, an exultant *"Eeyah-HAH!"*

And Domino uncoiled like a three-quarter-ton steel spring.

Conan was suddenly weightless, flying godlike astride this Pegasus.
Until the brutal fall from grace, when Domino hit the ground, like
an earthquake, and Conan hit the saddle, convinced every vertebra
was shattered, while Domino heaved skyward again.

It was like being caught in a film running at supernormal speed,
only there was nothing funny about the jerking, racking movements;
not with the mass of fifteen hundred pounds behind them. Domino
defied both gravity and equine anatomy, leaping, corkscrewing, kicking up his heels like a gargantuan lamb, while the buckaroos
chorused whoops and rough exhortations, goading his titanic frenzy.

Yet Conan stayed in the saddle, riding slick, hat in his left hand,
fanning, spurless boots automatically raking from shoulder to rump,
never once "pulling leather," so much as touching the saddlehorn,
and if he'd had time to think about it he might have called it a miracle.

Reflex.

That was the miracle.

Domino made four spine-wrenching turns to the right, each ending in a savage collision with the ground, then on the fifth turned
abruptly left, but Conan was ready for it, his body tuned to
Domino's, reacting at an instinctive level far faster than conscious
thought.

Reflex.

He gasped for air, breath crushed out of him under the impact of
yet another 10 G. landing, and as Domino flung himself into the sky

again, Conan leaned to the left, reins loose. A tight rein now would be suicidal.

Reflex kept him in the saddle, and the miracle was that he had been fifteen when he last sat an unbroken bronc. The body never forgets lessons pertinent to survival.

But Domino wasn't a bronc.

Weight to the right stirrup; heel down; keep the foot free. It was the rousing clamor of whoops from the buckaroos that fueled the stallion's fury, and that realization was also pertinent to survival.

Another succession of vaulting gyrations, gravel and dust exploding, while Conan drowned the impelling shouts with his own, using the reins now, but only to slap at Domino's shoulders, to reinforce the command of his heels digging into his sides.

A sidewinding turn caught him off balance and he nearly went flying solo. Domino didn't give up easily, adding a few variations to the allegro theme of vault, pivot, and crash land. Conan rode it out, still shouting, still insisting with heels and slapping reins on the command *forward*. And finally, climaxing the pas de deux with a last leap and an airborne about-face, Domino ceased his demonic, tectonic dance. He stopped bucking only to break into a full gallop, hurtling toward the closed gate where Mano was bolting for cover, leaving the gate locked, an impervious wall.

But Conan regarded that threat to life and limb almost with relief; Domino was only running out his hysteria. He stood in the stirrups, easing the reins to the right, mindful of the spade bit, and at that point, relief translated into anger. Linc was a fool to put a greenhorn on this horse with a spade bit. A true greenhorn could have torn his mouth to bleeding shreds.

The imminent collision with the gate was averted as Domino obediently turned and slowed his pace. Conan circled the yard twice, more to get himself under control than the horse, so that the little surprise he had in store for Linc was calculated, even if motivated by anger.

He approached the barn at a lope and didn't rein until he was within a few yards of the door, and Linc, Potts, and the hands began scrambling out of the way. Then a quick tug on the reins, and Domino sat back on his haunches, forelegs flying, one hoof striking so close, Linc dodged back, hit the barn wall, and slid clumsily to the ground.

As the dust settled, Conan dismounted, which had an immediate calming effect on Domino, who stood quivering and panting, and Conan sympathized; he wasn't at all sure of his legs. The buckaroos picked themselves up, but it was a slow process; they were doubled over with spasms of laughter.

That was also part of the game, a conciliatory signal. They were laughing at themselves, at the unexpected outcome of the trial. All except Linc. But Ted, watching from the barn door, was clearly enjoying himself.

Conan said dryly, "You were right, Linc. Ol' Domino does have a little spirit."

Linc pulled himself to his feet, glaring hotly, hands clenched into fists until Potts stepped in with a wry grin.

"Hey, Linc, you wasn't s'posed to be the one spittin' dust. You better have a talk with that pin-eared cayuse."

Linc could take that from Potts, and could even laugh.

"*You* wanta try sittin' that pin-eared cayuse, Gil?"

"I'll pass on that. He's already got the wind up. Mr. Flagg, mebbe we should sign you on; we could use a good bronc buster."

Conan flexed his back and grimaced painfully as he surrendered Domino's reins to Linc.

"Thanks, but I think I'll stick to Molly from now on."

That was also a conciliatory signal, and Linc's smile showed a hint of warmth for once. Conan took some hope from that, but the promised thaw didn't materialize. The smile vanished as a strident voice broke the brief détente.

"Linc, what the hell d'you think you're doin'?"

Aaron McFall was crossing the yard from the house, with Laura a few steps behind, her pace slowing as his quickened. The buckaroos, except for Potts, began making prudent retreats, mumbling excuses, Ted turned abruptly and went into the barn, but Linc stood his ground.

Potts put in apologetically, "We was jest havin' a little fun, Aaron. Didn't nobody get hurt."

"*Fun!*" He glared at Linc as if he, not Potts, had spoken. "You ain't got nothin' better to do? You don't get enough *fun* down to Burns ever' damn night of the year?" When Linc, red-faced and sullen, made no response, Aaron glanced at Conan and added, "Well, Linc, next time you figger to prune up a greenhorn, you damn well better make sure you got a real greenhorn first."

Conan set his teeth against an angry rejoinder. With that caustic counsel and derisive laughter, Aaron had destroyed all hope of Conan's achieving any rapport with Linc. That was verified in the cold look Linc sent him before turning away, jerking at Domino's reins.

"I gotta take care of this horse," he said, and stalked into the barn. Potts sighed and started after him.

"I'll give him a hand, Aaron. Be up to the house in a little while."

Aaron ignored that, turning a speculative eye on Conan.

"That was a purty good job of ridin', Flagg. Course, that damn plug ain't nothin' but a fancy-show stud." And with that he turned on his heel and set off for the house.

"Typical," Laura said flatly. "Aaron is incapable of giving a compliment without qualifying it with an insult."

She was wearing Levis and a Western-style shirt, but that only made him more aware of her model's face and figure; a city girl in country clothes. He remembered Bridgie's terse assessment: Laura didn't belong here. He was also remembering something else Bridgie had said: You couldn't expect her to be satisfied with country life—or a country husband.

If Laura *had* sought an alternative to her country husband, it would have been Linc. Her limited opportunities to meet other men would dictate that to some degree, and, as Bridgie had noted, Linc didn't belong here, either; they had that in common. And Linc had made his feelings clear enough already. Laura's feelings were still an enigma.

She turned, looking up at him anxiously.

"It *was* a good job of riding. Are you all right?"

He laughed and began walking with her toward the house.

"I think I've sprung my rib cage, cracked my coccyx, and dislocated my liver, but aside from that I'm fine."

"Well, there isn't much I can do for you except advise a hot bath and a couple of aspirin. And perhaps some liniment. I have a patent remedy highly recommended by the buckaroos, but I'm not sure whether they rub it on or drink it."

The humor was forced, but he laughed with her, surprised she was capable of it. He recognized the tightness around her mouth, the shadow of desperation behind her eyes.

"Are you serving as ranch nurse now?" he asked.

"Yes, and occasionally it's more like ranch *doctor*. Doc Maxwell's nearly an hour away at the least. Sometimes when you have an accident out here, there isn't that much time. In San Francisco I'd probably get arrested for practicing medicine without a license, but Doc just makes sure I have the necessary drugs and equipment. Anyway, it's been educational. And convenient for Aaron and George. I mean, not every ranch has a live-in nurse. In fact, we can almost claim two; Gil Potts had some paramedic training in the Army. But he's very considerate. Leaves the nursing to me, which seems to be my only claim to fame."

He caught an almost inperceptible slurring in her words, which with the careless cynicism made him realize she'd been drinking. That came as a surprise; when he first met her she was a virtual teetotaler. But that was five years ago, and not in the wake of sudden widowhood.

"Well, I'm glad you haven't given up nursing. RNs are too hard to come by these days."

"Oh, I haven't given it up; it's sort of my civic duty. I even teach a class in first aid for 4-H. Respectable Mrs. McFall, teaching the kiddies to set bones and suction snake bites." Too much bitterness was coming through; she paused, as if to get herself under control, then made a question of the comment, "Ted said you went out to the reservoir."

"Yes. It seemed the logical place to start."

"He was worried about you, and so was I. Crossing that property line now could mean getting shot at."

"Well, I did have to dodge a little lead."

She paled, eyes widening. "Alvin?"

"No. Bridgie. Fortunately, she wasn't shooting to kill." He stopped at the peal of a bell, startling in the evening quiet.

"The cocktail hour," Laura said.

"It's announced with a bell?"

She laughed and nodded thanks as he opened the gate for her.

"Actually, that's the dinner bell for the hands. The family whiles away the time until Irene gets them fed with a little tiddly or two. I introduced that citified custom; my one contribution to local culture. It's one of the rituals of life now; the family that boozes together . . ." She leaned hard on the stair rail as they climbed the steps to the porch. "Anyway, Gil makes an elegant old-fashioned; that's part of the ritual, too."

And apparently Potts was definitely part of the family. In the foyer, Conan watched her as she turned on a table lamp. Dusk came quickly here, but it would be a long time before the last light faded. Her hand was shaking.

"Is there anything you need, Conan? I left it to Ginger to get your room ready, and I haven't even checked it. I'm afraid I'm not much of a hostess."

"I've no complaints. Is there anything *you* need?"

She almost winced, turning away from the light.

"Need? Comprehension, perhaps. And . . . and a clear conscience. But right now, I think I need . . . *not* to talk about it. Not yet."

"All right, Laura."

"Thank you." She gave him a wan smile, then, hearing voices outside, squared her shoulders. "I must get some ice, and you'd probably like a little time to yourself."

It was a dismissal of sorts, and he accepted it.

"Well, I'd like to wash off some of the dust and horse, at least."

Once he closed himself in the guest room, he took time for more than cleaning up. He unlocked his briefcase—steel cased and secured with a combination lock—put the soil samples in marked envelopes, and filed them in one of the flaps with George's letter. The briefcase held the bare necessities of his trade, or avocation. Chemicals, fingerprint powder and tape, an ultraviolet lamp, microscope slides, a 12X magnifying glass, a case of tools to which few locks were impervious, a tape-recorder and an assortment of tiny monitors, a Minolta 35mm camera, a pencil flashlight, a pair of Zeiss shirt-pocket binoculars, and a Mauser 9mm automatic. The latter he seldom carried with him, but it was always loaded.

Before he left the room, he put the briefcase in the closet, one of the old-fashioned kind, copiously spacious, with double doors. He hung a tie across the knobs, apparently casually, but if the doors were opened, he'd know it.

Downstairs in the living room, the cocktail hour was well under way when he arrived; a tense gathering, and as he entered, a silent one. Aaron, wreathed in smoke from a panatela, again occupied the chair to the left of the fireplace. Ted was sitting near the door, working at an old-fashioned, while his brother stood at the front windows, brooding over the golden western sky. Laura was in the chair near the bar, behind which Gil Potts busied himself. She raised her glass with a mocking flourish.

"Conan, you've almost missed the first round."

Potts glanced at her, then put away his worried frown to give Conan a smile.

"Well, Mr. Flagg, the bar's open, and the drinks is on the house. What'll you have?"

"Laura tells me you mix a fine old-fashioned, Mr. Potts, and since that's what everyone else is having, she must be right."

Potts laughed and began preparing the drink with smooth, practiced movements, using a rosewood pestle to crush the sugar cube with the bitters.

"Far be it from me to doubt Laura's word, and you might as well leave off that 'mister' business. I don't hardly know how to answer to that." Then, when he garnished his creation and handed it to Conan, "Give that a try."

It was, as Laura promised, an elegant old-fashioned, but light on sugar and long on bitters. He'd been surprised that a mixed drink would find favor in a region where whiskey was traditionally served with no adulterants other than, if necessary, water. Aaron, he noted, took his without the fruit garnish, but still it was an unexpected concession.

"It's perfect, Gil, and you might leave off the 'mister' with me, too."

"Good 'nough." Then he added with an oblique smile, "That there's an o-o-old family recipe. Picked it up tendin' bar in Winnemucca a few years back."

Conan laughed politely, filing that information for future reference as he went to the vacant chair by the fireplace. Potts perched at one end of the couch, seemed to try to think of something to say to lighten the somber mood, then apparently gave up and turned his attention to his drink. Conan lit a cigarette, pointedly ignoring Aaron's intent scrutiny through puffs of cigar smoke. The only sound was the clink of ice as Laura tipped up her glass.

"I hear you been out to the rezzavoy," Aaron announced at length.

"Yes." Conan took a swallow of his drink, wondering whether Ted or Laura had been the source of that information.

"Damn fool thing to do. I told Joe Tate nobody from the Runnin' S ever set foot across Alvin's propitty line, and by God, I won't have nobody makin' a liar outa me."

"I'm not from the Running S, Aaron."

"What d'you mean? Ain't you stayin' here? Ain't you signed on for a job of work here?"

"You aren't responsible *for* me any more than I'm responsible *to* you. I made that clear at the Double D."

Aaron put aside his cigar for his glass, which despite its generous size looked as fragile as an eggshell in his callused brown hand. He might have argued Conan's responsibilities further, but curiosity got the better of him.

"You talked to Alvin?"

"Yes."

"Well? What'd he say?"

"Very little."

"Damn it, *what* little?"

"Aaron, you know, that's none of your business. You aren't my client." Then, seeing the angry flush moving up from his neck, he laughed. "But I'd like your response to something Alvin said. He mentioned a man named Foley."

"Sure. Hor'ce Foley. Runs the bank down to Burns. Harney Valley Bank and Trust."

"You bank there? I mean, for the ranch?"

He squinted guardedly. "Yep. Always have. Like to do business with the locals whenever I can."

"It's a small bank, then, and your account is sizable; one they'd be reluctant to lose."

"Jest what the hell you gettin' at, Flagg?"

"Alvin asked Foley for a loan to rebuild his dam, but he was turned down. He said Foley got his orders from you."

At first, Aaron was speechless, his glass in danger of being crushed in his grip, until he slammed it down on the table beside him, oblivious to the splash of liquid.

"*Orders!* Orders from *me?* That yellah-bellied— I didn't know a damn thing about Alvin askin' for a loan, so how the hell d'you figger I give Foley any *orders?*"

"I didn't say you did. I was only wondering."

"Well, you can *stop* wonderin' right now." He frowned at the spilled whiskey as he picked up his glass. "Damn. Laura, I need a napkin or somethin'."

She was already at the bar getting a towel, which she brought to the table and tractably cleaned up the spill. Aaron ignored her and glowered at Conan.

"Alvin have anythin' else to say?"

"He said he was sorry about George."

That predictably evoked another outburst. Conan let it run its course, watching Laura as she returned the towel to the bar, picking up her empty glass on the way, moving with an air of dogged containment.

Potts asked hesitantly, "You . . . uh, want me to mix you up another Potts special, Laura?"

"Thanks, no. I'll just freshen this up a little."

She freshened it up by at least three straight shots, then returned to her chair and began drinking it with the same dogged air. Aaron, quiet at last, watched her, something close to concern or even grief evident in the granitic lines of his face. He didn't comment on her consumption of alcohol, although his doubtful gaze strayed to her glass.

But when Linc went to the bar to avail himself of the whiskey bottle, Aaron's features settled into the familiar lines of frustrated contempt.

"Ain't you startin' a little early tonight, boy?"

Linc didn't look around nor stint as he poured.

"No, Pa. Too late. Too damned late."

CHAPTER 11.

Mrs. Mosely's announcement that supper was on the table was welcome not only as a diversion, but because Conan was by this time ravenous.

They crossed the hall to the dining room, where the evening meal was laid out family style, and for anyone unaccustomed to ranch meals, it was an impressive feast. A pot roast of profligate proportions; heaped bowls of green beans, stewed tomatoes, and creamed corn, undoubtedly canned from the summer's garden crop; airy, nubbly drop biscuits; a mound of butter and pitcher of cold milk supplied by the ranch's prize Jerseys; a small mountain of mashed potatoes with a tureen of gravy. As they seated themselves—Aaron at the head of the table—Mrs. Mosely, with her gray hair pinioned under a net, eyes a little redder than usual, put two oven-hot pies on the sideboard, with the terse explanation, "Apple and peach," then retreated into the kitchen.

Conan might have been a little embarrassed at his appetite, except that it attracted no attention at all; everyone was too distracted by personal considerations. There was little conversation to punctuate the desultory clatter of silver and china. Potts made an effort at small talk, but limited himself to matters pertaining to cattle or feed, and when that failed, engaged Conan in an uninspired exchange centering on the Ten-Mile and Henry Flagg.

Laura's dutiful attempts at conversation were notably unsuccessful; she was in that paradoxical state of sobriety resulting from too much alcohol consumed under too much emotional strain. No one here was immune to the strain, and at first Conan took no notice of Aaron's preoccupied silence or lack of appetite. But when he gruffly refused second helpings because his first were virtually untouched, Conan realized something was wrong, which was undoubtedly attributable to his emotional state but was more serious than bad temper. His leathery features had a gray cast, and his forehead was filmed with perspiration, although one of his few comments was a complaint about an unseasonable chill in the air.

Finally, when Laura got up to cut the pie, he rose unsteadily, bracing himself with a hand on the table.

"Laura, don't cut none for me. I'm goin' on up to bed."

She studied him a moment, frowning.

"What's wrong, Aaron? You don't look well."

"Nothin' wrong with me," he insisted. "Jest tired."

"You hardly touched your supper."

"I ain't hungry. You expect me to be hungry today?" At that, she turned abruptly, shoulders rigid, and his tone softened. "Sorry, Laura. Jest don't worry 'bout me. Nothin' wrong a little Pepto-Bismol won't take care of."

She managed a smile. "I know. Oh—I put some of those pills Doc left by your bed. You'd better take one."

"Pills," he muttered. "Ol' Walt thinks there's a pill to cure ever'thing." He had more to say on the subject, but it became unintelligible as he went out and stumped up the stairs. Laura began cutting one of the pies.

"Aaron considers taking advantage of modern medicine a sign of weakness," she said, apparently addressing no one in particular; it was only in such vague lapses that her consumption of alcohol was evident. "Like the digitalis. He's supposed to be on a maintenance. . . ." She frowned distractedly, then called up another forced smile. "Well, you have a choice of desert: apple or peach. Any takers?"

Linc was sitting with his hands in fists on either side of his plate, jaw muscles working. He looked up at her, but didn't seem to understand the question, then his chair scraped harshly as he rose and headed for the door.

"I'm goin' into town," he announced curtly.

Potts frowned, then hurriedly wiped his mouth and tossed his napkin down as he left the table.

"Uh . . . mebbe I better tag along with him, Laura."

"Yes, I'm afraid so. Thanks, Gil." She listened for the slam of the screen door, then turned to Conan and Ted. "Well, can't I sell any pie? Irene makes the finest pastries west of the Rockies."

Ted laughed politely as he, too, left the table.

"Mebbe later, Laura. I'm goin' out for some fresh air."

"All right, Ted. Conan?"

"Later for me, thanks."

She only nodded absently and began stacking the dishes, waving him away when he tried to help her.

"Irene and I will take care of this. Men in the kitchen make her nervous. Woman's work, you know."

And Laura didn't feel like talking.

"Well then, my compliments to Mrs. Mosely. I guess I'll get some air, too."

Ted was sitting on the top step of the porch. He didn't look around as Conan leaned against the post at the other end of the steps, but seemed engrossed in the rosy remainder of the sunset. The Mercedes thrummed at idle outside the main gate while Potts closed it. As soon as he got into the car, it rocketed down the road on a wake of dust.

"That's quite a little toy Linc has there," Conan commented as the roar died into distance.

"What? Oh. Yeah, toy's about it, too. That's all's left of Linc's music."

"His music?"

"He used to play gittar and do some singin'. He was damned good, Mr. Flagg."

"Conan—or am I to call you *Mister* McFall?"

Ted turned, watching him as he sat down on the step.

"Nobody calls me 'mister.' Okay, it's Conan, then. That an Indian name?"

"Irish. My middle name is Indian: Joseph."

"Joseph?" He laughed tentatively, and Conan smiled.

"For Chief Joseph. My mother was Nez Percé. Ted, has Linc given up his music?"

"Yes, I guess so, but he shouldn't have. He even wrote some songs; some real purty ones. Course, Pa couldn't see him makin' a livin' outa that."

"What did you mean about that car being all that's left of his music?"

He hesitated a moment, then shrugged.

"Oh, a couple years back he was all set to make a record of one of his songs; met a guy with connections in Los Angeleez. But he needed a lot of money for promotion, you know. Well, Pa knew he had his eye on one of them Mercydes, so he put it up to him. He could have his record or his . . . his little toy."

"A couple of years ago. Wasn't that about the time Charl Drinkwater died?"

"Yes. That jest took all the starch outa Linc. Mebbe that's why he settled for the car." Then he studied Conan, eyes narrowing. "Did you talk to Bridgie while you was over to the Double D?"

"Yes, and I know about you and Bridgie, but she didn't volunteer it."

He nodded, satisfied. "Didn't figger she would." His flat tone effectively closed that subject. Conan turned to another.

"George told me he was sure no one at the Black Stallion took part in this feud, but wouldn't it be possible for someone—one of the hands, maybe—to make raids on Drinkwater property without George knowing about it?"

"Oh, I guess it'd be *possible*, but it ain't likely one of us wouldn't get wind of it sooner or later."

"One of us? You mean the family?"

"Or Gil. And why would anybody wanta do somethin' like that, anyhow? Pa'd have reason enough now, but he didn't start this thing."

"Did Alvin?"

"Well . . . oh, hell, I don't know. I guess so."

"Do you know the Double D hands?"

"Sure. Good steady workers, and none of 'em has any reason to get a feud fired up between Pa and Alvin. Neither does any of *our* hands. It jest don't make sense; none of it. And George—" His voice faltered and he turned away. "You heard what Joe Tate said. He thinks George dynamited the dam, and I can't come up with any other reason for him bein' out there. But I jest can't believe he'd do somethin' like that. 'Specially not right after hirin' you to—to investigate this jackpot." He turned appealingly to Conan. "That wouldn't be too smart, now, would it?"

"No, and dynamiting dams wasn't George's style. Did he get along well with the hands here?"

"He got on real good with ever'body."

"Including the family?"

"Sure. We never had no trouble." The answer was too quick, and the emphasis on the "we" almost suggested that he meant specifically himself and George.

"And with Laura?"

Conan realized he had overstepped himself when Ted came to his feet and said curtly, "You been listenin' to too much gossip." He stood undecided for a moment, then thumped down the steps, hands in pockets, shoulders hunched.

"I'm goin' out ridin'. Tell Laura I'll be back in an hour or so."

Conan watched him go, irritably annoyed at himself; that question could have waited. As the desert silence closed in, he lit a cigarette and watched the burgeoning of stars. He heard Ted's departure on Molly, but afterward the only sounds were distant slammings of doors from the bunkhouse as the hands settled in for the night, and later the eerie harmonic chorus of a coyote pack singing the moon up. A wild sound full of echoes of years and millennia past, a cast of mourning in it that unexpectedly brought tears to his eyes for a man who had been vital and alive when the moon last rose. Or perhaps his grief was for the survivors; for the victims of some vicious and senseless game.

He had finished a third cigarette when he heard the screen door close behind him. Laura walked over to him, a shadow in the darkness.

"Woman's work is done. How about walking me home?"

He accepted that invitation with relief; some rapport still existed with at least one member of the family.

They walked around to the back of the house and under the breezeway connecting the back door with the cookhouse. There were lights in the bunkhouse and trailers, but except for a halfhearted bark from one of the dogs, the silence was unbroken. Behind the house was a trimly mowed lawn lit by a yard light haloed with motes of insects. Another light shone over the door of the house to the north; a relatively new building whose architecture would probably— ironically, perhaps—be called "ranch style." The door was unlocked, but Laura hesitated before opening it, and when they were inside, he understood why.

It was another world. San Francisco. This was the kind of house he'd expect of the Laura and George he had known in San Francisco. Fine woods and carefully chosen materials and accessories; paintings thoughtfully arranged on every wall. And books. Half a wall filled with books whose diversity indicated they were read and prized.

Laura stood with her arms clasped to her body, brown eyes haunted. Then she crossed hurriedly to the kitchen.

"Let me fix you a drink. Scotch? No, I—I forgot. Bourbon, isn't it?"

He started to decline, but thought better of it; she needed the drink. Another drink.

"Yes, it's bourbon, and when the whiskey's good, I prefer it on the rocks."

"Oh, it's good," she assured him from the kitchen. "Put some music on, Conan."

He went to the stereo and looked through the records, startled once by a sudden crash, followed by the assurance that she had only dropped a glass. She was all right.

He didn't argue that, nor go into the kitchen, but concentrated on choosing music that would have as few emotional overtones as possible—a hopeless undertaking. Finally, he put on a combination of Monteverdi, Mozart, and the Modern Jazz Quartet. Laura was pale when she brought his drink; she sat down at one end of the couch, focusing on her glass as if she were afraid to look around her.

Conan seated himself in an armchair near her, tasted his bourbon and guessed Jack Daniels, then lit a cigarette and waited for her to set the course of their conversation, but she remained tensely silent.

At length he asked, "Do you think you should stay here alone tonight?"

She tipped up her glass. "Would the old house be any better?" Then, as if the whiskey had given her courage, she looked around, and the fear haunting her eyes gave way to fathomless regret.

"You know, when we moved into this house I was so happy. I thought, there's hope now. A place that's all ours; not the ranch's, not the family's, not Aaron's." She took another swallow of whiskey, grimacing at it. "But it didn't work out that way. In the end, it was only all mine."

"You mean now?"

Her eyes flashed briefly. "No."

"What happened, Laura?" He wondered if she would answer that, or if it wasn't cruel to ask. He only hoped he was right in assuming she needed to talk and wouldn't feel comfortable talking to anyone else about George. And finally she did answer, although obliquely.

"Conan, I've thought of you so much this last year. Remember that day—it was right after George proposed to me—you dropped by my apartment in San Francisco, oh, so casually, for a big-brother talk."

"Yes, I remember."

"You tried to warn me. Very kindly, you tried to tell me I wouldn't just be marrying George; I'd be marrying George *McFall* and the Black Stallion. You talked about the land and the life, and I thought I understood."

"I know. Some things can't be understood until they're endured. It wasn't working out, then. Your marriage."

She laughed and raised her glass, drinking as if it were water and she was simply thirsty.

"You didn't even make that a question. Conan, I *did* understand part of what you tried to tell me; I knew it wouldn't be easy for me. I never was a country girl." She smiled faintly over the phrase. "But I thought if I had George I could adjust to anything. Only I—I found out I *didn't* have George. Not the same George. He didn't change, really. He only reverted to what he always was; to George McFall, heir apparent to Aaron McFall. It finally came through to me. The man I met and fell in love with in San Francisco wasn't the real George McFall; he was out of context. But here—" She stopped, tension choking off the words until she got herself under control with more whiskey.

"The attitudes, Conan. The roles. Woman's work and man's; husband's and wife's. And the ranch—the land—is everything, and there's no room for anything else. No room for music or art or curiosity; no room for tenderness. A wife is not a lover; it isn't respectable. And anyone bearing the title of *Mrs.* McFall must above all be respectable."

For a moment, when she said "Mrs. McFall," her self-control wavered. She bolstered it with the rest of her drink, then stared into the glass, rattling the ice.

"Empty. You want another?"

"No, thanks. Laura . . ."

She rose and went into the kitchen. "Don't lecture me about demon rum. I know it's not respic—respectable."

He crushed out his half-smoked cigarette, wondering if she'd had lectures on demon rum before. When she made her way back to the couch, she lifted her glass to him defiantly.

"Consider it medicinal. I won't take Doc's pills. Still nurse enough to know better than to mix 'em with booze, and I have faith in brother bourbon. I may get messy—not before you leave, I hope—but at least I'll sleep."

He nodded vaguely. "Laura, how did George feel about . . . about your marriage?"

"Bewildered." She gazed wistfully into space. "Once I asked him to go to Portland with me to a concert. We have a plane and he could fly; it would only mean one day lost. But it was branding time. Too busy. I told him we hadn't been off this ranch together for three years, and he just looked vaguely surprised. 'Honey, anytime you want to go to Portland or anywhere else, just say so. I can hire you a pilot.' *Hire* me—oh, Conan, my mind, my *feelings*, were turning to 'dobe, but he didn't understand. It just didn't make sense to him that I wanted more than room and board and a clothing allowance out of marriage; out of life."

Conan took a moment to taste his bourbon, watching her as she resolutely emptied nearly half her glass at once.

"Is that how it stayed between you?"

"Until a year ago. Then came the proverbial straw."

"What was it?"

"Money. Root of all divorces. But not in the usual sense. You see, Ted had been entrusted with twenty thousand dollars to buy new breeding stock."

"Yes, I heard about that." And he was relieved that she brought it up. "Some of the money disappeared, didn't it?"

"Two thousand dollars. Good God, that's chicken feed—literally —around here. It was the principle of the thing. *Principle!*" Her mouth twisted in bitter anger. "I don't know what happened to the money, and I doubt Ted does, but it was his first big responsibility, and he was so proud. And then—well, George found the discrepancy one night when he was working late in the office; he made a habit of working late. He told me about it that night; said he could see no explanation other than theft. I'm not sure he really believed Ted was guilty, but he said he'd have to talk to Aaron about it. I *begged* him not to tell Aaron; I all but crawled on my knees. But he didn't understand that, either."

"Did he tell Aaron?" It was more a cue than a real question; she was lapsing into brooding silence.

"Yes. The next day when the family gathered for the solemn ritual of the cocktail hour. Aaron—what's the term? Set 'im down. That's it. Set 'im down good." She closed her eyes, gripping her glass with both hands. "God, it was—it was like seeing someone flayed alive. The Assyrians used to do that. Called down the wrath of God. Maybe that's what it's all about, this feud. Wrath of God. Ted didn't have a chance to defend himself; Aaron had already tried and convicted him. I suppose the real reason he was so ready to condemn Ted was because he wanted to marry Bridgie. No—to marry *Alvin's* daughter. High treason. Hang him from the nearest yardarm. Or cottonwood."

"Did George take a stand either way?"

"Not against Aaron." Her voice was thick with disgust. "That would be like taking a stand against himself. I know then I couldn't go on living married to Aaron's alter ego. Moment of truth, Conan; that was mine."

"And Ted's?"

She sagged back into the cushions, frowning as she raised her glass again.

"He was so hurt, so wounded. I've often wondered . . ."

He waited, then found it necessary to cue her again.

"Wondered what, Laura?"

"Oh . . . it just seemed like—like this feud . . ."

"You think Ted has something to do with it?"

She hesitated, then shook her head emphatically.

"I'm as bad as Aaron. I despise him for condemning Ted without a hearing, and now I . . . Conan, I don't know. Ted seems so steady and dependable, and he is, but he has the McFall temper, too. I have no reason to think he might be involved. Maybe it's just that—that I think he'd be *justified*." Then she turned away with a long sigh. "Or maybe it's just the sort of spiteful thing *I'd* do."

"I've never thought you spiteful."

She tilted her head and laughed.

"Do you really know me that well?"

He admitted to himself that he didn't, and he had little faith in self-revelation.

"Was it spite that made you consider a divorce?"

Her eyes narrowed, then she laughed again.

"Touché. No, and I wasn't just considering it; I wanted it. That's when I found out the word 'divorce' is not in the vocabulary of a respectable *Mrs.* McFall. Impossible. That's what he told me, standing there like a stone wall. *Impossible.*" She mulled the word as if she'd examined it so often it had become meaningless. "And when I told him, 'I want my freedom,' he just said, 'Laura, I don't understand.'"

But Laura had her freedom now. Conan watched her eyes close, lashes trembling against her cheeks as she downed another medicinal draft.

"Would he have contested a divorce if you'd initiated it?"

"Of course, and I had no real grounds; nothing that would make sense in a Harney County court. I didn't even have any money of my own to hire a lawyer."

"And it was left at that?"

"For George, yes. Subject closed. Period. I went into a state of deep shock for a while, then I decided I'd go back to San Francisco. I'd still be Mrs. McFall, but the idea of marrying again didn't appeal to me."

"But you didn't go."

She shook her head slowly. "Inertia, I guess. Besides, I've a rather . . . comfortable life here, you know." And she began singing in a quavering soprano, "I'm only a bird in a gilded . . .'"

"Laura—"

"Sorry. Not very funny."

She was drunk, or should have been, but her mind refused to go out of focus. He wondered if she wouldn't simply get miserably ill before she achieved oblivion.

"None of this is funny."

"No. Well, anyway, I haven't . . . didn't go. It was partly this feud. George was so torn up about it, I thought it would be better, kinder—now, that *is* funny—kinder to wait until it was resolved. But it never . . ." She looked at him in mute appeal, as if he could explain the phenomenon. "It just kept getting worse, and so did the situation here. It ceased to be a family. We were all prisoners here, or—or inmates in some sort of insane asylum. I had the strangest feeling that nothing mattered, that everything was all over; my whole life, all over, and I was too numb to care. And now . . . he's gone. Dead. He's . . . dead."

She seemed to be trying to make sense of the word, and trying to respond to its implications, face contorted harshly, hand pressed to her mouth. But not one tear streaked her cheeks. Finally, she sagged limply, staring down at her glass before draining it.

"Empty. Empty again. Fill 'er up? Yes, thank you." When he

reached out and gently caught her arm as she started to rise, she jerked away from him. "Conan, don't do anything for my own good. Please!"

He pulled in a long breath, then stood up and took the glass from her tense grip.

"I'll get you a refill."

"You're a genuine gentleman. Always were. No water. I can still tell the difference."

"I don't believe in diluting good whiskey," he said lightly.

The bottle on the kitchen counter was almost empty, but he had no doubt another was available. When he returned, he sat down beside her. She seemed nearly asleep, eyes closed, listening to the music.

"That's lovely," she murmured. "Beautiful. George never did like Mozart. Oh, God, *listen* to me. *In vino veritas*." Then, seeing the glass, she smiled and took it from him. "Thank you, kind sir."

He winced at that; he didn't feel particularly kind.

"Laura, I'm going to ask you a very personal question, so feel free to tell me to mind my own business."

She laughed. "Don't worry, I will."

"Why didn't you and George have any children?"

For a moment, he expected her to accept his suggestion, then she turned to her whiskey and shrugged apathetically.

"You're good at finding the chinks in the armor, aren't you? Well, I guess it was blind luck the first two years, and since then I've been taking contraceptive pills."

"Without George's knowledge?"

"There you go again. Zingo. Right in the chink." She paused for a long time, staring bleakly into nothingness, then, "That was really despicable, especially with a man like George. Raises specters of impotence; fate worse than . . . despicable, respectable Mrs. McFall. If I can say that, I'm not drunk. Not drunk enough." She tipped up her glass thirstily as if to remedy that, then lowered it with a long sigh.

"Oh, Conan, it was a hell of a thing to do, but a—a child is an infant human being; a life in fragile potential. I just couldn't bring a child into the world—into *this* world—until I was sure I could make a home for it; a real home. But George—the idea that I might balk at bearing an heir to the McFall dynasty would have boggled his mind. He'd have considered it not only unreasonable but immoral."

Conan nodded. "It was a terrible decision to have to make, Laura."

"And I decided terribly, is that it?"

"You're asking my opinion? I think you were forced to choose the lesser of two painful evils."

She studied him doubtfully, then laughed.

"I've almost forgotten what it's like to talk to a man who isn't hung up on his . . . Thanks, anyway."

"Are you sure George didn't know?"

"Yes. He was always a little vague and embarrassed about anything associated with the female reproductive system. I used to think it rather boyishly charming."

"What would he have done if he'd found out?"

"He'd have killed me, probably." She wasn't joking, she was quite serious, yet entirely indifferent. "But he wouldn't have freed me, not even in disgrace. Ah . . . I'm finally beginning to feel this. Sweet soporific sauce; beautiful sauce of the evening." She emptied the glass and put it on the table beside her with some care. "So, now I'll get myself undressed while I'm still able, and crawl into my little trundle bed with my little trundle bottle."

"Laura, I . . . I don't like to leave you alone."

She laughed and reached out to touch his cheek.

"Then stay. Why not? Give people something else to talk about. Oh, Conan, dear kind sir, I'm sorry. I'm getting messy, aren't I? Well—" She came to her feet, finding it necessary to accept his supporting hand until she got her balance. "I'll see you to the door, kind sir, and don't worry about my being alone. In a very short time, I doubt it will even register."

She was amazingly steady on her feet as she went to the door and opened it with an ironic little bow. Then she took him entirely by surprise with her next words.

"Conan . . . kiss me."

He did, not knowing what to expect, or what she expected of him, and he could only describe it as tender.

"Funny," she said finally, "you look for—for proof of your own existence. . . . Never mind. Good night. Thanks for the broad shoulder for crying on."

But she hadn't cried. "Laura . . ."

"Good night."

He hesitated, then turned away. "Good night."

The door closed behind him as he crossed the lawn; there was a chill in the air, the scent of frost. No lights showed in the bunkhouse or trailers; even the dogs were silent in sleep.

In vino veritas. Laura had given Ted a motive for the feud and herself a motive for killing George. Revenge and freedom. But he was skeptical of truisms, and reminded himself again that he didn't really know her.

CHAPTER 12.

A light was on in the foyer, but the old house was as silent as midnight even though it was only a few minutes past eight. Conan went upstairs as quietly as possible in boots and on aged steps with a tendency to complain under pressure. He felt his way down the darkened hall rather than turn on a light and risk waking Aaron, whose fitful snores were audible through the open door of his room.

Conan closed the guest room door before turning on the light, then went to the south window. There was a light over the barn door, but no light or hint of life within; Ted hadn't yet returned from his moonlight ride.

The closet doors hadn't been touched. He opened his briefcase and took out the small flashlight, a notebook, and the tool kit; then, after exchanging his boots for a pair of soft slippers, he went back down the hall to Ted's room.

It was in the north corner of the house, where he could neither see the barn nor hear Ted's arrival. His work here must necessarily be done quickly, but he went about it with no sense of urgency. For this, and for the training that enabled him to search a room thoroughly, silently, leaving no evidence of his presence, he was indebted to G-2 and a hard-nosed perfectionist who had been his commanding officer.

He pulled the shades but left the door open and depended on the tight beam of the flashlight. It was a random search and the results were commensurately random. He might have drawn a personality profile of the occupant of the room: clean, orderly, little interest in clothing except in functional terms; earnestly proud of the trophies and ribbons rewarding his achievements in sports, animal husbandry, and rodeo competition; touchingly sentimental about his family as evidenced by the collected letters, cards, portraits, and snapshots. A few of them included Bridgie Drinkwater, laughing and exuberant, seeming much younger than the girl Conan had met at the reservoir today. Ted showed engaging spirit in these pictures, and even Aaron McFall was a different man. Conan paused over one snapshot. Aaron posing proudly with his sons, George no more than eighteen then, and all of them smiling.

When he finally closed the last drawer, Conan put the shades back exactly as he had found them. Psychological profiles were interesting, but he'd found nothing that seemed to have any bearing on the feud or on George's murder, with the possible exception of three items discovered in a drawer full of miscellaneous boyhood souvenirs: a handful of blasting caps; a Smith & Wesson .38 revolver, an old relic that might have been an antique, but appeared to be in perfect working order; and $1,824 in cash hidden in a cigar box.

The latter wouldn't have made him so uneasy if it were more than two thousand and not so little less.

He crossed to Linc's room, pausing to listen for the distant drone of Aaron's snoring, then went first to the window and looked out to the barn. No sign of Ted yet.

Linc's room would take longer, he realized, simply because he wasn't as orderly as his brother, and the detritus of his existence included books, magazines, and stacks of sheet music. Most of these, including some unexpectedly heavy reading ranging from Salinger to Shakespeare, were hidden away at the back of the closet. Two guitars gathered dust there, too; a Goya classic, and a rakish, bright red electric instrument. In the Goya's case he found a sheaf of sheet music, words and notes penciled in a strong, vertical hand. Linc's songs; the price of a Mercedes 450SL.

Linc did not share Ted's sentimentality. Conan had almost given up hope of finding any evidence of a personal life outside the closet, when finally one drawer yielded a small cache of memorabilia, all of it concerned with Charlotte Drinkwater. A studio portrait, autographed "With love from your Juliet," showed a beautiful girl with shining dark eyes and a piquant smile much like her sister's. Some snapshots and a newspaper clipping were pressed in a Crane High School yearbook, marking the pages chronicling the crowning of Charl Drinkwater as homecoming queen. The clipping was from the *Clarion*; the studio portrait, reduced, the smile fey beneath the headline announcing her death. The article told him more about Charl alive than dead; of her death, Jesse Broadbent had chosen to say only that she had died in a diabetic coma a few minutes after admission to the Burns Memorial Hospital.

Another drawer yielded another kind of memorabilia: the casual accumulation cast out of pockets. He smiled faintly at the number of traffic citations. The matchbooks surprised him; he hadn't seen Linc smoking, but a crumpled package of Camels was also lost at the back of the drawer.

He studied the matchbooks, taking particular interest in one advertising the Longhorn Bar and Grill, and another the Sage Vista Motel, both in Winnemucca, Nevada.

He also took note of the two checkbooks, one issued by the Harney Valley Bank and Trust: a personal account, the checks all in Linc's writing, a number to various bars in Burns, regular deposits of five hundred dollars on the first of every month. Salary or an allowance, probably.

The second checkbook elicited an uneasy prickling at the back of his neck. The Citizens Bank of Boise. Linc, unlike his father, didn't always believe in doing business with the locals. Boise was across the state line in Idaho, a hundred miles away, and the largest city in the three-state area. He wondered if a desire for anonymity had inspired the choice. The checks bore no printed name or address.

There were few entries—four deposits and four checks. He took out his notebook and recorded the dates, amounts, and the account number. The pattern was obvious, however inexplicable. Four deposits, all within a few hundred dollars, plus or minus, of six thousand, had been made at three-month intervals over the last year, the final one dated July 27. And without exception, a check for five thousand had been drawn to cash within a few days of each deposit.

He put away the checkbook, made a note of the addresses on the Winnemucca matchbooks, checked the barn again as he opened the shades, then left the room, frowning, but not so preoccupied that he didn't listen for Aaron's snoring. A bathroom opened off the short wall to one side of the stairway, and a glance verified his guess that a second door gave access to it from Aaron's room.

He went through to the second door and stood listening. Even with his eyes accustomed to darkness, he could see nothing except the rectangles of windows. He had no intention of making a search now; Aaron's sleep was too restless, but there was something he wanted to check in the bathroom.

He eased the medicine cabinet open. There were patent remedies in it that wouldn't have been available in city drugstores for half a century. He found what he was looking for behind a box of slippery elm lozenges: a prescription bottle of Digoxin, a digitalis preparation. One 1.5 milligram tablet, to be taken each day in the morning. The prescribing physician was Walter Maxwell; it had been filled at the Waite Pharmacy in Burns almost a year ago, but the bottle was still nearly full. Aaron was undoubtedly a difficult patient.

Conan returned to the guest room in time to see Ted ride up to the barn, then took his briefcase and went downstairs to the office. He turned on the light, although there was a window and an outside door on the south wall, and the light would be visible from the barn. But Ted wouldn't take exception to his being here; for this he had Aaron's sanction. A few minutes later he heard Ted come into the house and go directly upstairs.

The office was a small room crowded with a sturdy oak desk, three green-enameled file cabinets, an old Mosely safe, and a bookcase filled with ledger books and legal and accounting texts. The walls were decorated with photographs of prize bulls and ribbons from county, state, and national competitions. It seemed ironic that a million-dollar business was conducted from this cramped, styleless room.

Knowing George's orderly, accountant's mind, Conan almost expected the desk to be neatly cleared, but it wasn't. Several ledgers lay open, along with a scattering of invoices, receipts, and notes torn from a memo pad. He sat down in the wooden swivel chair, wondering what had induced George to leave his work so precipitately last night. Something unexpected. If he'd had five minutes' warning, or if his leavetaking had been a deliberate decision arrived at without outside influence, the desk would have been put in order.

So, what was the outside influence? Conan stared across at the door opening into the living room. Someone might have brought that influence through that door, or it could have come in the form of a phone call or radio message. All the ranch pickups were radio-equipped, and a transmitter sat by the telephone at one side of the desk.

Or there was the outside door. It was locked; he'd already checked that. And the window. A turn of his head to the left gave him a clear view across the open yard to the pool of light at the barn door.

Last night, sometime after eight, when a light was last seen in this window, George had left this room and crossed to the barn through that pool of light to saddle his horse and ride—where? Was the Spring Creek reservoir his intended destination? If so, why?

Conan vented a long sigh, lit a cigarette, and began studying the ledgers and papers. The ledgers contained stock inventories: cows bred, calves branded, calves, yearlings, and steers sold, breeding stock purchased, head counts of cattle left in particular summer grazing areas and BLM allotments, the number of known fatalities with notes of probable cause. Under that heading on this year's list was the notation "Thirty head (Benson Flat) Cyanide."

George had been comparing head counts with those of the previous three years. Conan generally avoided anything associated with accounting, but he was familiar with this kind of inventory, and a little study made it clear that this year's head count was running low. Still, all the cattle hadn't been brought down from the summer pastures yet.

He gathered the notes scattered on the desk; terse reminders, most of them routine, one particularly poignant: "Laura's b'day—11/5." Only three held his attention for more than a glance.

"Check w/Gil—hd. ct. Dry Creek Pstr." He frowned over the last abbreviation. Pasture. The other was clear enough. Head count.

The second note read, "Red car—L?" In association with "red car," the initial could only stand for Linc, but it still made no sense. It was even more mystifying because it was paperclipped to two other notes, the one on top reading, "Conan—Hol. Bch. 779-7070." The other was dated July 25. "Bert—Nev. lic. HUT710."

Bert Kimmons, who had succumbed to a heart attack while trying to bring two old friends together in a common cause: the possibility they were both victims of cattle rustlers. This would be the license of the cattle truck Kimmons saw.

The date rang a bell. Conan took out his notebook, and his frown deepened. July 25. Two days before the last deposit in Linc's Boise account.

He looked through the desk until he found the ranch checkbook, a large folder, five checks to a page. The monthly payments of five hundred dollars to Linc were there, along with equal amounts to Ted, eight hundred to George, and varied amounts to the ranch employees. Salaries. But nowhere was there a check to Linc or even to cash to explain the deposits in the Boise account.

He began a systematic search through the desk drawers, but found nothing unusual, nor any of the thoughtless leftovers accumulated by less orderly minds. He did, however, find something he considered a stroke of luck. Taped at the back of the bottom drawer was a paper with three numbers on it. He smiled at that. The safe combination. He had some practice at opening safes *sans* combinations, and the Mosely wouldn't have been beyond his skills, but this saved time.

He found six hundred dollars in the safe, a temptation no city businessman would risk, plus a sheaf of legal documents: deeds, the oldest dating back a century to the founding of the McFall dynasty; water and grazing rights; insurance policies; and two wills, George's and Aaron's.

He took the wills to the desk and smoked three cigarettes in succession while poring over the crotchety involutions of fine-printed legalese. George's will was relatively simple. Laura—"or their heirs"—was the chief beneficiary except for a few sentimental bequests, and the estate consisted mainly of life insurance policies. The ranch wasn't involved simply because in this "family run" business George had no legal claim to so much as an acre. Aaron McFall was sole owner of the Black Stallion.

Still, George's estate was impressive. Laura would collect from various insurance companies a total of half a million dollars. Now he could add that to a divorce George dismissed as impossible. Freedom *and* money. Two compelling motives.

Aaron's will was a labyrinth of provisions and codicils, and Conan recognized the first faint throbs of a headache, but the general purport was clear. On Aaron's death, ownership of the Black Stallion, a three-million-dollar empire, devolved upon the "eldest surviving son."

Linc was now the eldest surviving, and perhaps that also constituted a motive for murder.

He put the wills back in the safe, lit one more cigarette, and attacked the file cabinets, checking the suppliers and buyers with whom the ranch did business. Each company was alloted a folder marked with its name and address, but he found none with offices in Winnemucca.

At length, he closed the file cabinets, put the paperclipped notes and the one referring to Dry Creek Pasture in his briefcase, and locked it. He considered a judicious application of fluorescent powder but decided against it. Subjecting the family and employees to black-light examination would only arouse antagonism, and it would be closing the barn door too late. No one would be returning to this room now to cover any criminal tracks; there had already been ample opportunity for that. Sheriff Tate had been assured that the office hadn't been entered since George left it, but Conan had a handful of keys surrendered over twelve hours later, and even without a key the locks would be child's play to pick.

He climbed the stairs wearily, body protesting with assorted aches and pains its hard use this day. Eleven o'clock. At home, he would consider this the shank of the evening, but here it was the middle of the night, and Linc and Potts hadn't returned from Burns yet. He'd have heard the whining roar of the Mercedes. Linc's toy. A very expensive toy bought with a forfeited dream.

CHAPTER 13.

Conan woke to the sound of hoofbeats, and it became enmeshed in his dream, in which a stampeding herd of cattle was bearing down on the bookshop, while Miss Dobie assured him the rain would discourage them, and Meg played cat-and-mouse with a crumpled copy of his will.

When he recovered from the shock of waking in a strange bed and recognized the hoofbeats as the buckaroos riding out, he was faced with the realization that he was paralyzed from the neck down.

No, not paralyzed, or he wouldn't be in pain.

A few hours on Molly and a few minutes on Domino all in one day—it wasn't the best way to approach the saddle after an interregnum of several years.

Getting out of bed was the worst part. After that he hobbled to the bathroom and immersed himself in a stinging-hot shower, then subjected his knotted muscles to five minutes of agonizing calisthenics. By the time he had shaved and dressed, he was recovered enough even to anticipate breakfast.

It was seven-thirty when he undertook the descent of the stairs, but the house was empty, and he knew the ranch workday was already well begun. In the kitchen there was a residual odor of bacon, but the breakfast dishes were in the dishwasher, which emitted a steady, nerve-fraying roar. The room gleamed sterilely with enamel and chrome, betraying its age only in its old-fashioned generous dimensions.

He went out the back door to the breezeway where a water pump indicated that all the old ways hadn't been usurped. The men washed up there before going into the cookhouse for meals. But the kitchen in the cookhouse was another bastion of modernity, better equipped than most restaurant kitchens. Laura was there with Irene Mosely and Ginger Vasquez, producing pies with assembly-line efficiency. He'd forgotten the quantities of food working buckaroos consumed, and the hours necessary to its preparation. Laura, floured to the wrists, put aside her rolling pin to give him a warm smile.

"Well, good morning. How are you?"

He leaned against the doorjamb, hands in his pockets.

"Mobile, which is a small miracle. How are you?"

Her eyes flicked down. "I'm all right, Conan," she said, turning away to wash her hands at the sink. She'd gone to some trouble with her make-up, but it didn't hide the bruised puffiness around her eyes.

Then as she dried her hands, her smile restored, "Come on to the house. I'll fix you some breakfast."

He followed her back to the kitchen, giving up after a few attempts at helping. She worked with a nurse's efficiency, answering his questions without so much as a waste movement. Linc and Potts were alive and well, and she wondered how they managed it; she was sure they hadn't returned before midnight. They left half an hour ago for Jordan Valley—"Jerd'n," she ironically corrected herself—to look at some Durham bulls. Aaron and Ted had gone out with the buckaroos to ride fence; even without the feud, that was imperative at this time of year. Hunting season. The yearly toll of cut fences and strayed, lost, or wounded cattle was incredible. Aaron seemed to be feeling fine this morning. Good appetite, good color. His old cantankerous self.

And incidentally, since probably no one else would get around to telling him, the funeral would be tomorrow. Service at the Methodist church in Burns, burial in the cemetery at Drewsey. It would be the first time Aaron set foot in church since his cousin Jed's son was married ten years ago.

She answered his questions about Bert Kimmons with little indication of curiosity, adding nothing to George's account. When Conan asked if Kimmons had mentioned a red car, she frowned, scooped his eggs—sunny-side-up to perfection—onto his plate, and brought it to him before she responded.

"I don't remember Bert talking about a red car. Did George say something about one?"

"No, not exactly. Mm. I haven't had hashbrowns like these since"—he laughed—"since I left the Ten-Mile. By the way, I seem to be afoot here, or I guess ahoof. Do I need Aaron's consent to borrow a car?"

She laughed at that as she poured two cups of coffee and sat down across the table from him.

"You can use the Buick. It was officially George's and mine, but I used it more than he did. He always preferred pickups." Her light mood wavered only briefly. "Well, where are you off to today?"

"Burns."

"What will you be looking for there? Some vital clue?"

"Hopefully."

She studied him a moment, fleetingly surprised.

"Am I out of line asking that sort of question?"

"No, of course not."

"Does that mean I'm not among your suspects?"

He shrugged. "At this point everyone is a suspect, simply because I haven't enough evidence to eliminate anyone, but you're low on the list." A large rock would be an impractical murder weapon for her, which didn't eliminate her as an accomplice, but he didn't pursue the subject. Her hand was trembling as she reached for her cup.

"Laura, did George say anything recently about Dry Creek Pasture?"

"What? Well, I . . . no. Not that I remember."

"Where is it?"

"Oh, south beyond Jenny Butte. It's sort of a basin, I guess. Actually, I've never been there. It's rough country, and George used to call it a rattler reserve."

"How far away is it?"

"I think about eight miles from here. It's close to the K-Bar property line."

"K-Bar? That was Bert Kimmons's ranch?"

"Yes."

He nodded and concentrated on his breakfast. George had mentioned a county road running along the property line. Kimmons had seen the Nevada cattle truck on that road.

Laura rose, seeming ill at ease with his preoccupation.

"I'll get the car keys for you, and consider the car yours for the duration. If I need transportation, I have plenty of alternatives. I always said this place looked like a used car lot."

◇❋◇

The Harney County Courthouse was a sturdy, square, stone building of WPA vintage, its economic lines softened only slightly by plantings of arborvitae. The lawn was a little patchy at this time of year.

Sheriff Joe Tate occupied an office whose decor was in keeping with the architecture, an austere, heavily waxed shine about it, but Tate seemed a little ragged around the edges, tie loose, cigar well frayed. He had surrendered his files to Conan almost eagerly, an index of his desperation.

"That rock is the murder weapon; Doc says there's no doubt about it." The rock rested in inanimate gloom on his desk, a pocked hunk of black basalt weighing perhaps twenty pounds. "Doc says George prob'ly got hit before the dam blowed; there was dirt in the wound didn't come from that rock. But he can't say how long before."

Conan was glancing over the autopsy report a second time, his respect for Walter Maxwell growing. It was meticulous, objective, and thorough.

"Was there any evidence that George had handled dynamite?"

"Nope, but I s'pose he could've been wearin' gloves and took 'em off to light the fuse. That place was so tore up, it'd be easy to lose a pair of gloves."

Conan raised an eyebrow but didn't comment. Tate didn't seem too impressed with that explanation, either.

"You checked Drinkwater's explosives inventory?"

"Ain't nothin' missin'—accordin' to *his* records."

"What about the Black Stallion inventory?"

"Harley talked to Wil Mosely; he keeps all them records. Same story."

That wasn't particularly surprising. "Is there anyone around here who could do some soil comparisons for me?"

"Well, lessee, your best bet'd be Cliff Spiker. He's with the county agent's office downstairs. Cliff's a geeologist; been in Harney County near twenty years. I'll give him a call, tell him you're workin' with me."

"Thanks, that should grease the wheels a little. I'd like to have him look at this rock."

Tate puffed at his cigar a moment, then shrugged.

"Sure. You know how to handle evidence."

"That would be a little hard to lose."

He sorted through the sheets in the file, stopping at a report on the employees at both ranches. Ranch hands tended to be itinerant and rootless as tumbleweeds, but this group was relatively stable, most of them employed at the same ranch for periods of two to ten years. Only two men had arrest records: Pete Harkness of the Double D, with an A and B conviction, suspended sentence; Morgan Hayes of the Black Stallion, with a manslaughter conviction for which he spent two years in the state prison.

"Sheriff, do you know Pete Harkness?"

He gave a short laugh. "Yep. That A and B don't mean nothin'. Ol' Pete jest can't hold his likker; got hisself in a fight with a California dude. Most of the time he's 'bout as mean as a puppy dog, and anyhow he ain't too smart, y'know. Good steady hand, but he can't handle nothin' too complicated. And if you're wonderin' about Morgan Hayes, I know all about how he come to do that time in Salem. Woman trouble."

Conan looked up. "Who did he kill, the woman or the lover?"

"The lover. That wife of his weren't worth a hill of beans, but you couldn't tell Morgan. Then one night he come home and found Nancy keepin' their bed warm with somebody else, and he flew mad. Don't figger he meant to do more'n beat the feller up good, but he cracked his head on the bedstead. Since then, Morgan's been straight as an arrah."

"In other words, an unlikely candidate to mastermind a long-term effort like the feud or a premeditated murder."

"Premeditated?" He eyed him skeptically. "Can't argue that now. No, not Morgan. He jest don't think that way."

"Do any of these people?"

"No, and I know ever'body on that list. Most of 'em been around here a good long time."

"What about Gil Potts? He seems to be fairly new to Harney County." He studied Potts's employment record, a nomadic history: Idaho, California, Nevada, Oregon; generally buckarooing, but occasionally working in various towns, cooking, pumping gas, construction work. The job tending bar in Winnemucca was noted; from there he came to Burns, worked at a Shell station for six months, then another six months at the Double D. His four years in the Army was also on record, including the paramedic training Laura had mentioned.

"Ol' Gil done a lot of movin' around," Tate commented, leaning forward to dispose of his cigar in a chipped ashtray. "But he never got hisself in trouble, you notice, and never took no rockin'-chair pay. Lotta guys like Gil around; don't like gettin' tied down. But, y'know, since he signed on at the Runnin' S, he's sorta put down roots. I told you he took a likin' to Linc. Sometimes havin' somebody to look out for steadies a man down."

"He seems to be successful as a steadying influence on Linc. I wonder what happened between him and Alvin."

Tate shrugged. "I guess they got into it hot 'n heavy, but I don't know what set it off. Course, Gil signed on there not long after Charl died; Alvin was purty broke up."

"And cantankerous?" Conan asked absently, thinking of Aaron McFall's bitter grief. "What can you tell me about Charl's death?"

That called up a sharp and questioning look.

"Well, like I said, it was diabeteez. Nothin' out of the way 'bout it 'cept mebbe where she was found. She come to town that night for the Burns-Crane basketball game. We found her car in the school parkin' lot, but *she* was clear t'other end of town in a phone booth, out cold. Coma. That's what Doc called it. But he says people goin' into diabetic spells sometimes do queer things. Mebbe she forgot she even had a car and jest started walkin' for help. Doc's place is out to that end of town."

Conan's eyes narrowed. "But she was in a phone booth? Did she call the doctor?"

"Nope. Some feller phoned the hospital, says he seen her lyin' on the ground by the booth; didn't know if she was sick, drunk, or took some drug. He wouldn't give a name; jest passin' through town, he says."

"And didn't want to get involved, I suppose."

"Somethin' like that."

Conan closed the folder and returned it to Tate, then took some slips of paper from his pocket.

"I looked over George's office last night. I didn't find much of interest, except he was running a comparison of head counts for the last few years."

Tate nodded. "He was worried about rustlin', mebbe?"

"I think so. When I called him, he said something about Bert Kimmons and that rustling ring working out of Winnemucca. I found these notes." He handed them to Tate, who put on his glasses to examine them. "The three with the paperclip are exactly as I found them. My home phone, the license number, and that reference to a red car. The other was by itself, the one about Dry Creek Pasture."

" 'Check with Gil,' " he read. "You ask Gil about this?"

"Not yet." He didn't add that he probably wouldn't until he knew more about the lines of communication in the family. "Did you check that license with Nevada DMV?"

"Yep. Truck b'longs to a feller named Al Reems; runs a little spread near Winnemucca. He swears up and down the truck never left his ranch that night, and a couple of his hands backed him up." He unwrapped a fresh cigar, scowling as he bit off the end. " 'Nother box canyon, that. Talked to Sher'ff Culp down to Winnemucca. He says Reems is slippery as a greased pig."

"He thinks Reems is running this rustling ring?"

Tate sent out a pungent puff. "He *knows* it, but he can't prove it. Reems's son-in-law runs the meatpackin' plant in Winnemucca, by the way, and this ain't no penny-ante operation. They prob'ly sell the beef over to Reno and Tahoe; lots of reesorts and rest'rants 'round there."

"And probably most of them inclined to ask few questions. Did either George or Kimmons say anything to you to explain that reference to a red car?"

"No, not a word. Wonder if that L stands for Linc."

"Possibly." Then he added with an indifferent shrug, "It might be a reminder of something else George wanted to talk to me about. My name and phone number were clipped on top of those notes."

"Mebbe." His chair squealed as he leaned back. "Well, you find anything else while you was nosin' around?"

Conan chose his words, trying to avoid an outright lie.

"I'm just getting my bearings, and I don't seem to be too popular either at the Black Stallion or Double D."

Tate grinned wryly. "No, don't s'pose so. I heard you was over to the Double D. Wonder you didn't get shot at."

"Well, I managed to get on speaking terms with Bridgie. She told me about Alvin's fall from his horse Thursday night."

Tate accepted that as a question and at first seemed annoyed at it, but apparently it was the answer that disturbed him, not the question.

"Purty flimsy as alibis go, ain't it? Damn." He clamped his teeth on his cigar, sending out smoke like a small fumarole. "If I don't come up with somethin' else soon, you know what I'll have to do. I'll have to take Alvin in, and that rankles, Mr. Flagg; damn, if it don't.

Ben Kromer—he's the district attorney—he's been on my tail all day. Young feller, Ben; tryin' to make a name for hisself."

"Can he get a conviction on the evidence you have?"

"I don't know. Mebbe he jest figgers he's gotta do *somethin'*, one way or t'other. I guess he's got people ridin' his tail, too. Hell, this thing's hit ever' paper in the state and prob'ly a lot outside. I'll tell you what'll happen. There'll be a trial and a lotta talk th'owed back and forth, but if Ben lays it out like Alvin killed George 'cause he found him blowin' up his rezzavoy, there ain't a jury in Harney County'll convict him. He'll get off, but nothin's gonna get settled."

"Aaron won't be satisfied with that." And he wouldn't stop at that, not with his eldest son's death unavenged.

Tate sighed plaintively. "Om'ry cuss. *Both* of 'em. Jest plain om'ry. And I've got that funeral to worry about now, with all them reporters and photogerphers gawkin' around—think they'd have the common decency to leave people in peace to bury their dead."

"That's not what they get paid for." Then a look at his watch brought him to his feet. "I'd better get down to the county agent's office before the lunchhour."

"I'll give Cliff a call," Tate said, punching the phone for an outside line. "I ain't sure what you're after, collectin' dirt, but I hope to hell you hit the mother lode."

CHAPTER 14.

Burns was a prosperous town; there were few vacant stores along Broadway, its main street and the route of Highway 20. While the buildings presented earnestly "modern" fronts, a glance down the alleys showed backs of honest brick or stone, chinked and patched over the years, as unimaginative and as solid as their builders, but apparently a little embarrassing to second and third generations. The Arrowhead Hotel, however, displayed its weathered gray masonry on all four stories—which made it the tallest building in town—with little self-consciousness, although there was too much glass and tile at the entrance.

Conan had lunch at the Arrowhead coffee shop, reminiscently enjoying the passing scene along Burns's Broadway, while waiting for Horace Foley to return to his office at the Harney Valley Bank and

Trust. It was rather refreshing to learn that people still went home for lunch.

But he didn't find Horace Foley refreshing, and when that appointment was concluded, he pushed his way out the bronze-accoutered doors guarding the citadel of finance with his temper at high simmer. Still, the vested, purse-lipped banker had yielded him some satisfaction. Conan seldom used the Flagg name nor the Ten-Mile, but it was both expedient and necessary in this instance; he had certain business to transact with Foley beyond the answers he sought from him.

Conan crossed to the east side of Broadway and walked south, taking note of the Waite Pharmacy as he passed. Another modern false-front, its windows filled with Revlon glamor and Rexall remedies.

At least Cliff Spiker had not, to his relief, shared Foley's truculent attitude. He had been intrigued with the challenge of applying his geological expertise to the solution of a murder, and willingly undertook the analyses Conan requested, as well as supplying him with topographic maps. They had parted on Spiker's promise that he'd have some answers for him tomorrow, Sunday or not.

Conan turned into a stucco building painted an intense rose pink. On the door, in gold leaf, was the legend THE CLARION, VOICE OF HARNEY COUNTY. Inside, the fluorescent gloom vibrated with the clack of presses, and communication between the four staff workers was carried on in shouts. A counter provided a barrier to the public, and Conan waited there for some time before he succeeded in catching anyone's attention. Finally, a wiry old man with spatulate, ink-stained fingers came over and peered at him.

"Somethin' you want?"

"Jesse Broadbent. Is she here?"

"She know you?"

"Conan!" Jesse's stentorian call rang through the din as she emerged from a door at the rear of the shop. "Abe, you send him on back here."

Abe reluctantly opened the gate at the end of the counter, while Jesse motioned Conan to follow her into a glass-fronted office.

"Come on in here so's we can hear ourselves think."

She closed the door, cleared a chair of a drift of proof sheets, filled two mugs from a gurgling percolator, then sat down behind a desk that looked like the wake of a paper avalanche, grinning slyly at him as he eased into his chair.

"What's wrong, Conan? You feelin' a bit stove up?"

He reached for his coffee, which had the olfactory appeal of a seething caldera, and decided to let it cool, instead lighting a cigarette and offering her one.

"That has the ring of a rhetorical question, Jesse."

She took the cigarette, then after a brief, surprised hesitation, leaned forward to accept a light.

"Well, seems I heard somethin' about you takin' Domino on and stickin' with him down to the bell. Damn, you keep up with that sorta thing, you'll be a Harney County legend."

"I'll be in the Harney County hospital first."

"That's where a lot of our legends end up; that or the county jail. So, how's the detective business these days?"

"Another rhetorical question? You could probably give me an itinerary of my activities since my arrival."

"I could tell you what you was up to today, anyhow. You was at the courthouse to see Joe Tate, right? Then you paid a visit to the county agent, and I'd give a lot to know how come. Or how come you got ol' Foley in such a dander."

Conan shook his head in amazement.

"Word does get around. Well, I went to the county agent's office to see Cliff Spiker about some soil samples, and if Foley's in a dander, it's because I was interested in his reasons for refusing Alvin Drinkwater a loan."

She nodded, taking a swig of the scalding coffee without so much as flinching.

"What'd he say?"

"Only that 'someone close to Aaron' had advised him not to approve the loan. He wouldn't name his adviser."

"Uh-huh. Well, that's inter-estin', and don't bother buyin' a copy of tomorrah's *Clarion* to see if I put that little item in. Here—I got a ashtray some'eres." She uncovered one finally and pushed it toward him.

"Thanks. I have faith, Jesse, in your discretion, and very little choice. You're my only trustworthy source of information."

"You don't trust Joe Tate?"

"I doubt he has the kind of information I'm after."

She gave a short laugh. "What you're after's more like gossip, then, ain't it?"

"More like."

"Lookin' for some fire under a smoke?"

"I'm just looking for some smoke." He tried the coffee, found it still scalding, and guessed it would also serve very well as type cleaner. "What are people saying about George's death?"

"Oh, they're tellin' it ever' which way. Most of 'em figger Alvin done it, all right; that he jest flew mad when he come on George ready to blow up that dam."

"Tate says there's no evidence that George handled dynamite."

"That don't mean he didn't."

Conan shrugged. "No, but neither does it lock any doors. Are you on good terms with Bert Kimmons's widow?"

"Edith Kimmons? Sure. She and Bert was about the first friends me and Sam had when we come here. Why?"

"I found a note on George's desk. 'Red car,' then an L with a question mark. It was paperclipped to another note with Kimmons's name and a Nevada license number."

"Oh—that rustlin' thing. Red car and L. Offhand, that adds up to Linc, don't it?"

"Maybe. I was hoping you could explain it."

She laughed. "Well now, I ain't exac'ly an oracle, y'know. But come to think of it, I asked Edith what Bert had to say about all that, and there *was* somethin' about a red car." She frowned in fierce concentration, then nodded. "Sure. A little for'n car, Bert said; passed it a while before he come up on that truck. He thought it was kinda queer, seein' a car like that clear out in the tules. But it was goin' west; that truck was headed east."

"Did he think it was Linc's car?"

"He never said so to Edith. You figger it was?"

"I don't know." He took a swallow of coffee and tried not to grimace at it. "I've gotten the impression Linc has a penchant for women. For married women."

Jesse took a long drag on her cigarette, eyeing him.

"You're after some names, is that it?"

"If possible."

"When it comes to gossip, anything's possible. Lately, there ain't but one name; Linc usually jest takes on one at a time. Sylvia Waite, wife of the feller runs the drugstore up the street. She works there part time, if you want a look at her. Real purty woman, but that never kep' Myron home nights. Mebbe that's why she took up with Linc."

"How long has she been taking up with him?"

"Oh, three or four months. Won't last. Nothin' does with him since Charl died. But if he needs an alibi for Thursday night, he's got one. I ain't sure he'd wanta use it."

"He was with Sylvia Waite?"

"Yep. Y'see, there ain't many places 'round here people can go when they're lookin' for a private bed. There's a motel at the north end of town, the Sunset. It ain't fancy, but the folks runnin' it do a purty good business jest lookin' t'other way and keepin' their mouths shut."

He couldn't repress a smile. "But not shut to you?"

"Well, I always got on fine with Gladys Betzger, and Linc's one of their reg'lar customers. Anyhow, he was at the Sunset Thursday night; come in about seven-thirty."

"With Sylvia?"

"No. She come in later, by the back way, so to speak."

"When did Linc leave the motel?"

"I don't know. I mean, Gladys didn't know."

He nodded as he flicked the ash from his cigarette.

"Linc probably won't need Sylvia as an alibi. His story is that he and Gil Potts spent the evening touring the bars. Tate swallowed it, so I'm sure Potts backed him up."

"It's prob'ly true. Jest not quite *all* the truth."

"That's a rare commodity even in an incomplete state." He gamely downed more coffee before giving up on it entirely and finding a final resting place for the mug on a corner of the desk. "Can you tell me any part of the truth about that money Ted supposedly stole from the Running S?"

Both eyebrows came up, then went down in unison.

"No more'n you jest said. He *supposedly* stole it."

"Then can you give me an expert opinion? Do you think it likely he did steal it?"

"Well, lately I've sorta been on the outside with the McFalls, and Ted's jest a kid. Kids can change awful fast, and I don't figger Aaron made hisself too popular with him, the way he set his heels over him marryin' Bridgie. I . . . jest can't say, Conan. It don't sound like Ted. I mean, that ranch's been his whole life. But people change."

Conan considered that statement and her uncharacteristic hesitancy. People did change, especially under stress, and Ted had been subject to a great deal of that lately.

"What can you tell me about Charl Drinkwater's death?"

"What d'you mean? You think mebbe she didn't die a natural death?"

"Did she?"

Jesse dismissed the question with a weary shrug.

"Natural as they come when you're only nineteen years old. I talked to Doc Maxwell when it happened. He was all broke up over it; said he could've saved her if he'd got to her half an hour before, but he was out to the Riddle's place deliv'rin' a baby. I wondered if she wasn't tryin' to get to Doc that night. His office is in the north end of town, close to where they found her. You hear about that?"

"The phone booth? Yes, Tate told me about that and the anonymous caller. Where is that booth, by the way?"

"Right on the highway. Broadway, I mean. Lessee, Broadway and about Forty-fifth."

"I understand Linc took her death a little hard."

Jesse snorted. "A *little!* Poor Linc. I always figgered he'd be a differ'nt man altogether if Charl'd lived."

"I thought they separated before he went to college."

"Well, I ain't so sure they *stayed* separated. But that's *pure* gossip, or mebbe jest wishful thinkin'. I know Linc's a hellraiser, but I guess he has his reasons."

Conan put out his cigarette with slow jabs, wondering how far those reasons would drive Linc. Everyone involved in this case had reasons, it seemed; motives.

Then he rose, calling up a smile.

"Well, Jesse, thanks for the information. Or gossip. I'm sorry I haven't anything to offer in exchange."

"I figger you will, sooner or later." She sent a wry laugh after him as he went to the door. "But I got a piece of advice for you. Stay clear of Domino if you intend to stay on your feet."

"I'm way ahead of you there. Thanks, anyway."

CHAPTER 15.

When he reached the corner of Broadway and Forty-fifth, Conan parked the Buick and got out to take a close, and aimless, look at the phone booth. He wasn't sure why, except that it was the site of an enigma, and unexplained phenomena made him uncomfortable. He rationalized the stop by looking up Walter Maxwell's address in the local directory; his office and residence were listed under the same number.

Then his eyes narrowed, fixing on a faded signboard across the street. An arrow pointed east and promised that two blocks away, the traveler—or seeker of privacy—would find the Sunset Motel.

Conan found it: old paint over old stucco; narrow casement windows, all curtained; a frugal neon sign announcing an eternal vacancy.

He drove back to the highway, crossed it, and wandered an old but well-kept residential district where golden maple leaves paved the streets. Dr. Maxwell's house and office was marked with a small sign on the door. Conan wondered if he was married. No, he hadn't worn a wedding band; Maxwell was the kind of man who would, even if he was a widower.

Conan returned to the highway and continued north out of town, so preoccupied he almost missed the junction where Highway 20 turned east again after its dog-leg through Burns. For nearly twenty miles the highway stretched across the plain of Harney Valley, never deviating a degree until it reached the barrier of Stinkingwater Mountain. The next ten miles he regarded as one of the most awesome drives in the state, yet when he finally turned off onto the dirt access road, he could remember little of what he'd seen.

At the Black Stallion, he put the car in the garage, welcoming the poplars' shade and the cool scent of the sprinklers ticking out rainbows over the lawn. Mano Vasquez was tending the flowers by the gate, but otherwise the ranch seemed deserted.

"Hello, Mano. Where's everyone gone?"

His manner was diffident, but underlying it was a defiant suspicion subtly different from that of the family and hands; Mano was even more an outsider here than Conan.

"Mr. McFall and Ted, they are out with the bookaroos working the cattle. The women are in the cooking house, except Mrs. McFall. She has gone riding."

"Alone?"

"Yes."

He nodded and continued up the walk to the porch.

"Thanks, Mano."

"*De nada.*" The inflection was cold, but it didn't register; Conan was too distracted by another sound as he entered the foyer. Music. The style was distinctly Western; a plaintive solo accompanied by the rhythmic strumming of a guitar.

It was coming from upstairs, and it wasn't a recording. Linc. Conan started up the stairs, drawn by curiosity, but halfway up, stopped by wonder. A simple melody, as were all the great and haunting melodies in history, cast in a minor key, tapping the springs of joy and grief common to the human experience.

It stopped, but only for an experimental humming with a slight change in the chording, then began anew, and Conan moved slowly up the stairs, listening to the words.

> She never was a country girl,
> Was only love that kept her here,
> Made her stay the long, still nights,
> Say, oh, love, oh, hold me near.
> Every dawn she sang awake,
> The light made sunrise in her hair.
> All day long she rode the hills,
> Findin' nothing there to care.

All the hills, they turn their backs,
And the only voice she'd ever hear
Was the lonely echo of her own,
Every day and every year.

Oh, I want lights in the night
And laughter all around me,
The moon with neon stars
And a neighbor I can see.
Oh, love me, love; I love you, love,
But it's loneliness, loneliness kills,
And she never was a country girl . . .

Conan stood transfixed as the last chord died, trying to sort surprise and delight from regret and bewilderment. A country girl. He remembered Laura smiling over the phrase. Laura with her copper hair—did the light make sunrise in her hair? But Bridgie had described her sister with a strikingly similar phrase: hair like a sunset.

The song began again, and Conan felt suddenly uncomfortable, as if he were eavesdropping. The politic course would be to slip downstairs and come up again with enough noise to advertise his presence, yet he was drawn to the open door of Linc's room, and there he stood watching Linc make music of plucked strings as if it were an act of love. *Linc don't belong here.* Bridgie's words again. Where *did* he belong? Where do poets and makers of music belong?

The strumming stopped, and Linc's eyes turned on him, ice blue, taken by surprise and resentful, and Conan could only manage a lame, "That was beautiful . . . the song."

The muscles moved under the sunbrowned jaws, and a shadow of doubt flickered in his eyes. Then he laughed harshly and struck a clanging chord.

"Well, son of a gun! A *music* lover, a gen-u-ine music lover, ri' chere at the old BS. Well, boys, let's hear it for the lover! A-one . . . a-two . . . a-three . . ." And he launched into twanging song, foot stamping the cadence.

"Oh, bury me not . . . on the long praireee . . . where the wild coyooootes'll howl—"

His hands and foot went still, laughter and mockery stricken from his face, words like an echo he didn't hear.

". . . bury me . . ."

A moment of taut silence, then he put the guitar aside, eyes averted, and crossed to the door, passing Conan as if he were invisible, the retreating sound of his boots on the stairs like a tumbling boulder.

Only when Conan heard the slam of the screen door did he finally rouse himself. He went to his room, feeling in some indefinable sense defeated, opened the windows to alleviate the accumulated heat of the afternoon, then spread the topographic maps on the bed and forced himself to concentrate on them.

At first, they seemed only random networks of fine lines, but once he located a few familiar points, the lines began translating themselves into the reality of mountain and valley, river and road. Here, angling across the upper left corner of one map, was Highway 20, and striking east from it, the dirt access road that passed the Double D, continued to the Black Stallion, then wandered off the map. To the south, a patch of blue signified a reservoir now nonexistent. If lines were drawn between the blue patch and the ranches, they would form a nearly equilateral triangle.

He arranged another map so that its top border coincided with the bottom of the first and traced the east-west line of the county road that marked the boundary between McFall and Kimmons land. Rattlesnake Ridge, Carmody Flat, Riddle Butte, Widow Creek, Greenhorn Mountain. Dry Creek wound like a fugue along the road, turned northeast through a narrow canyon, then unraveled across a wide basin. Dry Creek Pasture. "Pasture" was undoubtedly a typical misnomer, but it would be open and offer good grazing, although the approach to it from any direction would be rough, except through a valley called Basco Gap, which angled from the southeast perimeter to the county road. He understood George's term, "a rattler reserve." The tortured, close-spaced elevation lines abstracted a battlement of steep escarpments and deep canyons; the kind of rocky terrain rattlesnakes thrive in.

He measured out distances roughly. The imaginary line connecting the Double D and the reservoir was about five miles long, and if it were extended another four miles, would go through the center of Dry Creek Pasture. The distance from that point to the Black Stallion was approximately eight miles. From the basin center south to the county road was about one mile—as the crow flies—and from the point where the crow would cross the road to Highway 20 was nearly ten miles.

His calculations were interrupted by the sound of hoofbeats and voices. He went to the window and saw Laura riding in on Molly. Linc was at the barn door to meet her. He helped her dismount, and a short exchange followed that Conan had to read in gestures and attitudes. Laura shook her head repeatedly, but it seemed more an indication of doubt than a strong negative response, and they were standing closer than would be usual in a casual conversation between friends. Linc put his hands on her shoulders once, gently, protectively. She turned, looking behind her, and after a few more words, walked away, apparently to her house. Linc watched her, then took Molly into the barn. A few minutes later, Conan saw what had distracted her: Aaron and Ted riding in with the buckaroos.

He left the window, eyes shadowed, oblique, and sought his cigarettes, lighting one as he returned to the maps. He was still poring over them when the cookhouse bell rang to call the hands to supper and the family to the cocktail hour.

◇❈◇

Predictably, it could be termed the "happy hour" only in darkest irony, and was a virtual repetition of the day before: Aaron brooding behind a cloud of cigar smoke; Ted locked in silence, casting resentful glances at his father that suggested the aftermath of a quarrel; Linc equally silent, preoccupied with his own thoughts; Laura preoccupied with drinking too much too fast; Potts busying himself noisily with bartending and sporadic attempts at conversation.

Conan wondered why they bothered to maintain the ritual, and was reminded of an observation made by his aunt Dolly many years ago in reference to the Flagg family ritual of breakfasting together no matter what individual schedules might be. "You never nail up a gate, Conan, whether you're usin' it or not. You might need it someday."

Aaron consumed his old-fashioned in bristling silence, but when he started his second, launched a vituperative attack on Conan, questioning him about his day in Burns and his progress on the case, temper flaring as Conan's evasions became outright refusals to answer. Aaron then turned to ranch business, aiming his questions at his sons or Potts. No mention was made of George or the funeral.

As Aaron reached the bottom of his second drink, it became apparent that his testiness was, again, more than bad temper. Conan watched him, noting his pallor, a slight tremor in his hands, the cigar put out before it was finished with a caustic comment on its taste, and when at length he stood up, it was with the unsteady caution of an old man.

"I'm goin' on up to bed."

Laura was also watching him. "What's wrong, Aaron?"

"Nothin's wrong. I'm jest tired, that's all."

"Is your stomach upset?" She studied him intently with a nurse's eye as he crossed to the door.

"I jest ain't hungry, Laura. Now, don't you start mother-hennin' me."

"Heaven forbid," she murmured into her glass.

Conan asked, "Aaron, did Dr. Maxwell prescribe something for your heart condition?"

He turned and scowled. "I don't see how you figger that's any business of yours."

Laura answered the question, looking up at Aaron with a curiously detached air.

"Doc prescribed a maintenance dose of Digoxin and a salt-free, low-cholesterol diet—which Aaron refuses to take or follow."

"Damn it, I can't be bothered with them fool diets and pills. I don't need 'em. I been feelin' fine."

"Have you?" she asked.

Aaron shrugged uneasily. "Well, I jest didn't sleep too good last night. That's all's wrong with me."

"All right, but I'd like to have Doc make sure of that. We could stop by his office tomorrow while we're in town for . . . the funeral. Please. Just to ease my mind."

It was revealing, perhaps, that he didn't argue, but only nodded absently as he shuffled to the door.

"Whatever you say, Laura, but he'll jest tell you the same thing. Nothin' wrong with me."

"Shall I bring you . . ." But he was out of earshot. She vented a sigh of resignation. "I'll fix some soup and try to get it down him."

Supper was also, in many respects, a repetition of the night before, the tension unallayed by Aaron's absence. Laura took a tray up to him, then called Dr. Maxwell, taking her place at the table when the rest of them were nearly finished. In answer to Conan's query, she shrugged, mechanically cutting a chop into mincemeat, forgetting to transfer even one piece from fork to mouth.

"Maybe it *is* just lack of sleep and indigestion. I wonder if he'll ever be honest enough to admit to grief."

That comment created a silence even Potts didn't try to leaven. Linc broke it with a complete change of subject, his hotly sarcastic tone reminding Conan that he, like Laura, had indulged heavily at the cocktail hour.

"Saturday night," he said, apparently addressing Ted. "The Grange is puttin' on a dance over to Drewsey, y'know."

Ted didn't look up. "I heard about it."

"I'll jest bet you did. Bridgie and her ma's in charge of the refreshments. You hear about that, too?"

Before Ted could respond, Potts put in mildly, "You figger you should go, Linc? I mean, tomorrah's the—"

"What d'you want me to do? Sit home and cry?" He sent Laura an apologetic look, then, undaunted, asked, "How 'bout you, Laura? We ain't missed a Grange dance for years."

She smiled stiffly. "Well, I think I'll pass on this one, Linc, and not because I feel obliged to sit home and cry. I'm a little worried about Aaron."

That reason pleased him no more than the other.

"Well, *I'm* goin'! You can set here and hold Pa's hand, and, Gil, you can set here and cry, for all I care."

He stormed out of the house, and in another repetition of the night before, Potts followed with a hasty apology to Laura. In the ensuing silence, Ted stared miserably at his plate, unaware of Laura's pensive, cognizant scrutiny.

"You know, Ted, he's right. There's no use sitting here crying. Why don't you go to the dance?"

He looked up at her, his face reddening.

"I—I jest don't think it'd be right. . . ."

"Because of George? Do you think he'd care? As for me, I'd be happy to see you have a good time." She didn't mention Bridgie, but undoubtedly knew that was the real, and compelling, attraction for Ted. But he still hesitated.

She turned to Conan. "I'll bet *you'd* enjoy it. A real Saturday-night shindig, a bit of vanishing Western Americana."

He took her cue, considering the possible advantages of an opportunity to talk to Bridgie and Emily Drinkwater.

"I haven't been to a Saturday-night dance since I was a kid. Ted, are you willing to be seen in the company of a rank greenhorn?"

He laughed uncertainly. "Well, I wouldn't exac'ly call you a greenhorn, Mr. Fl—uh, Conan."

"But I *am* a stranger here."

Ted pondered that and apparently found it a satisfactory rationale. He rose, signaling concession with a studied sigh.

"Well, all right, then. Laura, you're sure . . ."

"Yes, I'm sure. Now go on and enjoy yourself."

He was having a hard time restraining his anticipation.

"Thanks. We won't stay late."

CHAPTER 16.

The Grange Hall in Drewsey was a two-story falsefront of elegant proportions, which were generally lost on the residents, who also seemed blithely indifferent to the fact that since being bypassed by the highway years ago, the town was sinking not into oblivion but into the golden limbo of a ghost town, a concept more relevant to city dwellers, who viewed it through the rose-colored glasses of nostalgia.

On any other night, Drewsey would be as quiet as the hills around it, but tonight the sounds of revelry were audible to the farthest house. Conan had to park some distance away; every open space around the hall was filled with an assortment of vehicles ranging from pickups to Cadillacs. Light flooded from the windows and music gushed into the chill night. Local talent, Conan guessed; a fiddle, percussion, and a couple of guitars with an electric twang.

The cool air at the open door had attracted a cluster of revelers. Ted worked through the greetings and condolences nervously, repetedly introducing Conan as the reason for his presence at this festive occasion. Inside the hall, the music reverberated from the high ceiling, the wooden floor shook with the stamp of dancing feet, and conversations were carried on in amiable shouts. The style of dancing on this number, which had a strong, fast beat, varied from rock to jitterbug to fox trot.

Off the dance floor, the sexes tended to segregate, the women gathering around the refreshment table, elderly matrons in their flower-printed dresses, their daughters and granddaughters garbed in a variety of styles from conservative Sears-Roebuck to name-label chic. The men gravitated toward the doors and windows, cigars and cigarettes thickening the air; a few Copenhagen snuff or Bull Durham tins appeared. Occasionally, some of the men wandered outside to meet at the side of the building and pass a bottle around. No alcohol was served inside the hall, but the good spirits weren't due entirely to the music or convivial atmosphere.

Most of the men wore boots and Levis or twills with pearl-buttoned shirts, and some sported dress suits of the elegant, nearly Edwardian Western cut. String tie slides and wide belt buckles decorated with polished stones or fine silverwork were proudly displayed by men who would consider wearing bracelets or necklaces degenerately effeminate.

"There's some of the guys from Crane," Ted said, or rather shouted, looking toward a group of teen-agers gathered in one corner. Crane was the county's boarding high school; Ted's alma mater. Conan took the hint.

"Go ahead, Ted. I'll see what the refreshment table has to offer."

Ted hesitated, well aware that among its offerings was Bridgie Drinkwater, who stood beside her mother, filling paper cups with punch. But he turned the other way, apparently overcome by a case of adolescent nerves, and pushed through the crowd, which was dissolving with the cessation of the music, toward the corner and his school friends.

Conan made his way to the table, looking for other familiar faces. He saw Jesse Broadbent near the door and hoped she was distracted enough by the woman she was talking to not to notice him, but doubted it. Sheriff Tate was here, too, but two familiar faces weren't in evidence. Perhaps Potts had succeeded in talking Linc out of coming.

The music resumed, a slow number with a nasal tenor accounting a trucker's unrequited love, and the dance floor began filling again.

"Hello, Mrs. Drinkwater—Bridgie."

They both smiled courteously, but Bridgie's gaze kept straying past him toward Ted. Emily offered a cup of punch.

"Glad you could come to the party, Mr. Flagg."

"So am I; it brings back memories. But I had a hard time talking Ted into coming with me."

She glanced at Bridgie with a smile of fond cognizance.

"Well, I'm glad you got him to come. Time like this, a person needs a little leaven in life. How's Laura?"

"She's all right," he said, repeating Laura's own repetitious assurance. Emily's smile faded with a long sigh.

"I sure miss seein' her here. She was always one of our reg'lars at the dances. Why, her and Linc used to—" She stopped, succumbing to a flush of embarrassment.

Conan casually tasted his punch. "Dancing was never George's forte, but Laura loved it. I'm sure she appreciated having Linc as an escort."

That this was considered something other than a convenience was verified by her constrained attitude; a gentle woman, he thought, transparent as glass.

"Well, George wasn't . . . I mean, he—he never was one for kickin' up his heels much."

Conan spared her further explanation by turning to Bridgie and offering his hand.

"Well, *I'm* here to kick up my heels. Bridgie, would you dance with me?"

She accepted with the willing tolerance of youth for a surprisingly active octogenarian, and if she was a little stiff in his arms, he suspected it wasn't a reaction to him, but to Ted's presence. And perversely, perhaps, Conan set a gradual course toward the corner where Ted was pointedly engrossed in conversation with his friends.

"How's your father, Bridgie?"

"Oh, he's fine. He don't ever come to these parties, y'know. Most of the fellers 'round here never have time for dancin'. Least, not once they're married."

"Like George?" Then, when she only shrugged, "Look, I want a straight answer, that's all. I've heard the rumors, and I want to know if there's anything behind them."

She glanced around uneasily, but Conan was making sure they didn't stay in one spot long enough for anyone to overhear more than a fragment of their conversation.

"You mean about Linc and Laura. Well, Mr. Flagg, I don't rightly know, but there's been a lot of talk, and Linc—well, he didn't exac'ly act like a brother to her."

"How did Laura act toward him?"

"That's hard to say. I mean, I never could tell what she was thinkin'; not really. You sound like you're still . . . lookin' for answers."

He nodded, catching a glimpse of Ted moving toward the edge of the dance floor, alone, watching them intently.

"Yes. Did you think I'd give up so soon?"

"Well, no. You said you was stiff-necked." She gave him a side-long smile. "Least, a warnin' shot don't faze you. You—uh, havin' any luck?"

"It's a little early in the game yet."

"I guess so. I didn't tell my folks about you. I mean, about why you're here. Jest said you was out to the rezzavoy to see where—where your friend passed on."

"I appreciate that, Bridgie. Very much."

"Well, I figgered Pa's got enough to worry about right now. Oh, you might be inter-ested—Pa had a call this afternoon from Hor'ce Foley. I guess he changed his mind about that loan; said Pa could come in and sign the papers Monday."

Conan raised an eyebrow in skeptical amazement.

"Well, it's a relief to hear some good news occasionally. Did Foley say why he changed his mind?"

"No." She eyed him suspiciously, for the moment too intent to realize they were moving closer to Ted with every turn. "I figgered mebbe *you* might know somethin' about it."

"Me? I have a hard time getting the time of day around here." A few more turns; he held her attention with a direct look and an offhand compliment. "Except from you, and that's worth getting shot at. You're the image of a girl I knew—but that's a long story."

She laughed. "I'll bet it is, and prob'ly a good one."

"Well . . ." He shrugged, then, with a show of surprise, came to a stop. "Oh—hello, Ted."

He doubted he could have moved her from that spot if he'd

wished to, but at first she and Ted only looked at each other, both seemingly suffering a sudden vocal paralysis.

Conan said lightly, "There's Jesse Broadbent. I want to talk to her before she leaves. Ted, you'll have to take over the dancing honors."

Jesse was standing near the door but showing no inclination to leave, a fact that didn't register with Ted or Bridgie. Ted finally got out a few stumbling words.

"Bridgie, you . . . I mean, would you . . ."

She laughed and took his hand.

"Come on, Ted, before the music runs out."

Conan watched them dance dreamily into the crowd as he walked over to Jesse, who met him with a knowing half smile.

"You goin' into the matchmakin' business?"

"I'm a romantic at heart—or so I've been told."

"I believe it. Say, you hear the big news?"

"Probably not. I'm not wired into the local grapevine."

"Well, seems ol' Foley decided to give Alvin that loan after all. You know anything about that?"

"How would I? I just heard about it from Bridgie."

"Uh-huh. Well, I was jest thinkin' since you had that little talk with Foley this mornin' . . . Oh, Lordy, here comes trouble right through the front door."

Conan turned. Trouble was entering in the person of Linc McFall, his step unsteady, bleary belligerence in his set jaw and stiff posture. Gil Potts was with him, sober enough to show his uneasiness as Linc surveyed the room, then fixed on Bridgie and Ted, a cold smile twisting his mouth. He began pushing his way through the dancers, and Conan was close enough to hear him say, "Hey, jes' looka that, Gil. Looka the shtar . . . star-croshed lovers. . . ."

Conan took Jesse's arm. "Let's finish this dance."

"Why, sure. Best offer I had all night." The attempt at humor lacked conviction, and she showed a strong tendency to take the lead, but they were headed in the same direction. Out of the corner of his eye, he saw Joe Tate moving in unobtrusively.

At the center of the dance floor a circle of tension was growing, all movement, all conversation stopped within its expanding circumference. Linc was laughing sardonically, shrugging off Potts's efforts to draw him away.

"Hey, ain' this cute!" He draped an arm around Ted's shoulders and leaned close to Bridgie. "A roshe by any other name'd bed as swee'. Ain' that so, Teddy-boy?"

"Linc, you—jest keep your mouth clean, will you?" His face was red with embarrassment, which Linc seemed to find irresistibly funny.

"Dirt's inna ear of the beholder, li'l brother. Hey, come on, Bri'gie, baby—how 'bout a dance?"

She glared at him as she might a rattlesnake through the sights of a shotgun just before she pulled the trigger.

"Linc, you stay away from me. I'm dancin' with Ted."

"Oh, Ted!" Linc laughed in his face, and Ted turned away with a grimace of disgust. "Oh, Ted, Teddio . . . where the hell art thou, Teddio?" Then with a sweeping gesture that nearly unbalanced him, "Deny thy father, refuse thy name, 'r be but swore my love, an' I'll no longer be a . . . a *Drinkwa'er.*" And he sagged under helpless peals of laughter.

"What's he talkin' about?" Jesse asked Conan, but he didn't try to explain. Ted irritably extricated himself from his brother's arm.

"Damn it, Linc, you're drunk. Jest get outa here. Gil, for God's sake, take him on home."

"Take yourself home!" Linc retorted, pent anger erupting suddenly out of befuddled laughter, taking Ted and everyone else by surprise. The gathering crowd seemed to compress like a startled sea anemone, but Linc was oblivious to anything beyond his own irrational indignation.

"You can jest, take yourself and your damn little—"

"*Shut up!*" Ted lunged, not entirely succeeding in cutting off the final epithet. Bridgie held him back, both hands locked on his arm, bewildered and even frightened, and if she did hear the word Linc used to describe her, Conan doubted she'd ever heard it before.

Ted said thickly, "Get him out of here, Gil!"

He was rigid with the effort of containing his rage, and there was no hope of apology in Linc's pale, strained features. But it wasn't Potts who stepped in to avert the threatened explosion; it was Joe Tate.

"Okay, boys, now you jest cool down. This ain't the place to settle nothin'. Ever'body's here to have a good time. Hey, Pete, get some music goin'!"

It was only then that Conan realized the music had stopped, and when the fiddler struck up a lively tune and his amateur orchestra nervously joined in, everyone in the hall seemed to breath a sigh of relief.

Everyone but Linc.

Perhaps if he hadn't been so drunk, or so much like his father in his refusal to recognize grief, instead channeling it into aimless rage, the matter would have ended there.

"So, if this ain't the place to settle nothin', mebbe you'd like to go to the *right* place, Teddy-boy."

He seemed sobered by his anger, his speech clearer, muscular control restored, but Conan could see his eyes and knew this to be an illusion; he doubted Linc could even focus. But this escaped Ted, whose anger was fed not only by grief but soul-deep frustration accumulated over long months and centered on the girl who still clung to his arm, whom Linc had drunkenly described in gutter terms.

"We'll settle it!" he said through clenched teeth, then pulled away from Bridgie and strode to the door. "Come on!"

"Ted? Oh, no—Ted, please . . ." But he didn't hear her halting protest; the crowd closed in on her.

Conan and Jesse managed to stay in the front ranks as the erstwhile revelers thronged out of the hall, and the combatants and spectators joined under the cold blue light of a streetlamp.

No one seem shocked at the impending encounter, and Conan understood that; a brawl or two was expected at a Saturday-night dance, an outlet for high spirits volatilized by alcoholic spirits, regarded almost as an informal floor show.

But this was different. These were not only brothers, but McFalls, and the cause of their dissension was Alvin Drinkwater's daughter. An explosive situation, and none of the onlookers was unaware of it. Yet none of them made an effort to stop the confrontation.

Honor demanded a fair fight. Two brothers could beat each other into bloody insensibility—and the local ethic did not preclude below-the-belt punches, gouging, any kind of wrestling lock, nor the expedient use of those lethally pointed boots—and no one would consider stopping it until honor had been satisfied.

The contenders entered the lists amid a fanfare of shouts and whoops. Conan watched sickly as they went at each other, smelled the bitter dust raised by their scuffling feet, heard the grunts and stifled cries of angry pain, the smashing thuds of fists into flesh, and Joe Tate stood by, an unofficial referee, a rural sphinx, while the crowd recorded the progress of the tourney with partisan shouts, and Jesse, shaking her head, plaintively murmured, "Oh, mercy, oh, Lord have mercy. . . ."

Linc was getting the worst of it. The illusion of sobriety still maintained, but his reflexes were too blunted to match Ted's. He stumbled into punches, his own missing twice for every time he landed even a glancing blow, and with every failure he left himself wide open to Ted's fists. He sprawled in the dust, choking and blinded, again and again, and only once succeeded in grappling Ted down with him, but even then, Ted was back on his feet before Linc.

Ted pulled no punches, moving into every opening with cold

efficiency, his hands more bloodied than his face, knuckles broken against his brother's flesh and bone. And Linc masochistically kept coming back for more; the anger that impelled them both seemed to feed on his unreasoning obstinacy, and as long as he could keep his feet, this fair fight would not be called.

But Conan finally reached the limits of tolerance, seeing the blood, purpled by the light, mired with dust on those savage faces and battering rams of fists. Boys' games played with men's weapons; one too drunk to know he was defeated, the other too angry to recognize his advantage.

Gil Potts. He was also standing in the front row, wincing as Ted's fist plunged into Linc's belly, doubling him over like a puppet with the strings suddenly cut. Conan pushed toward him. Potts might be willing to get Linc under control if he would tackle Ted.

But Conan didn't reach his objective. A crunching impact, a wretching grunt; Potts scrambled to catch Linc as he careened backward against him, and Joe Tate finally reached the same conclusion Conan had: this fair fight had gone far enough.

Tate raised his arms, palms down, and Ted paused, hands still fisted, but his attention divided, waiting for Tate.

"All right, you boys," Tate said over their hoarse panting. "Now, that's about enough for— *Gawdamn!*"

Linc still wasn't ready to call it quits. Staggering, one eye swollen shut, a purplish stream running from his nose and into his mouth, he stumbled back into the arena.

But that wasn't what wrenched that startled expletive from Tate. The light gleamed icily on a metallic surface, a knife blade, and the onlookers loosed a concerted cry of chagrin. The blade flashed out, slicing across Ted's forearm.

Conan was stunned, but more by the knife than the wound; it was only a light cut. A switchblade. It was incomprehensible here, a ghetto weapon. A submachine gun would be no less appalling, and he wondered vaguely where Linc had gotten it, how it had come into his hand at this moment, or if he realized that he had conjured the specter of death here with that shining blade.

The desert night silence closed in, but it wasn't just the knife that elicited the silence. It was Ted's face.

He spun away when the blade struck his arm, and when he understood the wound and its cause, went dead white under the smears of dust and blood. The metamorphosis was instant and frightening. He had been angry and intent on violence to this point, but still recognizable; still Ted, steady, dependable Ted. But he was someone else now, a man intent on and capable of more than violence; a man capable of killing.

Perhaps Linc saw it, too, but he still wouldn't back down. For un-told long, taut seconds the brothers circled warily, crouching like predators in an unnatural encounter, until Ted attacked, teeth bared in an atavistic grimace.

He wrested the knife from Linc almost effortlessly, lithely dodged his flailing fist, doubled him with a solar plexus blow, sent him writh-ing in the dust with a knee to the groin, and still wasn't satisfied.

The knife flashed in a long downward arc.

As if it were planned, Conan and Tate moved in, Tate pulling Linc out of the way, the plunging thrust stopped with a hard slap as Conan caught Ted's wrist with one hand, aimed a snapping chop at the elbow with the other, and the knife flew from his hand. A light kick to the back of the knees, and he dropped to the ground to crouch staring at the knife glinting in the dust, his labored panting sounding strangely like sobbing.

◇❖◇

Tate surveyed the prone combatants, shaking his head, and at length said, "This looks to me like a draw. Okay, ever'body, we come here for a party. Let's get on with it."

He had to repeat that order several times before the spectators began retreating to the hall with dissatisfied murmurings, leaving the field of honor to the bloodied adversaries, their seconds, the referee, and a few interested parties: Jesse Broadbent, Bridgie and Emily Drinkwater.

While Potts helped Linc up and provided a handkerchief to stanch his wounds, Conan stood aside for Bridgie to get her fallen champion to his feet, and if her words of comfort included calling him a damn fool, there was still tenderness in them, and Ted was himself again; no evidence of the terrible metamorphosis he had so recently undergone. The McFall temper. Conan wondered if this was what Laura meant when she said Ted had the McFall temper.

Joe Tate leaned down to pick up the knife.

"Linc, where the hell'd you get this thing?"

He looked at it through one dimmed eye; the other was closed in livid swelling.

"I . . . I don' know."

Tate didn't believe him, but didn't argue, pocketing the knife with a weary sigh.

"Damn it, this is an *il*legal weapon. I could take you in jest for car-ryin' it around, but I ain't gonna bother."

"Why *ain't* you gonna bother?" Bridgie demanded hotly.

Tate looked at her, mildly surprised.

"There's been trouble enough already, Bridgie."

"And he's a *McFall*—is that it? Ol' Aaron might get mad, and the whole county'd be shakin' in their boots!"

Ted said tiredly, "Bridgie, jest shut up. Please."

"Well, it's true, ain't it? Anybody else'd be headed for the county jail right now, but Linc's a *McFall*, and Joe Tate don't dare touch a hair of—"

"Bridgie, *I'm* a McFall, too."

That stopped her. She stared at him, then without warning burst into tears and stumbled away. Her mother took her in a comforting embrace back to the hall.

Linc was sagging against the lightpost being wretchedly ill, his back to them, Potts supporting him.

"He gonna be all right?" Tate asked.

"Prob'ly." Potts glanced over his shoulder. "I'll look after him. And thanks for—well, goin' easy on him."

Tate only shrugged. "How 'bout you, Ted?"

"I'm okay," he said curtly, then with a glance at Conan, "Let's get outa here."

The drive back to the Black Stallion was tensely quiet, Ted responding to Conan's questions with reluctant monosyllables or total silence. His attitude was both cold and belligerent, and Conan found his own temper flaring. Ted seemed to hold him responsible for this disastrous evening, and had not a word of thanks or even recognition of the fact that he had stopped him from killing his brother.

But Conan withheld comment on that, knowing his temper was only the backwash of tension. The state of his nerves also made him more vulnerable, and tonight more than anytime previously, he felt the acid bite of grief.

These were George McFall's brothers, and he had loved them. Yet the grief born of their love for him had helped fuel the rage that nearly left one dead by the other's hand.

And he considered that rage, particularly Ted's. Linc at least had the excuse of drunkenness. Ted had been totally sober, and yet one brother was still alive only because someone else had intervened.

CHAPTER 17.

Conan made a point of staying out of the way the next morning, the day of George's funeral. He didn't emerge from his room until nine o'clock, but not because he was indulging in a few extra hours of badly needed sleep. He awakened at dawn with the ringing of the cookhouse bell, and no amount of self-cajolery would keep his eyes shut after that.

He found evasion easier than he expected, thanks to the stream of visitors passing in and out of the main gate, where Mano was again posted with a shotgun to see that no reporters or photographers slipped past with the sympathizers.

The friends and neighbors who were allowed through the gate almost without exception brought offerings of food, but he knew he was seeing only a fraction of the neighborly offerings here; most would be taken to the Grange Hall in Drewsey, where the mourners would gather after the funeral for a pot-luck dinner. An old custom, and perhaps its roots were in the Irish wake; or perhaps in a land where affluence was an innovation, an offering of food was a particularly meaningful expression of comfort.

When he left his room, Conan slipped past the living room, where the sympathizers congregated with the family, made a haphazard breakfast in the cookhouse kitchen, then spent the rest of the morning wandering around the ranch, avoiding even the buckaroos, but keeping an eye on the house.

Finally, he saw Laura exit by the back door and go to her house. He followed her, but stayed only long enough to tell her he wasn't going to the funeral, explaining vaguely that he was expecting an important call. The pretext seemed of no interest to her, nor did she seem hurt or surprised, but he doubted anything he said registered, or that she'd had an hour's sleep that night.

She didn't even ask what had happened between Linc and Ted at the dance, although the scars of that encounter were obvious. That, Conan had ascertained from a distance; the brothers seemed to be avoiding him as much as he was them, and he managed to stay out of Aaron's way until the family was getting into the car to leave for the funeral. Aaron wasn't as indifferent as Laura to his refusal to attend the funeral, considering it sacrilegious if not treasonous. But there wasn't time to argue.

With Gil Potts at the wheel, the black Continental moved toward the gate in ponderous dignity, a flotilla of cars and pickups in its wake; the ranch employees, trussed in suits and ties, sunburned faces suggesting sober embarrassment. Except for Ginger and Mano Vasquez, Conan would have the ranch to himself for the afternoon, and he intended to take advantage of it.

He began with Aaron's bedroom.

It was a peculiarly impersonal room; Aaron kept few mementos. Conan did find a faded sepia portrait of Carlotta McFall. Her dark hair and the sensitive contours of her mouth reminded him of Linc. Perhaps she hadn't belonged here, either; at least, she didn't survive bearing Aaron's third son. He wondered if Aaron had ever forgiven Ted that.

But the room contained nothing pertinent to George's death or the feud. As the sun moved past zenith, making the windless afternoon an echo of August, he extended his search to George and Laura's house. It was a time-consuming and distasteful process, but invasion of privacy was part of the job; murder was too often a private affair. But this house, so rich in civilized and civilizing objects, offered as little as Aaron's room in the kind of answers he sought.

His next exercise in futility was the machine shop. He found it necessary to pick the lock on the explosives storage room. Tate's deputy had already checked the dynamite inventory, and Conan expected to find everything in good order. Wil Mosely's careful records agreed in every respect with the inventory. Over the past year, dynamite had been taken from stock and signed for by Aaron, Linc, Ted, and Gil Potts, but there was no way of verifying whether the stated amounts were used for the stated purposes.

His search of the bunkhouse was equally perfunctory and futile. The worst that could be said of the buckaroos was that they smoked, chewed, drank, and indulged in poker and calendars depicting incredibly endowed, air-brushed females.

He ignored the Moselys's house; Irene and Wil Mosely had worked at the Black Stallion for twenty years, and nothing he'd observed or learned suggested their loyalty to the McFalls had wavered in the last year. The Vasquez trailer he ignored because of the brevity, rather than length, of service. They had been hired only six months ago.

At any rate, searching their trailer was out of the question today. Ginger was busy in the cookhouse, but Mano, as general maintenance and yard man, worked outdoors, and Conan was well aware that his activities were under suspicious scrutiny all afternoon.

That was why he put Potts's trailer off until last. It was between the cookhouse and bunkhouse, facing the yard separating the barn from the main house, and exposed to view from a number of vantage points. But finally he found a moment when Mano was working in the branding corral behind the barn. Potts's door was locked, but that delayed him only briefly.

It was typical working-man bachelor's quarters—bed unmade, clothes, beer cans, copies of *Argosy*, the *Police Gazette*, and *Sir* scattered negligently; a place where a man slept rather than lived.

Potts wasn't a sentimentalist, either, but he was a collector of sorts. Weapons. Guns and knives. Two shotguns and three rifles adorned the walls, and Conan found five handguns in a drawer, ranging from a serviceable Colt .45 revolver to an exotic Italian 9mm automatic. The drawer also contained an assortment of hunting knives and a battered bayonet. There were no switchblades, and the collection wasn't unusual for a man of Potts's background.

Conan continued his search, methodically and painstakingly, but only one other item attracted his attention. It was in a packet of letters from Potts's mother and sister in Spokane. A newspaper clipping, the same one he'd found in Linc's room headlining the death of Charl Drinkwater.

He was preoccupied as he finished his search; still, he remembered to look out the window for Mano before he left the trailer. But his timing was bad, and he swore under his breath as he closed the door at exactly the same moment Mano emerged from the barn.

When he reached the house, he realized the afternoon was nearly gone, and hunger did nothing for his temper. He took time for a sandwich and coffee, and thus restored went upstairs for his briefcase and took it down to the office.

There was no evidence that the room had been entered since he'd left it. The air seemed stale and dead; he opened the window, then settled at the desk with a cigarette, the topographic maps, a notebook, and the telephone. The call went to Cliff Spiker's home in Burns.

A quarter of an hour later, he hung up and lit another cigarette while he studied his notes, eyes narrowed with a subtle excitement he refused to recognize consciously, as if recognition might blight the budding hope.

Spiker had been given the rock—the murder weapon—the soil sample from the muddied hooves of George's horse, and the sample Conan had taken from the reservoir. The rock, Spiker assured him, did not come from any outcrop within a mile of the reservoir, but lava formations of its type were too common in the county for him to guess its source.

It was the sample from George's horse that kindled the hope. It was diatomaceous earth, which was easily differentiated from the clays, sands, and volcanic ash composing most of the soil in the area. The sample from the reservoir was of the latter type, and there was no trace of it in the mud from the horse's hooves.

That meant the horse hadn't been near the reservoir. George and the sorrel had parted company before he reached the reservoir, and it was unlikely the parting was voluntary; a man didn't willingly put himself on foot in this country.

And Spiker had more to offer. Because diatomaceous earth was of high commercial value in pure deposits, the location of known outcrops was recorded and mapped in some detail. So were water sources in this arid land, and mud implied the presence of water. Thus, Spiker could pinpoint several locations in the immediate area where George might have ridden through wet diatomaceous earth.

Conan checked the locations on the topo maps, quickly eliminating most of them because of distance. Between approximately eight and eleven o'clock, George had ridden to or through a wet deposit of diatomaceous earth, and then been taken, probably after the blow that smashed his skull, to the reservoir. He didn't ride there; at least, not on his own horse. At a walk, a horse could cover perhaps five miles an hour; less at night, in spite of the full moon.

There was only one place on Spiker's list that was close enough to both the Black Stallion and the Spring Creek reservoir to satisfy the limits of time and distance.

Dry Creek Pasture.

Conan took a slow drag on his cigarette as he studied the battlement of escarpments around the basin, counting seven box canyons or narrow defiles which could be fenced off easily. Finally, he reached for the phone and placed a person-to-person call to Johnnie Moss at the Ten-Mile.

"Johnnie, this is Conan. Any plans for tomorrow?"

"Nothing important. I don't have to pick Avery up at that convention till Tuesday. Why? You need a ride home?"

"No, not yet. I need a helicopter."

Johnnie laughed. "Okay, but maybe you'd better have a pilot, too. Remember that time you took the Cessna—"

"I remember, Johnnie. How can I forget with you to keep the memory fresh?"

"Sorry," he said, with no hint of apology. "Anyway, where are you?"

"The Black Stallion, but don't come here. I'll meet you at the Burns airport at five tomorrow morning."

"Are you sure you mean *morning*?"

Conan smiled at his incredulous tone.

"I'm sure. I want to check something, and it can only be done in the dawn's early light, or it might attract too much attention."

"Okay. Mind telling me what it is?"

"No, but not on the phone. I'll tell you about it in the morning."

"All right, I'll be there." He sighed audibly. "Damn, five A.M."

CHAPTER 18.

It was a classic rosy-fingered dawn, fragile streamers of cloud pink against a deep, transparent blue sky. Conan looked down from the roaring, Plexiglas capsule of the helicopter at a serrated landscape molded by the warm rose of the clouds on the eastern slopes, the cerulean of the sky in the western shadows, and resolved to make this flight someday just for the pure pleasure of it. He couldn't fully enjoy it now, and he found that annoying.

He'd found a great deal to be annoyed about this morning, beginning with the alarm that woke him at three, and had been unusually short with Johnnie Moss when he gave him his instructions. But Johnnie's equanimity seemed unassailable, and he didn't ask Conan to elaborate on his brief explanation that he was investigating the possibility that cattle rustling was involved in the feud. Johnnie knew all about the feud; since George's death, every front page and TV newscast in the state was a textbook on that.

Johnnie kept the 'copter at a relatively high altitude until after they crossed Stinkingwater Mountain. Much of this land fell under BLM jurisdiction, and residents were accustomed to helicopters and planes overhead embarked on endless government surveys. Conan was hoping his own survey, and his interest in Dry Creek Pasture, would escape notice.

"There's the county road," Johnnie shouted, pointing ahead. Conan only nodded. He'd already recognized it; the topo maps covering this area had been committed to memory. He also recognized Dry Creek. Apparently, it had been named at some point further down its course or in a drought year; the rising sun flashed on sparse threads of water. Where the creek turned north, he looked ahead to a wide basin; Dry Creek Pasture. Johnnie took the 'copter down to a thousand feet and shifted course, approaching the basin from the southeast, where Basco Gap provided the easiest approach from the road on foot or horseback. There were tire tracks skirling off the road and disappearing in the sage up the canyon, but in themselves they meant nothing; in the era of the ORV, even the most remote hills were tire-scarred.

The canyon narrowed, its walls rushing past uncomfortably close, then suddenly opened into the basin, a spectacular vista with the hills on the eastern rim casting blue shadows across a plain gullied by Dry Creek and its ephemeral tributaries. The soil bared in its course had a pink cast, but at noon would be glaring white, and Conan smiled. Diatomaceous earth. The ridges to the east and north were rust-black lava, but to the west and south they were snow white where the cover of grass and sage was torn by erosion.

Johnnie glanced at him questioningly, and Conan pointed to the eastern rim.

"Counterclockwise, Johnnie, low and slow."

The 'copter's shadow skittered over the ragged escarpments as he studied the terrain sliding under them. But the search was brief. Within half a minute he shouted to Johnnie to turn back and circle the box canyon they had just passed.

It was perfect.

The single outlet was narrow and cliffbound, but the floor of the canyon was wide and cut by a running stream, which meant a year-round spring that provided the grass and water vital to the cattle confined there; at least thirty head. It wouldn't be unusual to find a few strays missed in the fall roundup, but not this many in one place. If that hadn't caught his attention, the two horses pastured with the cattle would have demanded a second look.

"You want me to set her down?" Johnnie asked.

"Make one more turn." Conan was getting the Minolta out of its case. "I want a couple of pictures, then put it down outside the mouth of the canyon."

Johnnie found a flat spot a few hundred yards from the opening; the rotors whipped up a dust cloud as they beat to a stop, and Conan scrambled out of the cockpit.

"Come with me, Johnnie. I'll need a witness."

The cessation of the 'copter's roar left an aural vacuum. Their footfalls crunched in an absolute silence that made rational the feeling that they were the only human inhabitants of the world. Their breath came out in white puffs in the chill air, and Conan appreciated the sheepskin jacket, a leftover from the Ten-Mile, like the boots. The latter weren't designed for walking, but he accepted their shortcomings. The odds were high against any rattlesnakes showing themselves at this time of year and in the dawn cold, but he would feel uncomfortable without that leather armor.

And if any rattlers were out, it would be here among these volcanic ridges. Iron-stained black burst through the grass and sage as if drought had split the velvet skin. If the pocked rock he'd seen on Joe Tate's desk were left here, no eye could differentiate it.

The mouth of the canyon was set an an angle so that from the ground not one cow could be seen, and it was spanned with a barbed wire fence artfully concealed in drifts of tumbleweeds. They went under it, Johnnie swearing when he snagged his jacket. Conan took pictures of the fence, and when they came into the canyon proper, some general views and close-ups of the cattle, focusing on the brands. They weren't disturbed by the invasion, only regarding them with blinking, bovine curiosity. The total head count was thirty-four; five with Kimmons's K-Bar brand, the rest bearing the slanted Running S brand.

Johnnie shook his head as he gazed around the canyon.

"It's just a big holding pen, Conan. Water and feed to keep a few head until they collect enough to bring in a cattle truck."

He nodded. "And they'd only have to trail the cattle a mile down Basco Gap to the road. Let's get a good look at those horses; I want to see if they have any brands."

Getting that look took some time. The horses responded as if Conan and Johnnie approached with intent to saddle, and part of the ritual of saddling was giving the rider a workout on foot before he caught up with his transportation. But finally Conan was satisfied; there were no brands.

They paused to catch their breath as the sun tipped over the eastern rim of the canyon.

"Well, Johnnie, horses mean saddles, unless someone rounded up these cows bareback, and I don't recommend that. There must be a cache of some sort; a cave, probably." He pivoted, studying the rock walls. "Over there where the spring comes out. That looks like a likely spot."

It was likely, but, like the fence, the mouth of the cave was well camouflaged, and they almost missed it. Conan took pictures both before and after they cleared away the weeds, cautioning Johnnie as they entered to watch for snakes, at which he prudently let Conan precede him.

It wasn't in fact a cave, but a deep overhang about ten feet long, tapering back to a depth of six feet. Even at the opening they had to bend to avoid hitting their heads.

Johnnie said dryly, "Well, there's your saddles."

There were more than saddles here. Conan recorded photographically a gallon can of gasoline, two boxes of dynamite, and four salt blocks. He took scrapings from them; analysis would undoubtedly betray a high cyanide content.

The saddles had no identifying marks, but from the stirrup lengths, he judged that both riders were tall. The blankets and bridles were piled by the saddles, hemp ropes with leather hondos looped around the horns, and small toolbags containing wire cutters and gloves tied to the rawhide strings. One of the bits was a common snaffle, but the other was a spade. Still, there was nothing unusual about any of this equipment; nothing unique enough to be traced to an individual purchaser.

He found the real bonanza under one of the saddles. A small metal strongbox with a handle welded into the top, the hasp sealed with a padlock.

"Johnnie, I want you to watch me."

He crouched beside him as he took his tool kit from his jacket and gingerly tackled the lock, holding it steady with a small pair of pliers to avoid adding any fingerprints.

"I'm watching," Johnnie said. "Is this lesson number one for cat burglars?"

"No. Lesson number one for potential witnesses. Ah—" The lock surrendered with a sharp snap.

The contents seemed anticlimactic. Four carbon duplicates of receipts. He took them out and studied them, his initial disappointment turning to hope, then biting regret.

They came from the type of cheap receipt pad available at any office supply store and were written in a crude hand. Each was dated, and listed forty to fifty head of cattle, broken down into cows, steers, and calves, the total value within five hundred dollars, plus or minus, of six thousand.

He didn't have to check his notes to know that these amounts coincided exactly with the deposits in Linc's Boise bank account, and the dates preceded those deposits in every case by not more than three days.

Under the totals was the notation, "Paym't on acceptance," and the initials B.T. He could call up no name to go with them, but another set of initials at the bottom of each receipt and in a different handwriting did call up a name; one as familiar as the hand.

A.L.M.

Abraham Lincoln McFall.

Johnnie, peering over his shoulder, asked, "What does that mean —payment on acceptance?"

Conan was too preoccupied at first to respond.

"What? Oh. Acceptance of the beef at headquarters, I suppose, which is probably a certain meatpacking plant in Winnemucca."

"Isn't this sort of thing usually a cash-on-the-line deal?"

"Usually, yes." He laid the receipts on the ground and photographed them. "But in this case, payment is made to a bank account in Boise. By mail, I'm sure, and in cash with a numbered deposit slip."

"But why? I mean, wouldn't that be a lot more risky?"

"Insurance, perhaps, to keep the seller quiet. These are carbons. Someone has the originals, and along with the bank account, they make damning evidence."

"Blackmail, then?"

Conan paused. "Maybe."

"Those initials mean anything to you?"

"One of them—the seller. But he isn't in this alone. There are two horses, two saddles, et cetera." And he was remembering the five-thousand-dollar checks to cash from Linc's Boise account. If that money went to the unidentified partner in this enterprise, it was a strangely uneven partnership.

But whatever the nature of the partnership, the enterprise, or rather the threat of its exposure, constituted a clear-cut motive for murder. And Thursday night, George had ridden through the mud of Dry Creek; mud winter-white, white as snow in the blue light of a full moon.

"You know, it's funny . . ." Johnnie was squinting out into the sunlight, frowning. "We didn't see a single Drinkwater brand on those cows."

Conan looked up at him sharply, than laughed. He had also considered that fact "funny."

"True, Johnnie, and a very astute observation." He put the receipts back in the strongbox and carefully replaced the lock. "But observations are only points of departure. My aphorism for the day, and not bad for six in the morning."

Johnnie conceded that with a short laugh. "So, what are you going to do with this damning evidence?"

"Rip it off. And you're going to hold on to it so you can swear it never left your sight, and I had no opportunity to tamper with it."

"Now, wait just— *Damn!*"

"Watch your head, Johnnie. And don't touch the box; just the handle. Now, we'd better cover our tracks and take off. If we stick around much longer, we'll get caught in the last roundup."

At eight o'clock, Conan turned into the drive at Walter Maxwell's office-home. Johnnie was still holding the box with the air of one left holding the bag. He'd relinquished it only when he locked it in the trunk of the car while they breakfasted at a highway café where Conan called Maxwell.

The doctor was expecting them, and even expecting their entrance through the back door. Conan introduced Johnnie only by name, then Maxwell led them through the kitchen and down a hallway to his office and waved them to chairs while he sat down at an old mahogany desk nearly black with years of polishing.

"Well, what can I do for you, Mr. Flagg?"

"Provide a safe hiding place, I hope."

Maxwell eyed the box Johnnie clasped so nervously.

"That's what you want to hide? What's in it?"

Conan frowned and started to reach for his cigarettes, but there wasn't an ashtray in sight. No doubt Maxwell could order his patients to stop smoking, diet, or abstain from alcohol with the clear conscience of a good example.

"Doctor, I'd rather not tell you what's in the box, but you were at the ranch when I arrived; you know about my investigation. The contents of the box may be regarded as evidence, but I'm not ready to turn it over to Joe Tate yet. Facts in themselves can be highly misleading."

Maxwell laughed. "In my business, they're misleading nearly all the time. Why bring it to me?"

"I don't know who else to trust it to. All I'm asking is that you keep it in a safe place for a few days."

"And keep my mouth shut about it? Is that it?"

"That's it."

He pondered a moment, then reached into his pocket for a keyring and went to a cabinet behind his desk.

"All right. For a few days. I'll keep it in here; this is where I store any dangerous drugs I have on hand."

"Thanks. Johnnie, will you put it in the cabinet?"

He complied, breathing a sigh of relief when it was locked out of sight, and he and Maxwell returned to their chairs. Conan wrote Johnnie's name and phone number in his notebook, tore out the sheet, and handed it to Maxwell.

"If I can't reclaim the box within a week, give it to Joe Tate and tell him to call Johnnie. He can explain it."

"I hope by then somebody can explain it to *me*." Then he laughed. "No, not now; I have a feeling the less I know about it, the better. On the phone you said you had some questions for me—or was that just an excuse?"

"No, it wasn't. Laura brought Aaron in to see you yesterday. Can you tell me about it?"

"You mean Aaron's comments on the medical profession, or my conclusions on his state of health?"

Conan smiled faintly at that. "I can guess his comments. I want your conclusions."

"Well, I don't suppose I'd be betraying any medical confidences Laura couldn't, or wouldn't." He hesitated. "You *did* talk to her about it?"

"I asked her if you had anything to say about Aaron's health, but she was . . . rather vague." An understatement, and Maxwell would understand it. Laura had come home from the funeral in a state close to shock. But dry-eyed. The memory of it made him want to weep. A privilege, she told him later in an unguarded moment; tears were for people possessed of unsullied consciences, an enigmatic statement she refused to amplify.

When the family returned in the fading glow of sunset, Conan was waiting on the porch and heard Aaron's blanket condemnation of the journalistic "buzzards" at the funeral, which led into a diatribe on his embarrassment at his sons' bearing the trophies of a drunken brawl, and on the very eve of their brother's funeral. Conan caught some of the emotional flak, enduring in silence being charged with having no interest in George or his death beyond a fat fee.

The family then went their separate ways, Linc to his room with the door closed, Ted for a ride in the cold light of the waning moon, while Aaron chose to seek solace in work. With Potts tagging along uninvited, he went to the barn to pitch hay. Conan was a little surprised at that, and at the fact that Aaron showed no symptoms of the nervous stomach upset that had sent him to bed so early the preceding nights.

Conan accompanied Laura to her house and offered to stay with her awhile. Not offered; insisted. But she was equally insistent; she wanted to be alone, and he left her finally, recognizing the solace in solitude, and hoping it didn't include another fifth of bourbon.

He returned to the porch, and a short time later Gil Potts, no doubt discouraged by Aaron's short temper, left the barn and joined Conan on the porch step for a cigarette. Their conversation began on an antagonistic note, although Potts smiled and kept his tone light.

"Hear you was doin' some explorin' 'round the ranch this afternoon. Like inside my trailer."

Mano had wasted no time, Conan thought, but he only shrugged, matching Potts's light tone.

"In your trailer? How could I? The door was locked."

"How d'you know that?"

"I tried it." Mano hadn't come out of the barn in time to refute the lie beyond a doubt. Potts laughed, apparently satisfied.

"Well, next time I'll leave it open." Then he turned sober and hesitant. "Conan, I don't s'pose nobody else'll get around to sayin' it, so mebbe it's up to me. About last night, I mean."

"Saying what?"

"Oh . . . thanks, I guess. You gotta understand about the boys—I mean, it comes hard for them, sayin' thanks or apologizin'. The way they was raised, I s'pose, and they're both a little . . . well, tight-wound, y'know."

"I know."

"Anyhow, I'll say thanks for the boys. If you hadn't stepped in right when you did . . ." He shook his head in perplexed disbelief. "No tellin' what might've happened."

In the face of his earnest concern, Conan hesitated before asking the question, but a nagging suspicion still skulked at the back of his mind. That knife, the switchblade, had come into Linc's hand so suddenly, almost magically, and right after he had fallen into Potts's arms.

"Gil, do you know where Linc got that switchblade?"

There wasn't a false note in his attitude or tone.

"No. Never seen him with it till last night. Prob'ly picked it up in a poker game. Conan, he's a good kid; jest gets a little too much booze sometimes, and last night—well, he was kinda wrought up."

Another understatement, which recalled him to the present and Dr. Maxwell, who was looking at him inquiringly. Conan had heard the question but had to concentrate to recall it.

Laura. How did Laura take the funeral?

"Without a tear. I don't know, Doctor. She didn't want to talk."

An anxious frown deepened the lines in his forehead.

"I'm worried about her; she holds everything in too much. So does Aaron. At least, he holds in the things really bothering him." A pre-occupied pause while his fingers drummed on the desk, then, "As for his health, it's better than I anticipated. In fact, his blood pressure and pulse rate were low for him. When George died, I expected Aaron to go down with a heart attack, but he's a tough old man. You have to be to survive in this country."

"Which makes Aaron one of the evolutionary fit?"

He laughed. "I guess so. I've always thought of it as a centrifuge. This country sorts people out; the men from the boys, the strong from the weak. Of course, that depends on how you define strength and manhood, but I don't suppose you want to get into that now."

"I think we'd simply find ourselves in agreement. Did you know Aaron isn't taking the Digoxin you prescribed?"

Maxwell stared at him, perplexed.

"He what? But that's—Mr. Flagg, I'm afraid you're in error there."

"I doubt it. I found an old prescription in his medicine chest. It was a year old and the bottle was still nearly full, and he as much as admitted it night before last."

"I'm not doubting your word, it's just . . . odd. You see, I've written refill prescriptions for the Digoxin regularly since he first started taking it."

It was Conan's turn for a perplexed stare.

"I can't imagine Aaron going to the trouble of getting new prescriptions for something he didn't intend to take."

"He didn't go to the trouble. On a maintenance prescription like that, Myron Waite—he's our local pharmacist—just calls me and I okay a refill, then give him a written prescription for his records when it's convenient. And I know Aaron doesn't go to the trouble of picking up his own pills. One of the boys or any of the hands who might be in town running errands takes care of that."

"And Waite gives them to anyone who asks for them?"

"Anyone who has the prescription number."

"So anyone could've picked up the prescriptions?"

"Well, there's another possibility." He paused, then with a shrug went on, "I wouldn't put it past Myron to raise his profit margin a little by charging Aaron for prescriptions he didn't fill. I doubt he lists them individually on his bills, but he'd need the refill prescriptions from me for his own records; for Uncle Sam, that is."

Conan considered that explanation, not entirely satisfied, then frowned at his watch and rose.

"Doctor, you said you have an eight-thirty appointment, and it's almost time. As for the missing digitalis, I'll try to track it down. Meanwhile, thanks for your help."

Maxwell rose and offered his hand.

"Mr. Flagg, I'm glad I *could* help. And . . . good luck."

Conan drove to the airport in brooding silence, which Johnnie accepted with his usual equanimity. When he parked outside the hangar where the 'copter waited, he reached into the back seat for his camera.

"Johnnie, I have an errand for you. I want you to take this film to Ed Teeter in Portland."

"That makes kind of expensive developing, doesn't it?"

"But dependably discreet." He frowned; the film spool seemed to defy his fumbling fingers. "Tell Ed to hold the prints until I call him. I just hope to hell I won't need them."

CHAPTER 19.

Conan didn't wait at the *Clarion*'s counter, but went directly to Jesse's office and found her conferring with Abe over tomorrow's front page.

"Conan! Come on in. Abe, that looks good, but talk to Billy about that picture 'fore you set the funeral story." Then as Abe morosely departed, "Cup of coffee, Conan?"

"Uh . . . no, thanks. I've come to take you to lunch."

"Lunch? It ain't 'leven yet." Then with a quick laugh she plucked a jacket from a wobbly coat rack and shrugged it on as she headed for the door. "But it ain't ever' day a handsome young city dude asks me out. Come on. Abe, I'll be back in a little while. You like eggrolls?"

Conan was scrambling to keep up, but managed as a matter of principle to reach the front door in time to open it for her.

"Eggrolls? Well, yes, I like them, but—"

"But you figger any eggrolls made in Harney County's gonna be built out of jerky? Well, you'll see. Might 's well walk. It's only a couple of blocks."

The café was a flat-roofed, unimaginative building with big windows advertising high school football schedules and 4-H pot-lucks, but the sign was intriguing: HIGHLANDER CAFE spelled in neon over a green Chinese dragon.

They were early for the noon rush; only a handful of customers were there to exchange familiar greetings with Jesse. Still, he was about to hint at the advisability of privacy, but that proved unnecessary. She chose a booth in the corner by the window; the low back provided a clear view of the adjacent booths, and she let him take the side that put his back to the wall, a peculiarly Western nicety.

The Highlander's name undoubtedly derived from the high school tribal symbol, a cartooned and kilted Scot, which in turn derived from Burns's namesake. The interior was as uninspired as the exterior, its walls a visceral rose-pink coexisting in a state of armed truce with the blue-green plastic leather booths. But Conan forgave the decor when he took a close look at what adorned the walls, and he began to understand the derivation of the green dragon.

There were three glassed panels; three of the most exquisite examples of Chinese silk embroidery he'd seen outside a museum. One hung above their booth, and he craned around to stare at it. Two storks in the branches of a pine, bursts of needles, delicate feather patterns, all stitched in subtle gradations of gray, the only stroke of color the birds' scarlet crests.

Jesse watched him, smiling. "Kind of purty, ain't it?"

"My God, Jesse, it's beautiful. You don't suppose this one would be—" A waitress emerged from the kitchen, affording him a brief glance through the door, and he gave up all hope of making any of these silks his own. The chef wore Levis, but his face would fade effortlessly into a crowd in Peking. A descendant of one of the millions of Chinese imported to build a frontier nation's railroads, Conan speculated, who wasn't likely to part with these treasures of his heritage.

"You game for the eggrolls?" Jesse asked.

"I'm game if they live up to the art."

The waitress and Jesse exchanged pleasantries, Jesse pointedly ignoring the curious glances cast at Conan. When the order was recorded and coffee served in heavy-gauge restaurant cups incongruously decorated with chrysanthemums and dragons, Conan lit cigarettes for them. Jesse nodded thanks through a cloud of smoke.

"So, what've you been up to this mornin'?"

"Jesse, you probably know exactly what I've been up to."

"Well, I know you met a feller out to the airport early this mornin' and took off with him in a hellycopter."

"Some business came up at the Ten-Mile. I had to make a fast trip to Pendleton to sign some papers." That seemed to go down easily enough, and he went on lightly, "But you missed something. I came to the *Clarion* directly from a private interview with Sylvia Waite." She'd missed something else, too, but he didn't intend to tell her about his visit to Dr. Maxwell.

"Sylvia? How'd you manage a *private* talk?"

"She's working at the pharmacy today, so I just waited until Myron took a beer break. This is marvelous coffee."

"Mm. Little bit weak. What'd Sylvia have to say, and how'd you get her to say anything?"

"Well, she was quite cooperative when I mentioned Linc and the Sunset Motel."

"You checkin' on Linc's alibi?"

"That and some strayed digitalis. Maxwell prescribed Digoxin for Aaron after his heart attack, but he stopped taking it about a year ago. The problem is, Doc has renewed that prescription regularly since then."

"That's queer." She frowned after an explanation, then, "You don't s'pose Myron's jest takin' a little rake-off?"

"Doc suggested that, but Sylvia swears she's seen her husband make up the prescription several times. Of course, she had no idea who picked them up; her memory seems a bit selective. Maybe she's afraid to say anything that might get Myron in trouble. I gather he has quite a temper."

"Myron's a little man, Conan, body 'n soul. Seems to think hollerin' and beatin' up on his wife makes him bigger."

"Well, Sylvia has her problems, but so does Linc. She can't give him an alibi past eight-thirty. It seems Thursday was the night she chose to suffer qualms of guilt. She went to the Sunset, but only stayed long enough to tell Linc their grand passion was over. I guess he didn't offer much of an argument; she left within half an hour."

"At eight-thirty? So, you figger Linc had time enough to go out to the rezzavoy and bash his brother's head in?"

He shrugged, overlooking her skeptical tone.

"Linc had time, but George didn't have his head bashed in at the reservoir. His horse went to Dry Creek Pasture, and I'm assuming he went with it."

Her skepticism turned to mystification.

"What's this about Dry Crick Pasture, and where is it?"

"South of the reservoir, near the county road that runs between the Black Stallion and Kimmons's ranch."

"The road where Bert sighted that cattle truck?"

"Yes. I know George was worried about rustling, and I found a note in his office; a reminder to talk to Gil about Dry Creek Pasture. I don't know if he *did* talk to him, and I won't ask Gil. I'm not ready to show my hand yet."

"Well, what makes you think—" She stopped as the waitress brought their eggrolls, and for the next few minutes the conversation lagged as Conan surrendered to appreciation of the golden-crisp delicacies; they lived up fully to the promise of the green dragon and the embroideries.

Finally, Jesse paused in her own hearty appreciation, giving him a smug smile.

"They ain't bad, are they? Now, back to Dry Crick. How come you think George was killed out there?"

He explained Cliff Spiker's analysis of the soil samples, adding, "He also told me that rock, the murder weapon, did *not* come from the reservoir, but there are tons of that type of basalt around the pasture."

She ruminated on that, chewing stolidly.

"So, you figger George headed out that night for Dry Crick 'stead of the rezzavoy? I don't see how he'd have any more business out there than at the rezzavoy."

Conan applied a cautious dash of hot mustard to a forkful of eggroll while he considered how much to tell her.

"Jesse, nothing at the Ten-Mile induced me to take a 'copter flight at dawn."

She laughed. "You had business at Dry Crick?"

"Yes, but if you tell anyone I was out there, so help me God, I'll personally run you through your own presses."

"Conan, it's a bit late to fret about trustin' me."

"I know, and I learned one lesson the hard way: it isn't always smart to keep everything to yourself. A client of mine once spent two days in jail because I happened to be in a hospital, unconscious. Anyway, I found out someone else has business at Dry Creek."

"Like rustlin' cows, mebbe?"

"Yes. I found a box canyon furnished with a good spring, plenty of grass, a couple of horses complete with saddles and rigging, and thirty-four head of cattle."

Her eyebrows went up in unison. "What brands?"

"Running S and K-Bar."

"No Double D?"

"No."

She considered that for a moment, then nodded.

"You figger George found the box canyon, then somebody found *him* and made sure he wouldn't tell nobody about it."

"Then took his body to the reservoir and blew it up for the sake of confusion. There's dynamite stored in the canyon, by the way."

"But why'd he ever go out to the pasture that night?"

Conan leaned back, frowning.

"I don't know. He was worried about rustling and possibly in connection with Dry Creek Pasture, but I doubt that induced him to ride out there alone at night. I think it was a sudden decision; he left his desk in very atypical disorder. A phone or radio call, probably; a plausible story from someone he trusted or at least believed. That would mean he was deliberately lured there."

"You think it was Linc did the lurin'?"

The initials A.L.M. hovered in the eye of memory.

"I'm only saying it *could* be Linc, since Sylvia's blown his alibi."

"What about the alibi Gil give him?"

"You mean the alibi they gave each other."

"Well, a person could ask around the bars, see if anybody remembers seein' 'em together that night."

"Not *this* person. I'm an outsider, remember? I'd get whatever line Linc and Gil put out." He frowned irritably at an inadvertent overdose of mustard. "Anyway, I can't eliminate them from the suspect list."

"Who's on that list?"

"All the McFalls, and Gil Potts—who's one of the family—and Alvin Drinkwater. You know about his alibi?"

She snorted. "You mean that story 'bout him gettin' th'owed off his horse? It ain't much of an alibi. 'Sides, it makes you wonder, not findin' any Double D brands in that canyon."

"I know, and Horace Foley tells me Alvin's in a precarious financial position. At least, that was his excuse for refusing the loan before he finally admitted that Aaron has a ring through his nose."

"Well, it ain't no secret Alvin's had a couple of bad years, so mebbe he *is* cadgin' some cash rustlin' cows."

"But you don't believe it?"

She shrugged uneasily. "Oh, hell, Conan, I don't know what to b'lieve anymore, what with this feud 'n all."

"Yes, it's been quite successful in creating general doubt and confusion." He polished off the last of his eggroll and leaned back with a sigh of repletion.

"You think that's the real reason for the feud?"

He nodded, and seeing the waitress bearing their way with a pot of coffee, stopped to light a cigarette while she filled their cups, then continued on her rounds.

"Jesse, I think diversion is probably the primary purpose, but there's more to it. A vendetta; something vicious. But I'm sure the feud, the rustling, and George's murder are related; I just don't know exactly how. On the surface, it looks like he was killed simply because he discovered that box canyon, but too many people have other compelling motives, so I'm wondering if it's really that simple."

Her eggroll demolished, she accepted a light for her cigarette, letting it hang on her lip, bobbing as she spoke.

"What kind of motives you talkin' about?"

"Well, money, for one. Like the half million in insurance Laura will collect."

"Mm. Yes, half a million makes a purty good motive."

"She has another. Freedom. She wanted a divorce, but George wouldn't give her one, and if you believe the local gossip, her freedom could also be a motive for Linc. He has a financial motive, too. I saw Aaron's will. Ownership of the ranch goes to the eldest surviving son, and as a result of George's demise, Linc is now the eldest surviving."

Jesse frowned at that. "I never noticed him showin' much interest in runnin' the ranch."

"No, but it's worth a sizable fortune if he wanted to sell it, or if he opted to make a deal with Ted. He's the one with the interest in running it."

"Lordy, it's really gettin' complicated, ain't it?"

"It's even more complicated when you get to Ted. Maybe he made an agreement with Linc, or is simply banking on his lack of interest to make a deal with him in the future. Ted has his reasons to be bitter toward Aaron, because of his opposition to his marriage to Bridgie, but he also had reason to be bitter toward George. You know about the money he supposedly stole from the ranch. According to Laura, Aaron set him down good over that. She compared it to seeing someone flayed alive, and it was George who told Aaron about the loss. If Ted happens to be innocent, that would only make him more bitter."

"Yes, but . . ." She paused uncertainly and took a puff on her cigarette. "Conan, I jest can't swaller Ted rustlin' cows or bashin' George's head, even if he *was* bitter."

"Sure, he's such a nice kid; quiet, dependable, well mannered. And Saturday night you saw him on the verge of burying a knife in one brother."

"I saw it," she admitted reluctantly. "I guess you jest never can tell about people."

"Still waters run deep, as someone's bound to say." And he hadn't forgotten the $1824 hidden in Ted's room; still waters run much too deep sometimes. "But there's another possibility. Alvin has no one to take over the Double D except Bridgie—his son apparently signed up for life with the Army—and she wants to marry Ted, an excellent match if he had control of the Black Stallion; a dynastic merger in the grand manner. Consider the possibility of a conspiracy that includes the star-crossed lovers and this rural Capulet."

"You ain't sayin' Bridgie'd be in on this, are you?"

"I'm not saying anything; only speculating. Bridgie might be a conspirator, but she took no direct part in the murder. She says she was home with her mother that night, and I balk, even in hypothesis, at including Emily Drinkwater in the conspiracy."

"Glad to hear you balk some'eres. What about Laura and Ted? They was home, too. And Aaron? You leavin' him out?"

Conan laughed. "Yes. Aaron's done nothing to make himself popular with anyone, including me, but I can't come up with a motive for him to initiate the feud, assuming it's a diversion for the rustling, in order to sell his own cattle at half the over-the-counter price, nor to kill George, who apparently lived up to his expectations as son and heir in every way. But the fact that Ted and Laura were at the ranch that night doesn't eliminate them. Laura would have no trouble slipping away without being seen, nor would Ted."

"Damn, you should've been a lawyer." Then she frowned. "One thing, though, all this conspirin' over the Runnin' S ain't gonna do nobody no good long as Aaron's still alive 'n kickin', and he's such an orn'ry cuss, he'll prob'ly be kickin' for a long time to come."

Conan paused as he was about to light a cigarette, staring at her while the lighter burned futilely in the air. Then his eyes slanted as he made contact with the flame.

"Maybe you should've been a detective. With all my convoluted hypotheses, I lost sight of that little fact."

"Well, I'm sorry to blow holes in your hypotheses."

"You haven't. You've only given me something else to worry about."

"What d'you mean?"

"Aaron. About how long he'll still be kicking."

Jesse turned pale under her weathered tan.

"You mean somebody might . . . might try to kill *him*?"

"Possibly."

"Mebbe you oughta talk to Joe Tate about that."

Conan shook his head impatiently. "Even if he agreed with me, what could he do? Put Aaron under protective surveillance? It probably wouldn't help anyway—and can you see Aaron accepting a police guard?"

"Not hardly. So, what're you gonna do?"

"I don't know. Keep digging, I suppose."

"Anybody in particular you're diggin' for? I mean, you got any fav'rites in this conspiracy race?"

The initials A.L.M. came almost inevitably to mind, but with it a plaintive song that touched the heart. He wondered if he resisted accepting the possibility of Linc's guilt in the murder because he didn't like to believe a maker of songs could also be a killer. And the two horses, two saddles, the five-thousand-dollar checks to cash—Linc had at least one accomplice in the rustling.

Still, that wasn't what made Conan hesitate. There was more under the surface here, factors he sensed but didn't understand.

"No, Jesse, I don't have any favorites. Not yet."

CHAPTER 20.

He'd been cold enough for the heavy sheepskin jacket in the chill of today's dawn, but as he drove along the dirt road to the Black Stallion, wheels rumbling up a storm of dust, Conan was down to his shirt with the sleeves rolled up. Cottony cumulus clouds patched the landscape with shadow. Wind clouds, the natives would say. Not a drop of rain in 'em.

But again, he wasn't enjoying the scenery, his thoughts casting back over the events of the day. The conference with Joe Tate and Cliff Spiker was only a bone to satisfy Tate with his good intentions. Conan didn't mention his dawn helicopter flight, and Tate apparently hadn't heard about it. Dry Creek Pasture was referred to only as one of the many possible sources of the mud on the hooves of George's horse, and Tate seemed to find that piece of evidence inconclusive. Conan didn't argue the point.

After he left the courthouse, he drove west on Highway 20 to the cemetery where George McFall was buried, and stood awhile by the mound of withering flowers. There was no headstone yet. When he drove back into town, he wondered why he'd been impelled to the grave. Not to pay his respects; his debt to the dead could only be paid with answers.

He passed the high school, a rambling buff-brick building flanked by a parking lot full of shining machines, and he was reminded of another death: Charl Drinkwater's.

Her car was found here the night she died. She'd come to town for a basketball game, a very social event. How did she end up alone and on foot in a phone booth at the other end of town? People going into diabetic spells sometimes do queer things—Maxwell as quoted by Tate. But why was she alone?

He pulled into a Shell station across from the school, relieved that the attendant went about his business in taciturn silence. But as he idly examined the sign above the pumps, he frowned, and it was he who initiated a casual dialogue when the man collected for the gas. The sign announced the owner's name, P. T. Gormer, and it rang a bell.

"I know a guy who used to work here," Conan said as he handed him a ten-dollar bill. "It was a couple of years ago."

"Lotta guys used to work here; come 'n go all the time."

"His name is Gil Potts. Maybe you weren't here then."

"I was here. I own this place." He counted out Conan's change carefully. "Sure, I remember Gil. Nice feller. Customers liked him."

Conan got the impression Mr. Gormer didn't, but the arrival of another customer precluded further conversation.

It was nearly four-thirty when he reached the Black Stallion. As he made the double stop to open and close the gate, he saw Linc and Laura on the front porch, but by the time he put the car in the garage, only Laura was waiting for him there.

"Well, the wanderer returns. I was worried about you."

"About me? I told you last night I had to take care of some business at the Ten-Mile." He studied her, noting the brittle strain under a smile as carefully applied as her make-up. "I should've left a note this morning."

"No, I remembered what you said, even if I wasn't tracking too well. I'm afraid I was rather rude to you."

"You weren't rude, Laura. I'm only sorry there was nothing I could do."

"Thanks for trying, and I'm glad you're back. I decided you'd given up on the whole hopeless mess, and I wouldn't blame you. Let the inmates fight it out among themselves."

She'd been drinking, but it was evident only in her cavalier irony; otherwise, she was in perfect control.

"I don't give up that easy."

"No, I don't suppose so." A long pause, then finally, "Is it hopeless, Conan?"

"What do you mean?"

"I mean, have you found any answers?"

He shrugged and said lightly, "I've collected a plethora of facts, and perhaps some of them constitute answers."

"And you don't want to discuss it with me." She laughed and started for the door. "So be it. You're almost late for the cocktail hour."

"I didn't hear any bells."

"It's early today. On Mondays I disrupt all the hallowed schedules for my 4-H class in Burns. I leave at seven, so we have to get supper out of the way early."

"Can't you call off the class tonight?"

"I don't want to. My last class. Mrs. McFall's last act of civic duty in Harney County." She gave him a wry smile as he opened the door for her. "Don't worry, I'll be quite all right, and Ted always goes with me. The class isn't over till ten, and none of the gallants around here would let a mere woman drive alone at night. I might get r—have a flat tire. Well, Gil, that's an inviting lineup."

That referred to the old-fashioneds arrayed on the bar while Potts added the garnish. Linc and Ted leaned at either end of the bar, turning bruised faces toward them. Aaron occupied his customary chair, his overstuffed throne.

"Where the hell have you been, Flagg?"

Laura murmured, "Home sweet home," as she went to the bar. "All finished, Gil?"

"Jest one more slice of lemon . . . there, now. You wanta pass 'em around? That one's Aaron's. Hold the cherry, light on the sugar." He was putting up a convivial front—like a good bartender, Conan thought uncharitably—but sending uneasy glances behind his smile at Linc and Ted as they took their drinks and retired to separate corners.

Laura was also playing at conviviality as she presented Conan with a glass, then took another to Aaron, who still glowered at him, ignoring her smiling service.

"For you, Aaron," she said, "virtually fruitless."

Her irony escaped him. "Flagg, I asked you a question."

He leaned an elbow on the bar. "So you did."

"Damn it, a man's entitled to a civil answer in his own house!" This with a cold glance at his sons, and Conan realized he was getting some of the backwash of another argument. Aaron turned on him again.

"I want to know what the hell you been up to! Hor'ce Foley called me today, and *you* got some explainin' to do."

At that name, Conan's mouth tightened, and he was as angry as Aaron, but not at him. He knew why the banker had called. But this was *not* a family affair.

He still had his drink in his hand as he went to the office door and unlocked it, pushed it open, then said coldly to Aaron, "If you want any explanations, I'll make them in private. Otherwise, you can do without them."

Aaron digested that ultimatum in fuming silence; then, apparently realizing no compromise was forthcoming, he took his drink in one fist and strode into the office without a word. Conan closed the door and watched him seat himself in imperious command behind the desk.

"Sit down," he said, peevishly motioning toward the chair across the desk from him.

His tone inclined Conan to automatic resistance, but after a moment, he went to the chair and sat down, absently putting his glass down on the blotter near Aaron's.

"All right, Aaron, what did Foley have to say?"

"He told me all about that loan for Alvin. You're s'posed to be here to nail George's murderer. 'Stead of that, you're passin' out *money* to him behind my back!"

Conan laughed. It was either that or give way to futile rage. But he couldn't contain himself enough to stay in the chair; he rose and went to the window.

"Aaron, I understand why you like to deal with the locals; good public relations, and all that, but I'd advise you to find another bank. Foley has a big mouth."

"Ain't nothin' wrong with Foley. He jest figgered I had a right to know what you was up to."

"Especially after you told him *not* to okay the loan?"

His chair scraped back as he surged to his feet.

"I told you, I never said nothin' to Foley about—"

"That isn't what he told me. 'Someone close to Aaron'—his words —advised him not to make the loan. Who was it?"

"I don't know what you're talkin' about, and that don't change the fact that you're givin' out money to the man who murdered my son! And you called George a *friend!*"

"In the first place, I'm not *giving* money to anyone. The Ten-Mile is backing a loan at reasonable interest with the bank acting as a go-between. Secondly, you only *think* Alvin murdered George. You may be right, but so far it can't be proven. Thirdly, I've met Emily and Bridgie Drinkwater and found them very likable. They're part of the Double D, too. I see no reason for them to suffer because *you* think Alvin is guilty."

Aaron came out from behind the desk, his rancor sagging out of him as he picked up a glass. Like so many aggressive men, he seemed curiously satisfied at meeting real resistance.

"I got nothin' against Emmy or Bridgie." Then he scowled irritably into the glass. "Gil knows I don't like these damned dyed cherries." He tossed the offending fruit into the wastebasket and took a healthy swallow.

Conan frowned, remembering Potts's and Laura's comments on Aaron's fruitless drink, but the answer was simple enough: he'd picked up the wrong glass. Conan didn't bother to point out the error. Instead, considering a peace-making gesture timely, he went to the desk drawer, took out three keys, and a fourth from his pocket.

"These are the keys to the office, Aaron. I won't be needing them anymore. Thanks for putting up with the inconvenience."

"Well, I hope it done some good."

Conan ignored the suspicious question in his eyes, picked up the other glass, and went to the door.

"It did. Shall we return to the happy hour?"

They found Laura and Ted sitting on the couch sharing a gloomy silence, and Aaron demanded, "Where's Linc and Gil gone to?"

"To town," Laura replied; then before he could work up another head of steam, "Aaron, please, I have something to tell you. I told Linc, and maybe that's why . . ." She let the sentence hang, while Aaron sank uneasily into his chair and waited in stoic silence for her to go on.

"Aaron, I'm going back to San Francisco. I called a friend of mine last night, and she said there's a job opening at the hospital where I worked . . ." Before she met George; she didn't finish that sentence, either.

Aaron looked across the room at her and suddenly seemed old and tired, nodding mechanically, repetitiously.

"Well, I guess I knew you'd be goin', Laura, but you're always welcome here; you know that."

"Yes, I know. But I . . . I want to get back to work."

He nodded again, staring vaguely into space.

"Well, I can understand that. When d'you figger you'll be leavin'?"

"Oh, as soon as I can get my things sorted out and packed. A week, probably."

"I—we'll miss you, Laura." Then he added almost plaintively, "Ain't right, not havin' a woman around."

Dinner was an unexpectedly pleasant hour, with Aaron indulging in gentle reminiscences of early days on the ranch, in which Laura encouraged him, laughing and commiserating over problems old and happily resolved. Ted shared the spirit of placation, even asking for a few favorite stories. The tension was still there, but by mutual consent kept under the surface, and perhaps because of the peaceful atmosphere, Aaron showed a remarkably healthy appetite.

But Conan found his own lagging, and his stomach protested the foot he forced into it with queasiness that verged on nausea by the time dessert was served. He turned down a piece of dark, thickly iced chocolate cake that normally would have induced him to ask for a second helping, privately blaming it on accumulated anxiety and lack of sleep.

When Mrs. Mosely and Laura began the woman's work of clearing the table, Ted managed to slip off to the barn without having exchanged one direct word with Conan, while Aaron retired to the living room and the television to watch the news. Conan went out on the porch to watch the sunset and enjoy a cigarette and cup of coffee, but found neither enjoyable, giving up the cigarette after a few puffs, the coffee after half a cup. The evening chill seemed to accumulate between his shoulder blades and spread out under his skin.

He knew, finally, that his symptoms couldn't be dismissed as nerves or lack of sleep, but he didn't know how else to explain them, except as an incipient virus infection, and his initial response was annoyance. A bout with flu would put a cramp in his investigatory style, and if he must be attacked by a virus, it could have made its presence known this morning when he was in Maxwell's office.

Still, he said nothing to Laura when she and Ted left at seven, although as acting ranch doctor she could probably offer a choice of remedies. He couldn't explain his reluctance; perhaps it was simply a stubborn refusal to admit he needed a remedy.

Long after they were gone, he sat shivering in the fading twilight, listening to the mutter of the television and a distant exchange of voices that died as the hands retired to the bunkhouse. He should at least get a jacket if he was going to sit out in this freezing wind. No. He should go to bed. A good night's sleep. That's all he needed.

But he was so damnably tired; his body seemed an immense weight upon itself, and the prospect of climbing the stairs to his room was overwhelming. Just getting to his feet was too much of an effort to contemplate seriously. Maybe he could just rest here until Laura came home.

He pressed his folded arms against his body; he wasn't even thinking straight. The class wasn't over until ten. Laura wouldn't be back before eleven. A man could freeze to death by then. Anyway, something in him balked at the supreme discourtesy of vomiting in the neatly kept marigolds.

He reached for the railing and his hand slipped, setting his pulse into an erratic flurry. A startling sensation, and that only intensified the irregular pounding.

Still, it clarified something in his mind.

This was no virus. It was an imminent threat realized on the primal level of brute terror. A threat to survival; to his life.

He levered himself to his feet, panting with the effort, and clung to the railing. The wind had risen. Couldn't stand up against a wind like this. And rain . . . no rain in wind clouds.

But it was only dizziness and a chill sweat that seemed to freeze on his skin. He realized that at the same moment he realized he'd never make it upstairs to his bathroom, and Mano would have to forgive the desecration of the marigolds.

He sagged over the railing until his stomach's rebellion eased, but the dizziness didn't abate, nor did the alien rhythm palpitating in his chest. Help. He needed help. . . .

"Aaron!" The door was open. Light glowing in a silent haze. Yellow light. No answer; the television still muttered, and he angrily mustered the strength to shout again.

"*Aaron, for God's sake . . .*"

Yellow light. *Yellow vision*. That meant something. A clue; a veritable clue. And where was Aaron? Behind a cloud of cigar smoke, watching some foreign apocalypse, while he died on his doorstep?

"*Aaron!*"

"What the hell—?" A shadow against the yellow light, and Conan began shaking uncontrollably.

"Aaron, can . . . can you drive?"

"What? Well, sure." He turned on the porch light and came out for a closer look. "You sick or somethin'?"

Conan flinched at the light. Still yellow; even Aaron's hair was yellow, and finally the neural link closed.

He said dully, "Yes, I'm sick. I've been . . . poisoned. Get me to Dr. Maxwell."

"You've been *what*? Here—jest hold on to me, or you'll take them stairs head first. Mebbe I better call Wil or—"

"No." He felt Aaron swaying under his weight as they started down the steps. "Don't call—don't *tell* anyone . . . can't let anyone know . . ."

"But, damn it, boy, you're sick as a dog. Easy now. That's the last step. All downhill from here on out."

It seemed quite literally downhill to Conan; downhill and canting.

"Just get me to Maxwell. And don't let him send me to a hospital. Promise me. On your word. No hospital and no—don't call . . . call Tate. Give me . . . your word . . ."

"All right, all right, you got my word on it. Watch that gate. What the hell you got against hospitals? Or Joe Tate? If you ain't the orn'riest son of a gun I ever run into. Hold on, now. You go down, I ain't gonna pick you up by myself. Little bit further . . ."

Conan stumbled along, clinging stubbornly to Aaron and to consciousness. He couldn't surrender yet; not until he made sense of this. How . . . *how* did it happen?

When Aaron eased him into the front seat of one of the cars, he closed his eyes, concentrating on forming words.

"Aaron, tell Maxwell . . ."

"What? Tell him what?"

". . . digitalis."

CHAPTER 21.

"Mr. Flagg, are you ready to tell us what happened?"

Mr. Flagg wasn't ready for anything. He lay huddled under a blanket on the couch in Walter Maxwell's office, resenting the brevity of the respite afforded him while the doctor restored his examination room to antiseptic order.

Let the inmates fight it out among themselves; an eminently reasonable proposal. But pride is a hard and unreasonable taskmaster, and finally he pushed the blanket back and maneuvered into a sitting position, an effort that left him dizzy and aching. He rested with his elbows on his knees, head propped in his hands.

His feet were fuzzy. Everything was. But the yellow vision typical of digitalis poisoning was almost gone. The blurred vision was a side-effect of the atropine injection Maxwell had given him. A paradox, that; a poison as antidote for a poison, and both were medicines.

Maxwell had drawn up a chair by the couch, and when Conan finally raised his head, he held out a glass to him.

"You better drink this; get something in your stomach."

"After all the trouble you went to emptying it?"

Milk, beautifully chill; it seemed pure ambrosia. He saw Aaron sitting across the room by the desk, but ignored him until he reached the bottom of the glass. Aaron waited with unaccustomed patience, a phenomenon Conan regarded with some amusement. He had finally been shocked into silence.

But then he had reason enough to be shocked, having a victim of poisoning thrust on him, and the process of emptying the human stomach wasn't pleasant, either for the victim or the observer. Conan had yet another shock for him; one he hoped would reduce him to a cooperative frame of mind.

He handed Maxwell his empty glass and looked across at Aaron, futilely straining to focus on his face.

"Aaron, you owe me for this."

He seemed startled, as if he'd been physically prodded.

"I—I *owe* you . . . ?"

"This was intended for you, not me." Aaron's slack-jawed silence was a satisfactory index of shock, even if Conan couldn't read nuances of expression. He went on matter-of-factly, "Doctor, wouldn't you agree it took a sizable dose of digitalis to make me this sick? What would Aaron's survival odds be if he'd been given that dose?"

Maxwell frowned, his gaze shifting to Aaron.

"At his age, and with his heart condition . . . I don't know. I might've saved him if I got to him in time."

"In time," Conan repeated, still looking across at Aaron even while addressing Maxwell. "But it's an hour's drive from the ranch, and that has to be added to the time necessary to discovery. Now, Laura might have recognized the seriousness of the symptoms soon enough, but she was here in Burns for her regular Monday evening 4-H class, and Ted came with her, as he always does. Potts was trained as a paramedic, but he and Linc left early for Burns's taverns, another regular occurrence. Aaron was alone in the house except for me, but all I could do was bring him to you, Doctor, and with his history, would you have considered digitalis poisoning *soon enough?* Or would you have assumed heart failure?"

Aaron was recovering, and before Maxwell could answer, he spluttered angrily, "Will you talk sense, damn it! *You're* the one got poisoned."

"Yes, I noticed." He eased back into the cushions. "I was encouraged by that at first; I thought I must be getting close enough to the truth to be considered a threat. But when I realized *how* I was poisoned, I had a rude awakening. I wasn't regarded as a threat. In fact, the killer didn't hesitate to poison you right under my nose. Now, that's a blow to the ego."

"I still don't understand—"

"A little patience, Aaron. Just consider the *how* of the poisoning. That's the key. I ate nothing at the ranch today until supper, and that was served from communal bowls, boarding-house style. Even the milk and water were served in pitchers. If the digitalis was in the food, I wouldn't be suffering alone. So, it had to be in the cocktails. The old-fashioneds; perfect for disguising alien flavors because of the bitters. And it was only in *one* old-fashioned, or, again, I wouldn't be suffering alone. *Your* old-fashioned."

"*My* old-fashioned? How the hell d'you figger that?"

"Remember when we went into the office this afternoon, we took our drinks?"

"Sure, but what does that have to do with—"

"And you were annoyed because there was a cherry in yours?"

"Well, yes. Gil knows I don't like the damn things."

"He didn't put one in your drink; I know that as an observed fact. You picked up *my* glass by mistake. I didn't say anything; we hadn't touched our drinks, and it didn't seem important, so when we went back to the living room, I picked up *your* glass, and probably saved your life. The digitalis had to be in that drink."

Aaron needed time to digest that, and it went down hard.

"But there wasn't nobody there 'cept . . . the family."

"True, and the family doesn't include Alvin Drinkwater, your arch suspect. But take my word on this: the feud, George's murder, and this attempt on your life are all part of one grand scheme. The person who tried to poison you is George's killer."

"But that means it's . . . Flagg, you—you're *crazy!*"

Conan only laughed. "Am I? How do you feel tonight?"

"What? Well, I—I feel fine."

"No stomach upset or dizziness? None of the symptoms that sent you to bed early Friday and Saturday nights?"

"I told you, I feel *fine*, damn it."

"And you felt fine enough last night, in spite of the funeral, to pitch hay. But there was no cocktail hour yesterday. You missed your evening overdose of digitalis."

Maxwell leaned forward at that. "Are you saying this isn't the first time somebody tried to poison him?"

"Yes. Either the poisoner wasn't sure of the dosage, or, more likely, Aaron was given just enough to make him sick; to establish his ill health, so that when he died of 'heart failure' as a result of this last dose, no one would be surprised."

"That sounds like somebody knows a little about medicine," Maxwell commented.

"Or knows someone else who does. Aaron, when was the last time you took the Digoxin Doc prescribed for you?"

He glanced uncomfortably at the doctor.

"Hell, I don't know. Can't be bothered with them fool pills. Ain't took one for mebbe a year now."

Maxwell only sighed as Conan went on, "But the prescription has been renewed regularly, so by now someone has a good supply of digitalis on hand. In fact, it was on hand two months ago when Bert Kimmons died—at the Black Stallion, of heart failure." He didn't pause for them to voice their startled reactions to that. "The digitalis was available, Aaron, and getting it into your drinks wouldn't be at all difficult. Your aversion to cherries sets them apart, and it would only take a split second to drop some powder or soluble capsules into your glass."

Aaron was reduced to bewildered silence, and it was Maxwell who asked, "Who mixed his drink today?"

"Gil Potts. But that doesn't mean anything. When I came into the living room, Gil had the glasses lined up on the bar, and both

Linc and Ted were standing within easy reach of them, and Laura took Aaron's drink to him. I don't know who had an opportunity to add the digitalis Friday or Saturday; I arrived on the scene too late. Aaron, do you remember who handled the drinks?"

He sank deeper into his chair. "I didn't pay attention. But nobody was there but . . . but the family."

That plaintive repetition wasn't so much an objection now as a realization; an agonizing one, Conan knew.

Maxwell broke the brief silence that followed.

"Mr. Flagg, you still haven't told me why you're so set on secrecy, or why I shouldn't call Sheriff Tate."

Conan frowned and tried to focus on his watch.

"What time is it?"

"Ten till nine."

That didn't leave much time, but more than he expected; he'd have guessed it was closer to midnight.

"The secrecy is to make sure the killer doesn't realize the poison missed its mark. The attempt is revealing in its way, and that gives me an edge, even if it's a thin one. I can't afford to forfeit it by showing my hand now." He cast an anxious glance at Aaron. "As for Tate, he's an officer of the law, dutybound to uphold it. He'd be forced to take certain action which would cause a great deal of grief, but wouldn't convict the killer. It might destroy the grand scheme, Doctor, but the schemer would escape."

"I don't understand."

"I can't explain it fully. I'm sorry."

"Without causing grief? Is that it?"

"Yes."

Maxwell accepted that with a thoughtful nod, but Aaron seemed too numb for any kind of response. Conan thought bitterly that it was misleading to hint that grief could be avoided; there would be more grief for Aaron, for this divided "family."

But that was the price. The price of justice.

The doctor asked hesitantly, "Do you know who this killer and schemer is?"

"Yes." He looked down at his tensely interlocked hands. "Odd, the insights that come when you're afraid you might die. I was thinking of another death, and the keystone fell into place; the one fact on which the whole scheme depends. But I won't tell you who it is. That way, neither of you can inadvertently alert the killer. Aaron, don't start protesting. Acting isn't your forte, and you'll have your hands full with the role I'm going to ask you to play."

Aaron had roused himself enough to display some of his accustomed obduracy, but at that he hesitated, the flame-blue of his eyes banked in a dubious squint.

"You . . . got some sort of plan?"

"Some sort. I have no proof; nothing that would stand up in court. My only hope for real justice is to force the killer into an admission of guilt. I could blow this thing wide open with a few words to Tate, but before I'm reduced to that, I want to try to get that confession."

Aaron asked flatly, "How?"

"First we'll have to reassure the killer. You'll go into the hospital tonight with a 'heart attack.' Doctor, we can't pull that off without your help. For one thing, Aaron will need coaching. He'll have to play his role well enough to convince a trained nurse."

"Laura?" Maxwell frowned. "You don't think—"

"Did I say it was *her* conscience I hope to catch with our play? Are you willing to take a role?"

He mulled over his decision, but only briefly.

"Yes, I'm willing. Having somebody make a poison of a medicine *I* prescribed rankles, Mr. Flagg."

"Aaron, what about you? I'm asking a great deal, I know. I'm asking unquestioning faith."

He folded his arms and scowled at the floor.

"I guess . . . well, you was right, y'know. I owe you. And anyhow, George must've had a lot of faith in you, Conan, or he never would've hired you on, and I always trusted his judgment. All right, I'll go along with you. At least . . ." A hesitation, then he added firmly, "I'll go along."

It was a remarkable testament, and Conan was assured, particularly by Aaron's use of his given name. It was the first time.

"All right, then, the play's the thing."

CHAPTER 22.

" 'Bout a mile to go, Conan. You asleep?"

He raised his head. "No, Jesse, I'm awake."

The road ahead was a brown blur sweeping into the car lights. He turned and looked out the rear window, where another pair of headlights bobbed in a haze due as much to his impaired vision as the dust.

Abe. The faithful Abe following in Jesse's car. Conan wasn't happy about that in spite of Jesse's assurances of Abe's trustworthiness, but she couldn't very well walk back to town.

Necessity was the mother of this expedient. Conan had to get back to the ranch tonight because the next act of the drama he was directing must take place there. And he had to get back *with* the ranch car, or its absence might raise questions that could betray the entire scenario. But he was incapable of driving himself; he couldn't see past the steering wheel. So, Jesse was chauffeuring him, with Abe tagging along to provide her return transportation.

It wasn't that he didn't trust Jesse. She too had a part to play in his drama, and he welcomed the opportunity to explain it; at least, what he felt free to explain. He balked most at having Abe trailing behind, but only because it increased the risk that someone at the ranch might realize all was not what he wanted it to seem.

Still, the ranch hands were accustomed to Linc and Potts driving in at late hours, and it was nearly eleven, Laura and Ted's usual time of arrival. He could only hope that his own arrival—and Abe's—would attract no attention.

The gate was open; Aaron hadn't stopped to close it on his way to Maxwell's. Conan strained his eyes toward the bunkhouse, but saw no lights go on as Jesse swung left into the garage, where the bulk of the house blocked the view from the bunkhouse. Abe was right behind her, and, as instructed, turned off his lights and waited with the motor running.

"Conan, you gonna be all right?"

He put aside the heavy coat Jesse had provided as a makeshift blanket.

"Yes. Doc said I should be back to normal by morning."

"I hope he's right." She got out, closing the door quietly, and came around to meet him at the back fender. "Here's the keys. I'll be out to pick you up in the mornin'. 'Bout nine?"

"That's plenty of time. Thanks, Jesse. Just leave the gate open when you go. I'd rather have the hands complain about my greenhorn negligence than get a look at you or Abe closing the gate."

"Okay. You take care of yourself."

He heard their departure as he stumbled to the house and faced the ascent to the porch, then the Everest of the stairs to the second floor. Despite his hurry to get to his room, he stopped halfway up; it was either that or make a sudden descent backward. And he knew he'd never laugh at the plight of the seriously myopic.

When at length he reached his bedroom, he went first to the

south window. Ten people might be standing in the shadows of the bunkhouse porch and he wouldn't have seen them, but no lights had been turned on and nothing seemed to be moving.

Satisfied that his return—and Jesse's car—had gone unnoticed, he began setting the stage for the next act.

It was midnight when the sound of motors brought him to the front windows. His vision had improved enough for him to read his watch, and his general condition had improved enough for him to enjoy a cigarette. Still, he had spent most of the last hour resting in one of the chairs drawn up by the table in front of the windows. Not on the bed. It was hard enough to stay awake in a sitting position.

There were two cars: Laura's Buick and Linc's Mercedes. Apparently, Tate had succeeded in finding Linc and Potts to notify them of Aaron's critical condition. But Laura didn't drive home with Ted; she emerged with Linc from the Mercedes. After a brief conference, Ted and Potts walked together around the side of the house, probably to the bunkhouse to break the news to the buckaroos, while Linc accompanied Laura into the house. Conan went back to his chair to wait. The small light by the bed was on, but not the overhead light; his luggage was placed conspicuously near the door, which was half open.

He could hear their voices as they came upstairs, but no words until just before Linc's bedroom door closed, and Laura admonished him, "Linc, just don't worry—please."

Then the sound of her footsteps approaching his door.

"Conan?"

He rose and put out his cigarette. "Come in, Laura."

"Conan, Aaron's in the hospital. He—it's his heart."

"Yes, I know," he said tightly.

"You—oh, yes. Doc said you brought him in. I—I'm not thinking too well. Funny, I should've expected this. He wouldn't take the Digoxin, and diet—he doesn't even know what that means. Then with George . . . What—what's all this?" She was looking down at his luggage as if confronted with something alien and inexplicable.

"I'm leaving in the morning, Laura. At least, I'm leaving the ranch. My pilot is busy with Avery tomorrow, so he can't come for me until the next day, but I'll wait it out in Burns."

She turned her uncomprehending gaze on him.

"You . . . you're leaving? Now?"

"Yes, I'm leaving," he replied impatiently. "I've been *ordered* to leave. Ordered off the case and off the ranch."

"Ordered? But . . . I—I don't understand."

At the note of appeal in her voice, his tone softened.

"I'm sorry, I didn't mean to be short with you. Come, sit down; you look exhausted. Did you see Aaron?"

She sagged into a chair, eyes closing briefly.

"Yes, I saw him. It's serious, Conan. Doc's worried. You can always tell when he gets quiet and absentminded." Then she pressed her hands to her forehead distractedly. "Oh, I don't know why I should give a damn. He—he's so . . . these last couple of years, I've come to—to *hate* him. But when Doc called me at the school and told me . . ." A long pause, then she sighed. "I guess I *do* give a damn."

"Of course you do, Laura." Then he turned hesitant. "Did you . . . talk to Aaron?"

"Yes. Only for a couple of minutes. Doc didn't want him to see anyone, but Aaron was working himself into such a state, he decided it would be better to humor him."

"He asked to see you? Not Ted or Linc?"

She averted her eyes. "Just me. He didn't even want Doc to stay in the room, but he put his foot down at that. He stood by with the oxygen ready."

"Why did Aaron want to talk to *you?*"

"Oh, I—I don't think he was tracking very well, and you know how he is when he gets something in his head."

"All too well. What did he have in his head?"

Her attempt at a nonchalant shrug was negated by the nervous working of her hands.

"Nothing, really. Nothing . . . important."

At that, Conan made a show of annoyance, lighting a cigarette with a hard snap of the lighter.

"Laura, why are you being so evasive? Will I have to go to Dr. Maxwell to find out?"

Her eyes flashed, then she brought out a smile.

"No, of course not. I guess I thought he was only—I mean, it didn't make much sense."

"What didn't? What did he tell you?"

"Well, he said he'd hidden a—a strongbox in his room."

"Hidden it? Where?"

"I don't know exactly. He just said it was in his bedroom, and no, he didn't tell me what was in it."

"What *did* he tell you about it?"

"Nothing, except that if he . . . died, I was to find the box and dispose of it. Bury it, drop it in the ocean, anything, just so no one would ever find it. But if he lived, I was to forget about it. He said

he'd . . . take care of it himself. I don't know what he meant by
that." Then she looked directly at him. "Do you, Conan?"

He turned and went to the window as if driven by impatience,
eyes hooded and oblique as he took a long drag on his cigarette.

"I'm not impressed with the way Aaron 'takes care' of things.
Damn, I just handed it to him; dropped it right in his lap. Evidence,
Laura. A ray of light in the murk of ignorance and prejudice. But he
didn't like the way the light was turned. It didn't shine directly on
Alvin Drinkwater."

"Evidence?" She was watching him intently. "What kind of evidence?"

That seemed to rouse him; he shrugged uneasily.

"It doesn't matter. Aaron wants the case closed, and I can't keep
it open without his cooperation. He ordered me off the ranch and
even threatened to press trespassing charges, and I wouldn't put it
past him to do it. We . . . had quite an argument. That's probably
what triggered the heart attack. I won't enjoy having that on my
conscience if he doesn't recover."

"Oh, Conan, you can't blame yourself. Anything might have triggered it."

He studied her skeptically for a moment, then nodded.

"*Will* he recover, Laura?"

"I don't know. Doc kept saying he's a tough old man, but I think
he was trying to convince himself." She paused thoughtfully. "But,
you know, when I saw him, he looked better than I expected. His
color was quite good. Maybe Doc's just being pessimistic. I hope so;
I really do."

"So do I." He didn't want her to dwell too long on Aaron's apparent symptoms, and went on quickly, "But I'm formally washing my
hands of the whole affair. *Ecce* Aaron. Let him take care of it. I'm
only sorry I let you down. And George."

"Well, I think it was hopeless to begin with. Thanks for trying,
anyway."

She seemed to accept his capitulation with more relief than regret.
Conan jabbed out his half-smoked cigarette.

"Maybe it *was* hopeless. At least, that's a salve for my bruised
ego."

She laughed weakly and came to her feet.

"I'm sorry about your ego, but only the hardiest egos survive
here." She looked over at his luggage, her smile fading. "When are
you leaving? I can drive you into town."

"Thanks, but you'll have enough to worry about. I called Jesse
Broadbent; she'll pick me up about nine."

"Jesse? Oh. Well, I'll see you before you leave. I guess I'd better get to bed now. I'm tired and . . . oh, God, I need a drink."

She tempered that fervent declaration with a brittle laugh as he walked with her to the door. There he paused, looking across to Aaron's bedroom, frowning slightly.

"Aaron said he hid the strongbox in his room?"

"What? Why, yes. Conan? What are you going to do?"

He turned abruptly and crossed to the bed to pick up his robe, then to the table for his cigarettes. She was still staring at him perplexedly when he went out the door with her and shut it behind them.

"I'll consider the case closed when I go out the front gate in the morning. Tonight I'll sleep in Aaron's room."

"Why? To guard the . . . whatever he's hidden there?"

"I guess so. It won't matter a damn in the end, but I can look back on a total failure and say I did all I could. Good night, Laura. Sleep well."

"Yes. You, too." She studied him in the brighter light of the hallway. "You look . . . tired, Conan."

"I am. It's been a long day for everyone. And, Laura, I think it would be best for all concerned if you kept what Aaron told you to yourself."

Her flushed cheeks and averted gaze gave silent testimony that the warning came too late, but she only nodded and started for the stairs.

"Good night, Conan."

He went into Aaron's room and closed the door, listening to her retreating footsteps, hearing them stop outside Linc's door. Then a light knock, the door opening and closing on a whispered exchange.

Conan took a deep breath, enduring a brief resurgence of nausea, then secured the bathroom and hall doors with straight chairs propped under the knobs. It was all he could do. He stripped off his clothes and all but fell into bed, sinking immediately into a deep sleep.

He was a worthless sentry this night, but only he knew it, and that was what counted.

CHAPTER 23.

When Jesse dropped him off at the bus depot the next morning, Conan was carrying his suitcase and had reverted sartorially to dude status. His boots, Stetson, and the briefcase he'd left in Jesse's keeping.

He wasted little time at the depot; only enough to pay for a locker, which he left empty, putting the key in his pocket. Then he walked the two blocks to the Arrowhead Hotel, still carrying his suitcase.

He didn't make a friend of the hotel clerk, insisting on a room on the top floor in the corner away from Broadway, but facing the sidestreet; he didn't like his sleep disturbed by highway traffic, but he despised looking out on an alley. And he wanted the room next to his, too; he objected to strangers behind his walls. The clerk sighed and frowned, but found his foibles tolerable when recompense appeared in the form of cash.

Room 410 had been modernized perhaps thirty years ago; that is, it had a private bath with appropriate fixtures. But the walls were bedecked with baroque peonies, and the bleached-oak bedstead was built before the era of queen- and king-size. Still, the room was scrupulously clean and comfortably airy with its high ceiling and big double windows.

He took the reproduction of covered wagons retreating into an unlikely sunset off the wall, then went to the windows. Centered under them was a table on which the inevitable Gideon was piously displayed; to the left, a tired armchair sulked. He opened the windows and looked down at the junction of Third Street and the alley backing the hotel.

There were two ways to reach this room from the alley. A closed hallway connected the alley and the lobby, from whence the elevator, whose shuddering workings would send a victim of claustrophobia into hysterics, rose. Of more interest to him were the service stairs at the back of the building. Anyone using them ran virtually no risk of observation. Jesse had provided that information, saving him the time and effort of personal exploration.

But he had other preparations to make; another stage to set. He opened his suitcase and went to work.

Most of the preparations were made in the next room, where he set up a tape-recorder equipped with earphones, ran an extension into his room, concealing it under the hall carpet, then secured a mike in the molding behind his door. He turned on the television in his room to test his electronic eavesdropper; then, satisfied that it was functional, delved into his suitcase again for the compact Zeiss binoculars and a fifth of Jack Daniels. These he put on the table under the window, with two glasses from the bathroom. The last thing he took out was the Mauser automatic. He flipped off the safety, snapped a bullet into the chamber, and put it on the table. In plain sight, but ready.

The knock came as he was putting the suitcase into the closet. He checked his watch before he opened the door.

"Jesse, you're early. It's only ten till eleven."

She was breathing hard, a hand pressed to her bosom. When she saw the gun, she paused, but didn't comment on it.

"Lordy, I'm gettin' too old to climb up four flights of stairs. Didn't meet nobody in the alley, by the way."

"Good. Shall we break in this bottle?"

"Thanks, and don't bother waterin' it down." While he poured a couple of straight shots, she took possession of the armchair by the window. "You ain't heard from anybody yet?"

"No, not yet." He pulled a straight chair up to the table and arranged his cigarettes, an ashtray, the binoculars, and the Mauser on the end close to hand. "Relax, Jesse. It'll take time to search Aaron's room, and more to check the cache at Dry Creek."

"Relax. Sure." She tipped up her glass. "Well, if you can look so damned relaxed, I guess I can, too."

He laughed, knowing full well she wasn't deceived by appearances, wondering why so many of the things that might go wrong never occurred to him until it was too late.

The telephone rang at eleven-thirty. Jesse sat up as if her chair had suddenly become electrified, but Conan waited for a second ring before he answered it.

"Hello."

"Uh . . . Mr. Flagg? I—I want to talk to you."

"Yes, I thought you would, Linc. Where are you?"

"Down in the lobby."

"Come on up to my room. Four-ten."

He hung up and turned to Jesse, who was hurriedly emptying her ashtray, her hands shaking.

"Well, I guess I better get to my listenin' post. Conan, is it . . . is it really Linc?"

"Yes. It's Linc." He ushered her into the next room as a grinding creak in the elevator shaft announced its ascent. "Jesse, remember, don't come into my room for any reason unless I call for help."

She nodded distractedly, pausing only long enough before closing the door to whisper, "Good luck."

"Come in, Linc."

Conan had rinsed out Jesse's glass, and as Linc cautiously opened the door, he uncapped the Jack Daniels bottle and added a shot to his own glass.

"Can I offer you a drink? You'd better shut the door."

Linc did so with some reluctance, as if he didn't want to cut off his retreat. Still, when he came into the room he managed an air of cocky confidence.

"I'll have a couple of fingers, since you're pourin'." Then his confidence slipped, to be replaced by something cold and unfeigned. "You figger you need that?"

"What? The gun?" Conan shrugged and handed him a glass. "I don't know. Have a seat."

He probably would have preferred to remain standing, but finally went to the armchair, while Conan moved his chair aside and sat on the windowsill where the gun and binoculars were only an arm's reach away. The traffic was sporadic, each car heralding its presence with a muted rumble. He purposely displayed more interest in the view than in Linc, but was acutely aware of his every move.

Linc was new at this game and uncomfortable with it, and well he might be; he didn't fully understand either the rules or the object of it. Yet he seemed determined to play it out, sitting tensely at the edge of his chair, downing half his whiskey without seeming to taste it.

"I think you got somethin' that belongs to me, Flagg."

"Something like a strongbox? The one Aaron hid in his bedroom?"

He cast a resentful glance at him. "Yes."

Conan only nodded, watching a pickup pass below; but it was blue. He waited silently as Linc gathered himself.

"I guess you figger you got some kind of *reward* comin' for *findin'* it. All right, but I ain't hagglin'. I'm gonna make one offer, and that's it. Ten thousand. Cash."

Conan seemed to consider the sum, one eyebrow raised.

"You've accumulated about four thousand in your Boise account. Your cut, I assume, after . . . expenses. Where do you intend to get the rest of it?"

"Where the money comes from ain't your problem."

"No, and I suppose your wholesaler in Winnemucca would consider an advance advisable under the circumstances."

"You tryin' to pump me? Forget it. You wanta make a deal or not?"

Conan paused to light a cigarette so that he could take a close look at the dark station wagon passing below.

"Linc, I admire your moxie, but you're in a sellers' market. Yes, I want to make a deal. I'm just not impressed with your offer."

He slammed his glass down. "I said I ain't hagglin'! Ten thousand's all I can get, so take it or leave it!"

"I'll leave it." He blew out a stream of smoke, his eyes cold, his tone sharp. "Good God, Linc, whose idea was that? Not yours, I hope. Only a penny-ante blackmailer would assume *my* motive is blackmail. I didn't set up this meeting to squeeze a few dollars out of you—and I *did* set it up, right down the line. Just keep that in mind."

Linc, confronted with something totally unexpected, was reduced to suspicious uncertainty.

"Then, what . . . what d'you want from me?"

"Two things, and probably you'd prefer to deal in cash. I want the truth, and I want you to set yourself free."

He paled, and for a moment seemed afraid, but not of Conan. The word "free," perhaps. Then he picked up his glass and emptied it in one swallow.

"What're you talkin' about?"

"Well, let's start with the first part of the bargain. The truth. Tell me about Charl Drinkwater's death."

"*Charl?* What the hell does she have to do with this?"

"She has everything to do with it; you know that."

"I'm gettin' outa here. . . ." He rose and stumbled to the door, but Conan didn't move, nor raise his voice.

"And what will your good friend and boozing buddy Gil Potts say when you come home empty-handed?"

He froze in his tracks, then slowly turned, staring at Conan uncertainly for some time before he said coldly, "It don't make much differ'nce, does it? Looks like I'm goin' home empty-handed anyhow."

"Not necessarily. I'm willing to deal, but on my own terms." He leaned forward to pour more whiskey into Linc's glass, watching him as he moved like a sleepwalker back to his chair, seemingly drawn by the whiskey, but downing it slowly this time, never once looking up from his glass.

"I found the key Sunday, Linc, in Gil's trailer. A clipping: the *Clarion's* account of Charl's death. The key, and yet I passed it off without a second thought. Gil knew the Drinkwaters and you; her loved ones. It didn't seem odd that he'd keep that clipping. Then last night it finally came through to me. At the time of her death, Gil was living in Burns, and it hadn't been six months since he moved here from Winnemucca. He *didn't* know the Drinkwaters or you. Not then. So, why would he clip out an obituary for a girl he'd probably never heard of? Why, unless he knew something not about *her*, but about the subject of that article—her death?"

He didn't expect an answer to that, but hoped for a comment, or at least some recognizable reaction. But there was none. Linc didn't even seem to hear him.

Conan went on, "The night she died, Charl came to town for a basketball game and parked in the school lot, which happens to be directly across the highway from the gas station where Gil was working. He saw something; something connected with her death and with you. You're the one he's blackmailing. Those five-thousand-dollar checks to cash—that money went to Gil, didn't it? And how else would he coerce you into taking part in the rustling? You may be a hellraiser, but that kind of carefully premeditated larceny would never occur to you." Linc made no response, his whole attention apparently concentrated on his whiskey.

"What did he see, Linc?" Still no answer. "Damn it, I know both Alvin and Aaron had their backs up about you and Charl; reason enough to avoid being seen together. But enough for Gil to blackmail you into partnership in almost every major crime in the book? There's more to it. There *must* be. What is it he's holding over your head?"

Again he waited for a reply, but despaired of getting one. Linc sat staring into his glass, but he wasn't seeing it; he wasn't seeing anything except some remembered image that struck him numb with agony. Yet when he finally spoke, his voice was strangely flat.

"She was my Juliet . . . *beauty too rich for use, for earth too dear* . . . and I killed her. I killed Charl."

CHAPTER 24.

Once that terrible confession was made, the rest of the story followed with little prompting. Linc seemed in a trance state, under an irrational compulsion to have it out.

Jesse had been right in thinking that Linc and Charl began seeing each other again after he returned from college, but it was a secret thing because of family opposition. In fact, they had only a few clandestine meetings, and Charl was so maddeningly cool that at first he thought she was playing games with him. But it was only because she was so uncertain about him; about the two of them and their future.

The diabetes? Yes, he knew about that, but she didn't seem to take it seriously, and in answer to his questions, only laughed and made jokes about being on the needle; an insulin junkie. He knew so little about the disease, he didn't realize she was being dangerously casual.

The night of her death. Yes, he met her in the parking lot. She made an appearance at the game, then slipped out. He was waiting in his car. They stood outside for a while; yes, under the lights. A warm night. He suggested a drive and stopped at the gas station first for something to drink, parking to the side in the shadows.

She asked for Fresca. No sugar. He understood that much about the disease. The soft-drink machine was inside the station, and while he was there, out of Charl's line of sight, he took out a hip flask and laced both bottles with at least three shots of vodka.

A kid trick. A stupid kid trick, but she was being so damned cold and skittish, acting like a cheap teaser, and he wasn't too sober to begin with. That's all he ever learned at college. Boozing. So, he poured in the vodka, making jokes with the station attendant about its relaxing effects. Gil Potts. He didn't know his name then.

No, Charl didn't seem to notice any difference in the taste, and it *was* relaxing. She admitted she still loved him. Enough to marry him, whatever her father thought.

They went to the Sunset Motel. It wasn't the first time; only the first since his return. Not that Charl made a habit of that sort of thing. She wasn't that kind of girl.

"She loved me. God help her, she loved me. . . ."

It seemed the narrative might stop then, but the compulsion to confession was unrelenting, even though the words had to be forced out, one by one.

All their differences and fears seemed resolved that night; everything true and free. Afterward, he dozed in innocent relaxation and thought she was only asleep, too, until he realized it was late, and he'd have to take her back to the game. She might be ready to confront her father with her intent to marry him, but a rendezvous ending at the Sunset Motel must remain secret; she'd been adamant about that.

But she wasn't just asleep. She was unconscious. He guessed it must be the diabetes, and because he knew so little about it, he was terrified. He tried desperately to rouse her, even slapping her face, but she didn't respond.

Doc Maxwell. That was his first thought. Doc could be trusted to say nothing about their being together.

Linc dressed her as best he could, then carried her out to his car and drove to Doc's office. Only a few blocks from the motel. But he wasn't there. Delivering a baby somewhere; he learned that later.

There was only one alternative. The hospital. Yet he was still inhibited by her insistence on secrecy. If he took her to the hospital himself, Alvin would hear about it sooner or later. A trivial concern, but only in retrospect.

Thus, the anonymous phone call to the hospital, and Charl left in the booth while he hid his car around the corner and waited. The ambulance arrived within ten minutes. He was shaking with relief when it took her away. Then, sure she was safe, he drove back to the ranch and went to sleep to dreams of golden optimism, like any man so deeply in love he'd reached the brink of marriage.

He didn't know Charl was dead, that she died a few minutes after reaching the hospital. Dr. Maxwell called Laura the next day; it was she who told him. He asked her about diabetes, and how and why it could kill. She gave him a lengthy dissertation, but only two facts stayed in his memory. Diabetes in adolescence could be severe and extremely difficult to control, and that was the case with Charl.

The second fact was that alcohol had the same effect on insulin balance as sugar.

And Linc knew then that he might as well have poured cyanide into Charl's Fresca; it would have been no less lethal to her than the vodka.

He ended the confession as he began it, his voice still flat and stripped of life, hard, brown hands locked on his glass. His eyes were fixed still on that remembered image, blue and depthless as the desert sky, and as empty.

"I killed her. I killed Charl."

Conan turned away; that grief was intolerable. *Past hope, past cure, past help!* Yet it was two years old now. What had it been when it was fresh? When Gil Potts began capitalizing on it, began blackmailing Linc?

It defied comprehension that one man could prey so callously on another's agony. Gil Potts at the gas station, laughing with Linc over the relaxing effects of liquor. Conan could picture that, and Potts reading the newspaper account of Charl's death, cutting it out, probably still laughing. Cutting it out for future reference.

It wasn't enough that Linc had unknowingly laced her drink with what was for her a deadly poison. His misfortune was compounded because he'd done it in the presence of a man with enough medical training to know what those few ounces of alcohol would do to a diabetic; who came to the same conclusion Linc did—that he killed her —and made Linc the goose that would lay golden eggs for him forever.

Conan looked down into the street. Even during Linc's recital, he had responded to every passing car; it became almost reflexive. But he was jarred to alertness when he saw the black pickup with the white lettering on the door.

He reached for the binoculars and hurriedly focused on the door, recognized the Running S brand, then shifted to the license plate. ATL580. His eyes narrowed to slits as the pickup turned into the alley behind the hotel.

Then he put the binoculars on the table and studied Linc, still wrapt in his irremediable grief.

"Linc, I'm . . . sorry."

He was roused by that and turned to stare at him.

"Sorry? Sure. Tell me about sorry." Then he tossed down the last of his whiskey. "All right, that's the truth. Now, what about your part of the deal?"

Confession was obviously over for him; back to the business at hand. But he had two years' practice at self-anesthesia. Conan wasn't deceived by that sudden shift, but he needed a moment to collect his thoughts and made it by offering more bourbon. Linc refused it.

"I had enough, and mebbe I said enough."

Conan shrugged. "You know your capacity, but you haven't yet said enough. That's only part of the truth. The worst part." He paused, leaning back against the windowframe. "Was Charl a country girl?"

Linc turned away, his answer slow in coming.

"No. Not in her heart. I wrote that song for her."

"Not for Laura?"

"Laura and me was *friends*. That's the way *she* wanted it, and she was the only friend I had after—after . . ."

Conan believed that, perhaps because it satisfied some baseless and romantic preconception about Laura. She loved George; at least, she loved the man she married.

"Linc, George asked me to come here to find the truth about the feud, and I stayed to find his killer. I've done both, and yet I can't prove anything. That's why you and I are haggling over a piece of evidence I should turn over to Joe Tate. But those receipts by themselves will only put you in prison; they won't convict George's killer."

Linc frowned in bewilderment. "His killer? What do them receipts have to do with—with George?"

Conan didn't entirely understand the question, or rather, why he asked it, and with no hint of subterfuge.

"I'm talking about the second part of the bargain. His killer will go free unless you're willing to undertake it; willing to set yourself free."

"What d'you mean?" he asked tightly.

"Free of Gil Potts."

"*Free?* Free of Gil? I'll never shake loose of him. He *knows*. Don't you understand that? He knows about Charl." He pressed his fists to his forehead. "Alvin—God, he'd kill me if he knew, and he'd have ever' right to. Hell, if I had any guts, I'd kill myself. Gil's got me right where he wants me, and I guess that's where I'm gonna stay."

"Even if it means being an accessory to grand theft and murder?"

He looked up, startled, and again it seemed genuine.

"Murder? What're you talkin' about? Okay, we got the feud started, and the rustlin'. You know about that."

"Part of it. Was it Gil's idea?"

He nodded slowly. "Ever'thing was Gil's idea. Damn, it started off so easy. Jest a hunderd here, a hunderd there; seemed cheap enough at first to keep his mouth shut."

"When did it start?"

"Right after he signed on with us. George hired him. I didn't even recognize him from the fillin' station."

"He didn't contact you while he was working for Alvin?"

"No. Mebbe he had his finger in a sweet enough pie there to keep him happy till Alvin caught him."

"I assume a hundred here and there didn't satisfy him."

"Not for long, and I never had much money of my own, but Gil was good at thinkin' up ways to get hold of more."

"Like the money Ted was accused of stealing?"

Linc didn't move except to close his eyes wearily.

"Damn, my own brother, and I jest stood there and watched Pa rip him apart. Gil was set to pounce if I even opened my mouth. Y'know, I thought Ted was gonna kill me Saturday night." He looked around at Conan. "Does he know?"

"I don't think so."

"He should've killed me. Alvin should kill me." A bitter laugh, then, "Wouldn't you think somebody'd put me out of my misery?"

Conan didn't comment on that, his attention attracted to a creaking sound outside the door; someone walking carefully on old floorboards. Linc didn't seem to hear it, but he hadn't been listening for it.

"When did Gil come up with the idea of the rustling?"

"Right after that business with Ted and the money. That scared him good, even if Ted took the blame for it. So . . . well, he knew this feller in Winnemucca. Only a few head now and then; Pa'd never miss 'em. Jest like ever'thing else, it started off nice and easy."

"Did Gil set it up with this friend in Winnemucca?"

"Gil? Hell no. He give me a couple of names, and sent *me* down to Winnemucca to make the deal. That, and them receipts, and that bank account—I know what they're for. To keep Gil's nose clean, and get me in that much deeper."

"Yet you accepted those terms?"

"I couldn't very well turn 'em down, now, could I?"

Conan reached for his glass, frowning.

"Is that when you and Gil started the feud?"

"Yes. Gil said it was jest to call attention away from the rustlin', but I knew better. He had it in for Alvin ever since he fired him. So, we started it up, then it sort of took off on its own steam."

"What do you mean?"

"Well, once Pa and Alvin got it in their heads anythin' happened to one of 'em was the other's doin', they kep' it up on their own. I mean, it *had* to be that way. I ain't lifted a hand against the Double D for six months, and I never touched any Runnin' S property."

Conan stared at him, nonplussed. He *believed* Aaron and Alvin had perpetuated the feud. His bewildered reaction to the questions about George's death began to make sense, and Conan recognized a correlative delusion: the delusion about George's killer.

"Linc, how could Aaron or Alvin possibly maintain the feud without someone finding out?"

"Mebbe the same way Gil and me started it. He's foreman; he always knew where the buckaroos'd be."

"And where you and your brothers and Aaron would be; Aaron

keeps no secrets from the *family*. But Gil does. You said *you* bowed
out six months ago, but did Gil? What about the gasoline and dynamite at Dry Creek? And the salt blocks? I'll take any bets they'll
show a high cyanide content."

Linc came to his feet, suddenly angry.

"They ain't nothin' but plain salt blocks. Gil brought 'em in for
the cows we pastured in the canyon."

"Did he? Then why didn't he put them out where the cows could
make use of them?"

"Well, I—we jest never got around to it."

"And you never got around to facing the truth—about Gil or
about George's death. How do you explain *that*?"

"That was *Alvin's* doin', and, no, I don't think George planned to
blow up his rezzavoy. I think he was jest out checkin' the fence and
found it cut, but Alvin saw him and thought he done it."

"And in a fit of rage, crushed his skull with a handy rock, then
tried to cover his guilt by blowing up his own dam. Is that it?"

Linc hesitated, backed up by his cutting tone.

"Sure, that's it. It must be."

"Ignoring the improbability of George riding fence at night, how
do you explain the fact that the mud on his horse's hooves came from
Dry Creek Pasture—*not* the reservoir? Did his horse go to that rather
inaccessible spot on its own whim?"

"I don't know, and I don't give a damn! What the hell do you
want from me?"

"Your help, Linc. I want Gil Potts to pay for his crimes, and some
of them, at least, are punishable by law."

"By . . . by law? You want me to—to *testify* against him?" His incredulous tone suggested that Conan was asking him to jump out
the fourth-floor window.

"That's the only way you can set yourself free, even if the cause of
justice doesn't move you."

At that, Linc laughed, a harsh, hopeless, grating sound.

"Oh, damn—set myself *free*? Flagg, I been all through that.
When Bert Kimmons died, I got scared; he was so damn close. I had
a bellyful, and I wanted out, but Gil set me straight." He paused,
sagging down into his chair. "This is how it'd be: I go to Joe Tate,
tell him about the rustlin' and the feud, and how my friend Gil was
in on it from the start. State's evidence. Ain't that what they call it?"

"Yes."

"Well, that's about when ol' Gil starts shakin' his head and
lookin' hurt. Won't know a damn thing about any of it, and you
know what? Joe won't find any proof anywhere to back me up. It'll
be my word against Gil's, and ever'body knows what a nice feller Gil

is, how he looked after me like a brother. The Winnemucca outfit? I can give Joe a couple of names, but they're jest stable hands, and I got nothin' to connect 'em with Gil. But once Joe got a look at that canyon, or that bank account and them receipts, I'd be up a crick, and jest because you got the receipts now don't mean nothin'. They're carbon copies. Gil wants 'em back, but not to keep me outa jail. We got a sweet set-up, and he don't want it messed up."

"You mean he'd rather not kill his golden goose," Conan put in sourly.

"You mean me? Right. But if his goose gets cooked, *he* ain't gonna get in hot water. So, what happens? I end up in jail, with Gil on the outside laughin'. And talkin'. I know him. I know what he's like when he gets crossed. He'll talk his head off. About ever'thing, about . . . Charl."

That final realization seemed to bear upon him like a tangible weight; he sat hunched and defeated, while Conan stared at the door, equally oppressed. Linc considered his situation hopeless, yet he didn't understand *how* hopeless because he refused to understand George's death.

The rustling operation at Dry Creek provided a motive for George's murder, and Conan held the evidence that would tie that motive to Linc. Even if he chose to withhold it, someone else still had the original receipts.

Motive was one thing. Tate still needed opportunity.

"Linc, can you account for your time Thursday night? I mean after eight-thirty; after Sylvia Waite left you."

His head came up, and at first he was angry, then he relaxed with that bitter, hopeless laugh.

"Word gets around, don't it? Why d'you wanta know?"

"It was the night George was murdered."

"You figger *I* done it?"

"I want to know if you *could* have."

"Sure, if I sprouted wings. How the hell d'you figger I'd get out to the rezzavoy without a horse? There ain't a road within five miles."

"Not the reservoir; Dry Creek Pasture. The county road comes within a mile of it. Not a bad walk on a moonlit night, and there are horses available in the canyon. Linc, just take my word for it; George was killed at the pasture."

"But that don't make sense. What would Alvin be doin' there? He didn't know nothin' about that."

Conan sighed. "Never mind. Just tell me what you did after Sylvia left you."

He thought back, then shrugged.

"Well, I got drunk. Surprise."

"Where?"

"I drove out to the cemetery and sat on Charl's grave with a .38 in one hand and a fifth of booze in the other."

"Oh, God. Alone, of course. How long were you there?"

"Till I finished the fifth and Gil found me. I was tryin' to work up the nerve to put myself out of my misery, but I never made it." He pulled a crooked grin. "Know why? Sylvia. She called ever'thing off that night. Well, I figgered if I blew my head open then, she'd think it was because of *her*, and damn it, her kind's a dime a dozen."

"You said Gil found you at the cemetery?"

"Yes. He knows I go out there sometimes."

"How did he get there? Didn't he drive into town with you? And where was he while you were with Sylvia?"

"I dropped him off at the Peacock Bar, and he borrered Lex Dailey's pickup."

"When?"

Linc hesitated, looking at him curiously.

"Early in the evenin', I guess. Gil's got a life of his own, y'know, and he always had a way with the ladies."

"Is that what he told you? That he met a woman? When did he come for you at the cemetery?"

"I don't know exac'ly, but it had to be after two-thirty. I got it in my head I wanted to stop for another drink before we went home. Gil had to drive past the Peacock to show me it was closed. They shut down at two-thirty."

Conan stared out into the street, brows drawn. Now he knew Potts's mode of transportation to the county road, and knew he had time to reach the canyon, kill George, carry his body to the reservoir, and blow it up by eleven, then return to find Linc at the cemetery after two-thirty.

The only trouble was that Linc would also have had time to make the same trip after eight-thirty, and couldn't prove he hadn't. Tate could add opportunity to motive.

"Linc, was it Gil's idea to tell Tate the two of you were together all Thursday night?"

"Sure. He said what we did and who we did it with wasn't nobody's business."

"Especially if *his* business was with George?"

Linc came to his feet, glaring at him.

"What're you tryin' to say? You think *Gil* killed him?"

"Would that surprise you?"

"You're crazy! Sure, we was rustlin' cows, but it's a long way from rustlin' to murder."

"What's wrong, Linc? You can't accept Gil's guilt because it makes *you* an accessory to murder? Not an accidental death, but *premeditated* murder. George was worried about Dry Creek, but that doesn't explain his going there that night. Gil probably phoned him with some plausible invention, and George agreed to meet him there."

Linc only repeated doggedly, "You're crazy, Flagg."

"Well, here's more insane raving. You underestimate Gil's ambition. He intends his goose to lay bigger and better eggs than his take from the rustling. Have you seen your father's will? Ownership of the ranch goes to the eldest surviving son."

"I know that, but what . . ." He stopped, the light of understanding kindling in his eyes.

"Yes. You're the eldest surviving now. When Aaron dies, you'll own the ranch, but Gil owns you, and for all intents and purposes, the ranch will be his. And now he has more than Charl's death, more than vandalism and theft, hanging over your head. Murder one. Your brother's murder."

"But, he—he can't—what about . . . Pa . . ."

"What about him? He's in the hospital now, in critical condition, but it wasn't a heart attack that put him there any more than a heart attack killed Bert Kimmons. It was digitalis poisoning."

Linc was reeling mentally, his taut features glistening with perspiration.

"Poisoning? You got any proof of that?"

"I can't prove Gil put the digitalis in Aaron's drink."

"Then, how—what d'you expect *me* to do about it?"

Conan looked over at the door again.

"Stop him. Even if Aaron survives this attempt, do you think Gil won't try again? And sooner or latter he'll succeed. Then what about Ted? If he challenges Gil's right to the Black Stallion, I doubt Gil will hesitate at burying another McFall. But you're his golden goose; you're Aaron's heir. Without you, all his grandiose plans collapse."

"Without me?" He stared fixedly out the window. "What am I s'posed to do? Try workin' up the nerve to put myself out of my misery again?"

"Good God, no. Go with me to Joe Tate. Do what you wanted to do before; turn state's evidence."

His eyes shifted, focusing icily on Conan.

"We already been through that. You know what would happen if I went to Joe."

"But something's been added. Murder. Murder past and future; George's murder and Aaron's. And there's more hope than Gil let you believe. On the basis of what you tell him, Tate may be able to find evidence to substantiate your story. He'll have both the Oregon and Nevada police working with him, and there's at least a chance some proof against Gil *will* be found."

"A chance?" He laughed contemptuously. "You wanta give me odds? Meanwhile, I'll be one well-done goose, and there won't be nobody in the whole damn county doesn't know all about—about Charl."

"The alternative is making yourself a conscious accessory to Aaron's murder. You can't plead ignorance now."

"The hell I can't! I'm s'posed to swaller all this just because *you* said it? Who d'you think you are? You been talkin' about proof— you got any *proof* against Gil?"

"If I did, it would be in Tate's hands now."

"Sure, 'long with that strongbox. So, take that to Joe! You want Gil's golden goose cooked, *you* do it!"

"Linc, wait!" He was already at the door before Conan caught up with him.

"Get outa my way!"

"Damn it, will you listen to me!" Conan pushed him back against the wall until he finally subsided, glaring hotly at him, his breath coming fast and hard.

"All right, Linc," Conan said wearily. "You win."

"What—what d'you mean?"

"I won't go to Tate without you. I only hope . . ." He took a deep breath and reached into his pocket. "It isn't my choice. It's yours."

Linc stared blankly at his hand. "What's that?"

"The key to a locker at the bus depot." He gave Linc a moment to absorb that, then asked, "What were your instructions once you got the strongbox?"

"Instructions? You mean from Gil? What differ'nce does it make?"

"None. I was just surprised he trusted you alone on this mission."

"Oh, Gil trusts me. He stayed home at the ranch."

"Are you sure?"

"Now listen, you—"

"Never mind. Here, take this."

He took the key only after a long hesitation. Conan opened the door for him, then leaned against the jamb, taking a casual look up and down the hall. It was empty, but the door to the service stairs was only a few yards away.

"Linc, good luck."

He studied him skeptically, then struck out for the elevator, the key clutched in his hand, making a fist of it. Conan wasn't proud of the deceit involved in that key, but it wasn't Linc who inspired it. He closed the door and leaned close to the monitor.

"Jesse, the hook is set. Keep listening."

CHAPTER 25.

Conan had his gun in hand when he heard the footsteps outside the door. He opened it without waiting for a knock and found Gil Potts standing there, hands in his pockets, sunburned face creasing in a slow grin when he saw the gun.

"Howdy, there, Conan. Ain't you gonna ask me in?"

"Why should I? Your errand boy accomplished his mission." Then he added sarcastically, "You *did* overhear that part, didn't you?"

Potts only laughed. "I heard."

"Of course. So what do you want?"

He pushed back his hat to scratch his forehead.

"Well, I jest figgered mebbe you and me better have a little talk, friend."

"About what?"

"About Linc. Y'know, I worry 'bout him. He's high-strung, that boy; jest like a fine-bred stud. Now, we don't neither one wanta see him hurt hisself, do we?"

Conan seemed to consider that transparent pretext, then with an indifferent shrug stood aside and waved him in, closing the door after him. Potts homed in immediately on the bourbon and helped himself, using Linc's empty glass.

"Don't mind if I do, friend," he jibed, "but I sure wish you'd stop wavin' that fancy popgun around."

"It might come in handy."

"To use on me?" He took a swig of whiskey and laughed. "Well now, you might have a hard time explainin' that; shootin' down an unarmed man who never done you no harm."

Conan was willing to disarm himself—at least temporarily—to play to Potts's vanity, but he displayed obvious reluctance as he put the gun on the dresser beside him, only inches from his hand. He didn't ask for proof of Potts's lack of arms, despite the bulky sheep-skin jacket he wore.

"You don't call killing a friend of mine *harm?*"

"Depends on how good a friend he was." Again he laughed, relishing Conan's apparent frustration. "Ever'body always said ol' George was so damn smart; had a fancy college degree to prove it. Now, me, the only degree I ever had was a PHD. Know what that means? PHD? Post Hole Digger. Get it?" He tipped up his glass, then licked his lips through a malicious grin. "Yep, ol' George was so damn smart, all I had to do was pick up a phone, and he come run-nin' right to where I was waitin' for him, jest like you said. You figgered that one out real good, Conan. I take my hat off to you." And he did so, with a mocking bow.

"You mean you *admit* it? You admit killing George?" He seemed incredulous, and Potts was enjoying himself.

"Sure, I do. I killed him. There y'are. I figger you got that much satisfaction comin'."

"What about Bert Kimmons? Will you give me *that* satisfaction?"

"Why not? Jest between you and me, anyhow. Well, ol' Bert had one foot in the grave already, what with his bad heart. I jest kinda give him a push on in."

"Put him out of his misery?" Conan asked caustically.

"You might say I done him a favor that way."

"And Aaron?"

Potts downed more whiskey, frowning sourly.

"Damned ol' codger. Should be dead already."

"But, as Doc says, he's tough. How much digitalis did you give him, anyway?"

He shrugged, grinning again, eyes sliding up to Conan's.

"Enough. I take off my hat to you on that one, too, friend. Nice piece of figgerin'. Damn, if it wasn't."

Conan restrained himself with an evident effort.

"You said you were worried about Linc. Why? He had no part in George's or Kimmons's murder—or Aaron's poisoning. Or did he? Maybe he plays the game better than I thought."

At that, Potts bridled as if he'd been insulted.

"Hell no, he didn't have no part in any of that. Why, somethin' like that'd scare the pee-waddin' outa him. And he can't spill any beans he don't have." Potts seemed to recover his sardonic humor then; he put down his empty glass and stood grinning, thumbs hooked in his belt. "Matter of fact, I ain't worried 'bout Linc spillin' *any* beans. I got that boy hog-tied, and I figger on keepin' him that way. Justice, friend. If he's gonna pay for his sins, *I* plan on doin' the collectin'."

The muscles of Conan's face were rigid in anger; his hand moved nearer the gun as Potts sauntered toward him.

"Then what *are* you worried about, Gil?"

"What're *you* worried about? You think mebbe I'm packin' iron after all?"

"I think that's an unusually heavy coat, considering the temperature."

"Oh, so that's it. Well now, if it'll make you happy, I'll take it off, and if you figger I can hide a gun anywheres else on me, you're welcome to look for it."

Conan watched him strip off the jacket and toss it onto the bed, his suspicion unfeigned now. It was inconceivable that Potts had come here without a weapon. He had only been dallying with his prey, and there was an element of sadism in that, but Conan let him enjoy himself because it served his own purpose; those casual confessions were on tape now.

But he knew Potts's obvious course; knew why he was here, standing grinning and relaxed only a few feet away, apparently unarmed. He considered Linc's mission accomplished, the strongbox safe. Conan was only a liability to him now.

A knife, perhaps, like the switchblade so adroitly slipped into Linc's hand Saturday night; another act of sadism. Or perhaps a small handgun . . .

"You wanta frisk me, Conan?" Potts held his arms out from his sides, eyes glittering in malignant anticipation. "Have at it. Don't want you worryin' yourself none."

"Shut up, Gil. No, I don't want to—"

"Oh, I forgot. My hat. No tellin' how many six-shooters I got hid in this ol' Stetson."

It was beautifully done, and Conan might have admired the sleight of hand under other circumstances. Potts, loose as a rubber band, suddenly snapping taut, sweeping Conan's gun aside with one hand, the other arcing toward him, cobra-swift and armed now; terrifyingly armed.

It wasn't a gun hidden in the hat, but perhaps something equally deadly.

A hypodermic.

Its contents were an unknown quantity, and that more than the lightning attack threw Conan's timing off.

He twisted away, the shining needle skimming within an inch of his arm, its lethal potential the whole of his awareness, and the chop to the wrist that should have sent it flying only deflected it as he stumbled backward and slammed unexpectedly into the wall.

Potts swarmed to a new attack, his panting like laughter, left hand groping for Conan's eyes, his body pressed close, a heaving, cumbrous weight against him. The needle was still Conan's consuming objective. Head down, elbows thrusting up to fend off the attack on his face, his hands closed on Potts's wrist, and every muscle in his body strained in a lunging turn to propel the needle into the wall.

A crunch of broken glass, an angry howl hot in his ear, but Conan allowed himself a split second too long in shivering relief. If it had been a gun or knife, he wouldn't have dropped his guard for an instant, but he was so intent on that needle, he left himself wide open and off balance, and Potts's reflexes weren't slowed by pain.

His left hand was free, shaped into a pile-driver plunging toward the solar plexus, crashing home before Conan's locked-fist sweep could even create a distraction.

He doubled convulsively, recognizing in the paralyzing impact the shock of bone giving way. He didn't even see the next blow coming.

CHAPTER 26.

The first sensation he could identify, other than pain, was the acrid taste of old carpet and blood. He couldn't yet locate his body spatially, and the sounds were a senseless cacophony, until the savage explosion of the gunshot.

But before that was the crash of the door hitting the wall, angry voices shouting, unidentifiable thuds and tramplings.

Then the shot.

Yet he felt nothing. Nothing different. That neural and systemic shock he would feel.

A new voice joined the clamor; one he recognized. He clutched the bedstead and levered himself to his feet, groaning at the pain in his chest. Iron maiden. That's what it was called, that medieval instrument of torture. His head and the left side of his face seemed on the verge of exploding with every pulse beat.

In the corner by the window, an incomprehensible tangle of bodies. Jesse. It was her voice he'd recognized. Jesse vainly tugging at Linc McFall's shoulders, shouting pleas that fell on deaf ears. Linc had Potts against the wall and was methodically beating him into bloody anonymity.

Linc finally understood, had passed a tolerance threshold, and he would kill Potts if someone didn't stop him.

Conan staggered to Jesse's aid, but when he reached Linc, he offered no resistance; instead, his head fell back, his knees buckled, and Conan would have fallen with him except for Jesse, but together they managed to get him to the armchair, Linc murmuring, "I'll kill him . . . kill him . . ." And the object of that lethal intent, eyes turning up under the lids, crumpled in an insensible heap on the floor.

"Lordy, Conan, he's bleedin' like a stuck pig."

Conan leaned over Linc, jarred into sudden mental clarity, his own pain if not forgotten at least submerged. The wound was in the left thigh, toward the outside. He tore away the Levis, his hands turning red with the welling blood that soaked the cloth and spread a dark stain on the chair. But there was no pulsation in the flow; the bullet hadn't hit an artery.

Jesse began administering frontier first aid—a shot of straight whiskey—while Conan went to the door and closed it. The gunshot hadn't attracted anyone; not yet. He went into the bathroom, pulled every towel off the racks, and returned to Linc, noting in passing that Potts hadn't moved.

"Jesse, call Dr. Maxwell. But first, talk to whoever's on the switchboard downstairs. Tell them there's been an accident, but everything's under control. I don't want anyone coming up here to investigate."

She started for the phone. "What do I tell Doc?"

"Just that it's an emergency."

He knelt by Linc and pressed a folded towel to the wound, feeling his body go rigid on a jerking breath.

"Linc, I'm sorry. I've got to stop the bleeding."

"I—I know. You . . . all right?"

"No, but I'm in better shape than you are. Why did you come back here?"

His white features constricted with pain, or perhaps it was anger and remorse.

"I jest . . . got to thinkin'. Ever'thing you said. I knew in my heart you was right . . . about Gil. And George. I—I come back to tell you I wasn't goin' after that strongbox. Not unless you'd go with me and take it to Joe Tate. But when I got up here, Gil . . . he was gonna . . ."

Conan turned the scarlet-stained towel and pressed it to the wound again, listening to Jesse's subdued conversation with Maxwell.

"You saved my life, Linc."

He stared at him for a long moment. "I . . . *saved* . . ."

"Yes, so put that in your scales. Jesse?"

She hung up, nodding. "Doc'll be here in fifteen minutes, and I got ol' Perry down to the desk quieted down. He had a couple of calls from the third floor. Guess I better call Joe Tate."

"No—not now," he said, more sharply than he intended. "I'll call him later, but first—" A groan came from the crumpled pile that was Gil Potts, and Conan frowned. "Jesse, you take over here."

She knelt to fold a clean towel, judiciously examining the wound. Potts groaned again and stirred, but when Conan leaned over him, his eyes were still closed, his bleeding, gashed mouth gaping.

Judas, Conan thought bitterly. No. Worse than that. Judas's betrayal was a destined necessity, and he was capable of remorse. Conan had the means to bring Potts to justice now: his recorded confession, with Jesse as a listening witness taking down every word in shorthand. The play had been successful in catching if not his conscience at least his confession. But Conan found no satisfaction in that success now.

When he designed the trap, he had recognized the price Linc would have to pay to bring Potts to justice, and had considered it unfortunate but unavoidable. It became intolerable while he stanched the blood from a wound inflicted by a bullet that would have lodged in *his* heart or head if Linc hadn't taken it. And he was haunted by a wistful melody. *But its loneliness, loneliness kills* . . .

He couldn't hang Gil Potts without hanging Linc; not by the law; not through Joe Tate. It seemed a poor bargain now. Linc had paid, and was still paying, so dearly for his sins.

Conan pulled in a careful breath, dark eyes opaque.

But Potts must hang, one way or another, or *he* would hang Linc. And enjoy it.

He saw his gun under the dresser and went over to pick it up, sniffing the barrel. It hadn't been fired. Potts had used another gun on Linc; he had come here doubly armed. Conan put the Mauser in a dresser drawer, then got down on his hands and knees. Under the bed, he found the Italian automatic he'd first seen in Potts's trailer.

He rose, head pounding, teeth clenched at the serrated pain in his chest, but he refused to think about it except to make allowances for it. Potts was coming around, coughing and mumbling. Conan removed the clip from the automatic, emptied it into the dresser drawer, snapped it back into the grip, then put the gun on the floor under the table where it might have been overlooked in the confusion. But it was within Potts's reach.

Then he returned to Linc, putting his back to Potts. Linc was resting with his eyes closed, but Jesse had watched Conan's every move and gave him a long, questioning look, which he chose to ignore, concentrating on taking Linc's pulse.

"A little weak," he commented after counting a full minute, also choosing to ignore the sounds of movement behind him, "but fairly steady. How do you feel, Linc?"

He blinked, taking a halting breath.

"Better. I'll be . . . all right. . . ."

"Conan!"

There was a hint of accusation in Jesse's cry of alarm, but he was slow in responding, asking, "Jesse, what's wrong?" before he turned and saw Potts staggering to his feet, the gun in his hand, his battered face nearly unrecognizable, but his desperate rage obvious as he felt his way backward toward the door.

The words slurred viciously through broken teeth.

"Don't nobody move or I'll blow you all to hell!"

"Gil, don't be a fool," Conan protested. "I—I've already called Tate. He'll be here in—"

"Jest shut up, damn you! He ain't here yet. I'm gettin' outa here, and anybody gets in my way—"

"You don't stand a chance! He'll have every road in the county—"

"Don't bet on my chances, Flagg!" He stumbled and fumbled his way toward the door, every breath rasping painfully. "And don't try follerin' me, or gawdamn it, I'll put a bullet right in your guts and watch you die screamin'!"

"Gil, wait—*Gil!*"

But he had reached the door. His footsteps pounded along the hall, another door burst open, the thump of his boots clattered away down the stairs, and Conan stood listening to that retreat with an ambiguous mix of doubt and hope.

"Ain't you goin' *after* him?" This perplexed query came from Linc, straining to rise while Jesse held him back.

Conan frowned absently at his watch. "Relax, Linc, or you'll make the bleeding worse. Jesse, there's something you'll have to take care of, and we haven't much time." He jerked the mike loose from behind the door and followed the thread of wire into the hall.

Jesse was right behind him. "Conan, I hope to hell you know what you're doin'."

He laughed at that, wincing.

"I hope so, too, but I haven't time to explain it."

"Well, I guess you figger you owe Linc some. You gonna call Joe Tate?"

"I'll call him, but first I want you to get this recording equipment out of here. Lock it away somewhere—your office, your car—I don't care; just so it's safe."

She bent to finish picking up the wire.

"I'll lock it in the trunk of my car. It's parked jest a block down the alley. You want me to come back here?"

"Yes, you're our star witness, but we'll have to decide exactly how much you witnessed before Tate arrives, so don't tarry along the way."

"You jest leave this contraption to me. I'll be back in . . . well, give me ten minutes."

Linc was holding a reddened towel against his leg, too preoccupied with pain to comment as Conan poured bourbon into the two glasses and pulled up a chair.

"I think we could both use this. Can you handle the glass?" He paused to be sure, then, "Doc will be here in a few minutes. We have to get a few things lined out."

Linc brought his glass to his lips with a shaking hand.

"I don't understand. Gil . . . you jest *let* him go."

"Of course I did. You know damn well he won't go down for the count on this without taking you with him."

"I guess I . . . I deserve goin' down with him."

Conan's hand wasn't so steady, either, as he took a medicinal swig of whiskey, grimacing at the sting in his lacerated mouth.

"Deserve it? For what? For Charl? Is there any punishment equal to that crime, or any punishment worse than you've already suffered? You made some damn fool decisions, but I consider grief a mitigating circumstance, and grief loaded with guilt is a formula for insanity. You made your first sane, cognizant decision today when you decided to go to Tate; when you came back here."

"But you said there wasn't but one way to make Gil pay, to give Joe any—any proof against him."

Conan nodded, frowning into his whiskey.

"Well, maybe I was wrong. About Gil's paying, I mean. And maybe . . ." He shrugged, immediately regretting the unthinking movement. "I owe you, Linc. I owe you my life. I can't ask you to pay the price of that proof. Not now."

"It—it jest don't seem *right*. . . ."

Conan said sharply, "You could end up with a ten to twenty year sentence before Gil got through talking. Spending the best years of your life in prison is one way to expiate your sins, but I doubt you'd come out of it a whole man, and your one real sin you can never expiate. You'll pay for that every day until you die, but I can't help you there; no one can." He looked down into his glass, away from that drawn, ashen face, as he added, "You can't undo anything, Linc. You can only balance the scales with the rest of your life. How you do it is up to you."

Linc gazed silently at him, his desert-sky eyes remarkably clear; he said nothing, and after a moment Conan assumed an attitude of studied indifference.

"Besides, you might get a little rusty at the guitar in the state pen, and that would be a hell of a waste. You're not bad, you know. Not bad at all." Then, with a glance at his watch, "But if you prefer expiating your sins in prison, I need to know now, so I can call my lawyer."

That aroused him to startled question. "Your—your lawyer? What do *you* need a lawyer for?"

"Well, I've made myself an accessory after the fact."

Linc laughed weakly and finally nodded.

"I guess I better plan on workin' off my sins outside of prison, if it means you goin' in with me. I don't figger you'd exactly blossom behind bars."

"No. And I'm not through with Gil Potts yet. All right, our first problem is to get your story straight. The idea is to stay as close to the truth as possible; we'll just leave out a few details, like your involvement in the feud, the rustling, anything Gil forced you into."

"What about that money? The money Ted took the blame for? I can't leave Pa callin' him a thief."

"Gil stole it. He admitted it to me. And Jesse, who was . . . uh, hiding in the closet. You knew nothing about the theft. Maybe you were suspicious of Gil, but you had no proof."

"Oh. That's how it works, then."

The outlines of the edited story had been established by the time Conan heard the warning creak of the elevator, and he hoped that was how it *would* work, racking his brain to anticipate the questions Joe Tate might ask.

"Linc, one more thing—you said Potts gave you two names in Winnemucca. I want them."

He frowned questioningly, then shrugged.

"Well, there's Ben Tatum. He drove the cattle trucks."

The grinding of the elevator was getting louder.

"I suppose Tatum works at Al Reems's ranch."

"Yes, but how'd you know—"

"Never mind. Who else?"

"Pete Butell. He tends bar at the Longhorn in Winnemucca. But I told you, they're jest stable hands."

"They can deliver messages. You've had more dealings with Tatum. He'd recognize your voice. Would Butell?"

"Well, prob'ly not, but how come you—" He stopped at the sound of a knock on the door, and Conan rose, leaving Linc's unfinished question unanswered.

Walter Maxwell hesitated when Conan opened the door, looking quizzically from him to Linc.

"Which one of you is the patient?"

"Both, but I'll get in line. And right now I'm going downstairs to the pay phone; I don't like talking through a switchboard."

Maxwell leaned over Linc, frowning as he removed the red-soaked towel.

"I hope you're calling Joe Tate, Mr. Flagg. This is a bullet wound."

"I'll call Tate." But that would be the second call.

"Well, tell him to send an ambulance."

CHAPTER 27.

Conan opened his eyes into a glare of morning light, wondering where he was and what had awakened him. He moved his head on the pillow cautiously. The left side of his face seemed a pulsing balloon; the pills Laura had given him had worn off.

Laura. Yes, that was it. He was back in the guest room at the Black Stallion.

"Mr. Fl—uh . . . Conan? You awake?"

Ted was standing near the bed, repeating his hesitant query. That was what had awakened him.

"Yes, I'm awake. Damn!" This as he tossed back the covers and tried to sit up. From the base of his sternum to his waist, he was corseted in interlaced bands of tape.

"You all right?" Ted asked anxiously.

Conan made a second, more considered attempt to rise.

"I'm all right. Where's my robe? Oh—thanks."

Ted, still solicitous, helped him into it.

"Sorry to have to wake you up, but Joe Tate's here. He wants to talk to you."

"Does he always call so early in the morning?"

"Well, it's eight o'clock." And obviously the middle of the day, in his mind.

Conan looked over at the bottles Laura had left on the bedside table, reached for the one marked Darvon-N, then settled instead on the aspirin, and went into the bathroom for a glass of water. His face didn't look as bad as he expected it to; at least, not as bad as it felt.

"Ted, how's Linc? Have you heard from Doc?"

"Well, not this mornin'; Doc said he'd call soon as he seen him today. But I stayed at the hospital yesterday evenin' till he got out of surgery and come around enough to know who he was talkin' to."

Conan found his cigarettes on the table by the window. He looked out into the golden mosaic of leaves as he lit one, thinking about what Linc might have said while still groggy from the anesthetic. Ted hadn't returned to the ranch until well after Conan had surrendered himself, at an unusually early hour, to bed.

"How was he, Ted?"

"He was okay. Still hurtin', but, y'know, it was like a load was took off his shoulders. I guess he had his suspicions about Gil for a long time, but he couldn't prove anything, and he figgered nobody'd believe him, anyhow. Prob'ly right, too. Whoever would've thought ol' Gil . . ." He let the sentence hang, as if the enormity of Potts's crimes defied expression.

"Did Tate have any news about Gil?"

"Don't know. All he'd say was Gil was 'took care of.'"

"Well, that sounds encouraging." He was turning his thoughts to the impending interview with Tate, but something in Ted's attitude distracted him: an air of uncomfortable determination. He had a purpose here beyond announcing Tate's arrival. Conan waited, taking a leisurely puff on his cigarette, looking out into the blaze of leaves, while Ted gathered himself.

"Conan, I . . . I had a talk with Pa last night. He waited up for me." That seemed to amaze him.

"What did he say?"

"It was about that money. Y'know, the money he—he thought I stole. Well, Joe Tate talked to Pa, said that was one of the things Gil told you and Jesse *he* done."

"He told *me*. He didn't know Jesse was hiding in the closet, nor did he plan on my living to be a witness."

Ted nodded. "Funny he'd even tell you, though."

"He was proud of himself. What did Aaron say about the money?"

At that, he paused, again amazed.

"He . . . he apologized. Pa apologized to me."

Conan smiled, fully sympathizing with Ted's amazement.

"He's an honorable man, however cantankerous."

"Well, he come right out and said he was wrong. And he said he lost one son, but found out he had two more; said he . . . he was proud of us." With the last words, his face took on a crimson glow.

"He should be proud of his sons."

"Mebbe. Anyhow, I—I wanted to say thanks for findin' out about that money. And there's somethin' else." He looked up at Conan resolutely. "It's about Saturday night. About that . . . fight."

Conan gave him an oblique smile.

"I chalked that up to genetic spleen."

"Whatever it was, it scared me pink. I almost—almost killed Linc. I didn't want to talk about it, or even think about it, and I still don't know what happened. Jest ever'thing let go all at once. Well, I guess you can't thank somebody for somethin' 'less you're willin' to admit it happened. But it did, and I—well . . . thanks."

Conan said soberly, "I appreciate that, Ted, but Linc deserves an apology more than I do thanks, and you deserve an apology from him. He was asking for trouble."

Ted grinned and shrugged. "Damn, if he wasn't. Well, him and me got that settled out last night."

"Good. Well, maybe your gratitude will make some advice tolerable. That eighteen hundred dollars you have socked away in your room—you were saving it to replace the money you were accused of stealing, I suppose?"

Ted's jaw sagged. "How'd you know about that?"

He sidestepped the question, admitting, "It had me worried at first. Anyway, my advice is to take part of that money and buy the best diamond you can find for Bridgie."

His cheeks began to glow hotly again.

"Well, I . . . I been thinkin' about that."

"Then it's good advice." He looked out the window, smiling to himself. "Willful girl. Just like a Roman-nosed bronc, always ready to buck, but she loves you, Ted."

He could only nod, tongue-tied, and Conan didn't pursue the subject, but purposefully put out his cigarette, then checked the time as he slipped his watch on.

"Well, I'd better not keep the sheriff waiting. Tell him I'll be down as soon as I dress."

"Okay. Oh—Linc wanted me to tell you somethin'. He asked me to bring his gittar when I go in to see him today. He said mebbe you'd like to know about that." There was a hint of a question in his tone, but Conan only smiled.

"Yes, I'm glad to hear that."

◈

Laura was just coming out of the kitchen when he reached the foot of the stairs.

"Conan, how do you feel? Oh, dear, you *look* awful."

"Colorful, at least. *You* look extraordinarily good."

"I—I feel good. I'm at the stage where I start crying at the drop of a word, but I can deal with that. Conan, thanks for staying with it; for being so damned stubborn."

He kissed her cheek, laughing.

"It's an equivocal virtue. Now, I'd better see what Tate has on his mind."

"Oh, yes. Come on. He and Aaron are polluting the atmosphere in the living room."

When they went in, Ted was leaning on the bar, while Aaron occupied his usual chair, Joe Tate the one to the right of the fireplace, both puffing at panatelas.

Aaron eyed Conan through a pall of smoke.

"Well, Flagg, you finally got yourself up outa bed. 'Bout time, too."

Conan laughed as he eased himself down on the couch.

"Your hours are a little stringent for a greenhorn."

"Mebbe you oughta stay on. You ain't half bad handlin' horses, and I'd get you shaped up in a couple of weeks."

"I nearly didn't survive this one week. How are you, Sheriff?"

"Not bad, considerin'. How 'bout you?"

"Not bad, also considering. Any word on Linc?"

"I phoned Doc; said he was doin' fine. I'll stop by the hospital later. Never got a chance to talk to him yesterday, but I don't figger he can tell me much more'n you and Jesse did."

"I doubt it, but he knew Gil better than anyone else. He might have some idea where he'd go now."

"Well, we know where he went."

"You found him?"

"In a way, yes, we found him."

"Well, what did he say? Would he talk?"

Tate gave him a sphinx smile and adjusted his Stetson.

"No, he didn't do no talkin', but we learned a lot."

"What do you mean?"

"Well, I'll tell you what happened. Kind of a long story, though."

Conan said irritably, "I'm not short on time."

"No. Well, first we put out an APB. Too bad you didn't know what kind of rig Gil was drivin'. Had to check with the ranch, and he had a hell of a head start by then. Anyhow, I called the state patrol and Sher'ff Culp down to Winnemucca, and he got his boys and the Nevada patrol on it. We set up road blocks, but there's a lot of country out there, and a lot of miles of back roads. Ain't no way we could cover all of 'em without callin' out the Army."

"You didn't pick him up at any of the road blocks?"

"Nope. Did I tell you Ira Culp had his eye on a feller named Al Reems?"

"Yes. Didn't Culp say he thinks Reems is kingpin of the rustling operation?"

"Doesn't think it, knows it; jest can't prove it. Well, yesterday Ira told me he was right next to certain Gil was on Reems's payroll, one of his top hands, back before he left Winnemucca. Would've saved a lot of trouble if I'd knowed that, but I never had any reason to ask Ira 'bout Gil."

"Is that why he left Winnemucca? Culp was making it too warm for him?"

"Could be, but Ira never had any proof against him."

"It seems no one ever did."

"Least, nobody did and stayed alive, 'cept you and Jesse, and I don't figger neither one of you'd be alive if Linc hadn't come bargin' in." He looked over at Aaron as if to make sure he understood that.

Aaron muttered, "Well, I'm glad he finally put his fists to good use."

Conan put in, "And I'm glad he was smart enough to see through Gil; at least, suspicious enough to follow him to my hotel room. Gil turned out to be a little more than I could handle alone."

Aaron didn't comment, but he was finding it difficult to maintain his glower as Tate resumed his narrative.

"Anyhow, Ira figgered Gil might head for Reems's place, so he sent some of his deppities out to look around the ranch in a hellycopter; thought they might spot that black pickup. They did, too, jest about sundown. Reems has this cabin way to hell and gone in the hills north of his place. It's an old homesteader's shack; he keeps some grub and a couple of bedrolls there for the buckaroos when they're out workin' cattle, or sometimes he uses it for huntin'. Ira thinks he uses it for a hideout, too, if any of his boys gets into trouble. There's a road up to it, but it ain't much more'n a cow path, and out there in them hills, a jackrabbit'd have to pack a lunch to stay alive. Well, when Ira's deppities flew over the cabin, they spotted *two* pickups; the Runnin' S truck and one of Reems's."

Conan leaned forward. "Reems was there?"

"Sure was." He paused to emit a portentous cloud of smoke. "Him and two of his boys with their hands full of shovels, and Reems with the gun still on him."

The question had to be forced out.

"What . . . what gun?"

"The gun he shot Gil with. That's what the shovels was for. They was buryin' Gil Potts."

Conan leaned back, well aware that Tate was watching his reaction closely, but he'd be hard put to assess it; Conan himself wasn't sure of his feelings.

"So, he's dead."

"Yep, and no city lawyer's gonna talk Reems outa that one. That's what you call gettin' caught red-handed."

"Well, there's . . . justice in it, I suppose."

Tate was still watching him. "I guess so. I never did like that eye-for-an-eye business, but I ain't sorry the way it turned out. Mebbe we could've locked Gil up with that confession he give you and Jesse, but it'd mean a trial, and a real rip-snorter. I seen too many people hurt that way; people who got somethin' to hide that ain't really nobody's business. But it all comes out in a trial. The law ain't choosy, y'know; dredges up the minnahs with the sharks."

Conan caught the quick, ironic glint in his eyes, and knew without a doubt that Tate read him to the last line. But he offered no hint of acknowledgment.

"Well, Sheriff, I guess that closes the case."

"I'm willin' to call it closed; grateful, even. But there's still somethin' bothering me." He crossed his legs, frowning critically at the teetering ash on his cigar before he tapped it into the ashtray.

Conan conceded the cue. "What bothers you?"

"Well, what I can't figger out is why Al Reems wanted to shoot ol' Gil."

He shrugged. "Dishonor among thieves, I suppose."

"Maybe. More likely, Reems was afraid of what Gil might tell about his beef wholesalin' business if we ever caught up with him. But Ira says Reems took real good care of his reg'lar hands, and Gil wasn't the kind to pull leather. Reems'd know that. Besides, I seen a good lawyer make mush outa better cases than we had against Gil. So, how come Reems was so quick to bury him?"

"I hope you don't really expect me to answer that."

He laughed. "No, I'm jest wonderin' out loud. I guess Reems *must've* thought Gil was gettin' loose in the mouth, and I'm wonderin' where he'd get an idea like that." He paused, then when Conan offered no comment, "I figger it this way—*somebody* got to Reems and put that idea in his head about Gil, but Gil didn't know it, so when he went to his boss for help, he set hisself up for a fast funeral."

"Well, that sounds reasonable, Sheriff."

Tate pulled a slow grin as he put out his masticated cigar, that cool irony still glinting in his eyes.

"Sure does. Well, I guess that's somethin' I'll never know—who got to Reems. But the case is closed, and like I said, I'm grateful."

He rose and readjusted his hat. "Well, I gotta get back to town. Anytime I can lend you a hand, Mr. Flagg, you jest holler. Nice seein' you, Laura; you too, Ted. Aaron, you take care of yourself."

"That's all I been doin' lately," he grumbled, rising to see Tate out. "But I'm grateful, too, Joe. Mebbe now we can get some work done around this place."

Laura looked over at Conan, and when the screen door banged behind Aaron and Tate, she broke into a laugh.

"He'll never change."

"Probably not. Ted, when are you going in to see Linc?"

"This afternoon. Visitin' hours start at one."

"Do you mind if I go with you?"

"Glad to have you." Then he frowned at his watch and started for the door. "Talkin' about work, I better get out to the barn and get them leppie calves fed."

Laura rose. "And I'd better get *you* fed, Conan. Do you feel up to some breakfast?"

"I may start on lunch, too. I'm starved."

But they didn't make it to the kitchen. In the foyer, they encountered Aaron coming back in from the porch.

"Flagg!"

Conan stopped, waiting impatiently while Aaron hooked his thumbs in his belt, mouth compressed sourly, the furrows lining his forehead deepening.

"I jest wanted to say—well, you done a damn good job." That admission seemed to necessitate a pause for recovery. "Damn good. Whatever you charge for your work, you got it comin', and I . . . I'll take care of the doctor bills myself."

For that, Conan needed a pause for recovery, then he put on an amiable smile.

"Thanks, Aaron, I'm glad I could finish the job. And I'll tell Doc to forward my bill to you."

He blinked, but had no opportunity to comment on the quick acceptance of his offer. There was a pounding of footsteps on the porch, and the screen door swung open, propelled by a panting and wide-eyed Mano Vasquez.

"*Señor*—Mr. McFall! They—they're here! They have come *here!*"

"What the hell're you gabblin' about, Mano?"

"The Dreenkwaters—they just now drive up!"

"The *Drinkwaters?*"

"Yes, sir, they are all come. Outside, you can see—"

"Damnation!"

He pushed past Mano to the door and stared out incredulously. Conan looked over his shoulder and saw Alvin, Emily, and Bridgie

Drinkwater emerge from a dusty sedan, then stand side by side, nervously adjusting hats and coiffures.

Aaron demanded of no one in particular, "What the hell is Alvin doin' *here?*"

"*Alvin* is with his family," Laura said tartly, taking a stand only inches from his nose. "And *I* invited them."

"You . . . you *invited* 'em?"

"Yes." Then, with a glance at Conan, "My last act of civic duty in Harney County. Aaron, the feud is over, and Alvin was as much a victim of Gil Potts as you were. Don't you think it's time the two of you faced that together?"

He looked out to the car, where Emily was apparently engaged in a similar argument with her husband. But Bridgie was smiling, and without a word to her parents she walked away toward the barn. Conan didn't find it at all difficult to guess what drew her there.

Aaron loosed a gusty sigh and squared his shoulders.

"I guess as long as they're here . . . Well, go put on the coffeepot, Laura."

"It's already on."

He nodded once, then with his jaw set resolutely, he marched out onto the porch like a soldier, a general, into battle, while Alvin Drinkwater began his advance toward the picket fence.

Laura glanced up at Conan. "Do you mind waiting awhile for your breakfast?"

He was already halfway out the door. He laughed and took her arm.

"Come on. I wouldn't miss this for anything."